I0789009

DARK ANGEL

RUBY JEAN JENSEN

Gayle J. Foster

SPIRIT WORLD

Gladys followed closely, feeling her power in the growing effect she had on Peri Lee. Like an invisible bird in the growing dusk she flew silent circles over her head, faster and faster, wearing her down, down, down. Making her helpless, unable to stay in control of her own brain.

And now to enter—where? The most vulnerable, the most tender—the throat? Yes, the throat. Where the blood throbbed and pulsed visibly in the girl's fear and flight.

Peri Lee's dark eyes widened and darted in her helplessness, her chin trembled. She pressed for a moment against Dale, as though the contact would drive away the other thing. Dale's arms closed on her tense body...

Gladys stayed with her, closer and closer about her in the spinning flight, feeling the resistance of the girl's fear as if it were a psychic wall thrown out for protection. Gladys fought desperately against it, trying to edge through, while Peri Lee's hands dropped the reins and came out to claw at her. But the hands were helpless, of a different substance, and could only fling themselves uselessly at the air around them. Peri Lee swayed in the saddle, never quite falling, and the horse raced with his belly low as if he knew what was needed of him and exactly where he was to go. Gladys pushed at her power of mental resistance, that invisible something that was far more powerful than the hands. She finally began to melt through because her own desperation and need to live, to be beautiful and to be loved, was stronger than Peri Lee's fear of the unknown thing that was Gladys.

Both hands reached up to clutch her throat, pressing it free of Gladys, bringing with it added psychic resistance; the hooves of the horse left the pasture as he stretched long in a high jump over a white stockade fence.

First printed 1978 in the United States of America.

Published by: Gayle J. Foster, Carrollton, Texas

Library of Congress Control Number: 2022906470

Cover art: SelfPubBookCovers.com / Viergacht

❀ Created with Vellum

PROLOGUE

She was born beautiful. The only daughter of a beautiful couple, the baby sister of a handsome little boy. The setting into which she came was deserving of her. Green fields, irrigated by streams from the magnificent mountains of the Great Rockies. Her home was large, many-roomed, built by an ancestor; closed off from surrounding fields by tall rows of trees, lawns with specimen ever-greens, flower beds, rose gardens, kept neat and perfect by gardeners from the city of Denver.

Her future would be assured. As her mother before her, she would attend the modern brick and glass schools in the small town a few miles east and graduate high in her class, a physically flawless young woman who had never known the anguish of sickness or poverty, the lack of popularity or good looks. From there she would go on to the University of Colorado, and return to marry the son of another wealthy area farmer.

They named her Peri Lee.

In her first year of school all the little boys fell in love with her long dark curls, her dark eyes, her sweetness. She treated her friends as gently as she treated her pets at home. She had never seen unkindness, she didn't know to be unkind.

She was growing up, becoming aware of all things in a new way. And usually the feeling was good. She knew that beyond her sheltered world among the big farms there were other less pleasant worlds where people lived in fear and poverty, only strange, dark words in her mind; and at age ten she decided she would dedicate her life to helping those people. At age ten she also experimented with her mother's makeup. She was sent upstairs to her room to remove it. Her big brother's comment, just before her dad deported her from the dinner table was: "Peri Lee looks like a caricature of Mom." Laughing.

And all of it right in front of Dale Larson, whose dad owned the farm next to the O'Brion land. Tall, golden-brown Dale who was two years older than her brother, Gene. And he was laughing a little too.

Peri Lee didn't often get mad at her brother, but she wasn't sure what caricature meant, and it sounded bad. Besides, he had said it in front of Dale, and made him laugh.

"Well, you're just an old caricature of Dad!"

Her dad pointed a stern finger. "Off with it."

Her mother said gently, "You used too much, dear. Makeup should be subtle."

Peri Lee went to her bathroom and washed off the mascara, the eyebrow pencil, the rouge, the liquid makeup, the lipstick. It took a while: The more she washed the more it smeared.

She looked up caricature in the dictionary.

That was when she made up her mind to go away and devote herself to people in poverty—whatever that was—and just let her brother miss her. And Dale? Well, someday he'd fall in love with her, but she'd be gone and he could grieve. Forever.

She went back downstairs, but Dale and Gene were not there. "Where'd they go?" she asked, face still pink from fierce scrubbing.

Her dad said, "Now there's daddy's beautiful little girl. Come here, kitten, and sit on my lap. One of these days you'll be too grownup to hold."'

She went to him and slid one arm around his neck. "Did they go horseback riding?"

"Probably."

"Why didn't they wait for me?"

"I guess they didn't know you wanted to go."

"Oh yes, they knew. They're just big smarties, that's all." She was still thinking of caricature. "I didn't want to go with them anyway."

Later she saddled her own pony and rode to the farm on the other side of the O'Brion land and went riding with Sherry, the freckled, red-haired friend who loved sunshine, summertime, and riding on the hay lift.

It was Sherry who talked her out of going away. Unintentionally.

"I'm not leaving here when I grow up," Sherry said as she guided her pony down the driveway, "I'm going to marry Dale Larson."

Peri Lee was shocked at the admission. "But you can't! I'm going to marry him myself."

"Oh. Then I'll marry Gene. Let's tie our ponies at the fence and go ride the hay lift."

So that was settled.

On that day Peri Lee O'Brion knew she would marry Dale Larson.

But Dale didn't seem to know it. He seemed hardly to know she was around. He double-dated with Gene, girls who were already old enough and big enough to wear bras.

Finally, when Peri Lee was twelve, her mother gave her a ribbon-wrapped package and Peri Lee tore it open to find her first bra. Gene and Dale just happened to walk into the room then, at the wrong time, to see Peri Lee gaping in pleased surprise at this evidence of growing womanhood. Gene stopped.

"Hey—what's that?"

Peri Lee folded its tiny softness into her hands, too late. "None of your business."

Gene was beginning to laugh, Dale was smiling. "A bra?" Gene said. "What are you going to do with it? Now don't tell me, let me guess. Put it on your Barbie doll?"

Peri Lee suddenly was aware of a new truth. Her brother teased her only because she was annoyed by it. So, she wouldn't be annoyed anymore. *He* might not know where she was going to put the bra, but she knew, and that was all that mattered. She lifted her chin, put a small and secret smile on her lips, swung her long hair back from each shoulder and walked sedately past them, up the long stairway to the balcony. She paused and looked over the banister. Both young men stood staring up at her. And neither of them was so much as smiling now.

She felt quite mature.

When she was thirteen there was no longer any doubt where she put her bras. It was all in growing evidence.

By age fourteen boys were asking her for dates, and her dad was beginning to erupt into occasional explosions. And, paradoxically, her brother Gene was treating her like an equal most of the time, babying her at others, never teasing her.

He, and Dale, went away to college. Life became less interesting when they were gone, less exciting, and another new truth came to her. More happiness and excitement were generated in her life by Dale Larson than by anything else. Even though he seemed to look upon her as his own sister, she felt stimulated by his presence. Just knowing he was there, on the farm next door, made her feel great.

Without him, life seemed uneventful.

At age sixteen she won a local beauty contest. Her dad didn't really approve.

"You what? You paraded around in that nothing thing you call a bathing suit? Can't you find anything better to do with your time?"

"It was for charity, Dad. The proceeds go to help people who need help, that's all."

"Well, just so it doesn't become a habit."

He kissed her.

She went up to her room to get ready for a date. The dress she chose was a soft, two-piece burgundy with a narrow white check. The skirt had the new feminine fullness that was coming into style now after years of mini-skirts. Her dad would like it, she thought, smiling. Around her neck she tied a sheer, white scarf that had a scalloped burgundy edge. From her collection of jewelry she chose gold earrings and bracelet. She finished with a soft spray of Joy.

The day was gently warm, early summer. The date was for the afternoon and early evening. A drive into Denver, and then dinner at a good restaurant, and possibly a movie. The boy was someone she'd gone to school with.

She went down the stairs, one hand on the banister, and was halfway down when she saw the man standing motionless in the foyer below. He was looking up at her. She stopped, became as motionless as he. A dream, intruding into reality of the average day. Someone who had been out of her life for over three years.

She laughed joyishly and started running down the stairs. "Dale! Dale Larson!" Laughing, close to tears, she flung herself into his arms. He seemed pleasantly startled, and his arms closed tightly and instinctively about her. "Dale, I didn't know you were home. When did you come back?"

She tipped her head back and looked up at him, and without answering her question he lowered his face to hers and kissed her.

It was, in a way, her first kiss. What others there had been, from the boys she had dated, became nothing in comparison. Her first real kiss. Her first love.

And her last love.

She had no premonition of the horror that would enter her life in the shape of Gladys Evelyn Swartz.

CHAPTER 1

G ladys. Gladys Evelyn Swartz.

She hated her name. It was a name that a mother would give the baby daughter she secretly disliked, as if she knew the daughter would never grow up to be like her other daughters. As if she already knew this third child, this unwanted child, would wander out from under her feet and onto the long back stairs that clung to the back of the tall apartment house like a loosely attached branch of ivy to fall screaming down those steps. As if she already knew it would then turn into a sickly child, a whining thing who would succumb to diseases, whose bones would grow twisting like the ivy vine stairway, never straight, never strong; whose face could be as ugly as the name.

She didn't bother with makeup, Gladys Evelyn Swartz. It was hard enough to look at herself long enough to see that her hair was neat and her collar lay flat. The hatred for what she saw in the mirror curled in her throat and stomach like an over-ripe snake, and she had to turn away before she was sick again. Mama grew tired of coming to the bathroom after all these years and asking, "Gladys are you sick again?" Mama never tried to be solicitous and loving, and Gladys could hear the weariness in her voice and see the blankness in her eyes. And

Gladys hated Mama sometimes because it was from her body, and her not caring, that her own existence had come.

Often Gladys closed her eyes and wondered how it would feel to open them and look into the mirror to find a face and figure of beauty beyond belief; to know that she had simply awakened from a nightmare of loneliness and ugliness, that life had never been that way for her. With her eyes closed against the cruel reality of life she felt the strength and power of desire that came near to frightening her, as if it could grow to possess a life of its own.

But then many things frightened her when she finally looked upon life as it was. Her own hatred of what she *was* frightened her. People frightened her, a crust of fear around an unspoken need.

And so she was sick again. Deep down sick.

But Gladys kept her sicknesses to herself now.

She couldn't reach out to an unwilling mother anymore and cry wet, ugly tears and whine at her, "Mama, I feel sick." Actually she was pleading, "Mama, love me the way I am." There had come the time when she had to grow up, and even go out into the world and take a job.

An ugly job, of course. What else for an ugly person?

She got her mind off herself and began to hunt up the paraphernalia she carried along. Her name tag and number pinned to her blouse. Necessary to get into the factory, even after fifteen years. As if no one ever knew you. And why should they, when over a thousand women worked there? Of course she was easily distinguished from all others because she was the only one whose legs hadn't grown straight, whose spine was twisted and shortened. Sometimes, on those days when she despised herself most, she thought herself hunch-backed. Or nearly so. Really, she was lucky to have the job at all.

Her purse, too. With tissues because she had a head cold as usual. One doctor had said she must be allergic to something. He didn't seem interested. Another said she simply was susceptible. Disease prone. He was even less interested.

Gladys wasn't interested either. Just get life over, and done with.

And then what? When she thought of what came afterwards she

was afraid again because of the rise of something within herself. The terrible, terrible power of desire to be more than she had ever been.

As if she could be if she dared try.

But that was the dream and this was life, and she had to get on to work because, as Mama said, she was lucky to have the job at all.

In the dark and dreary kitchen her lunch waited in a brown paper sack. A thick sandwich. Potato chips. Cookies. She didn't have to watch her waistline because there was no waistline to watch. It was lost somewhere in the twist of her bones.

"Goodbye, Mama," she said.

"Goodbye, Gladys." She didn't look around. She was busy frying eggs for breakfast for two.

Gladys never said goodbye to her papa, because he never got up until the breakfast was on the table.

The day was cold, and the bus late. Gladys waited on the corner, her neck drawn down into her heavy, knitted scarf, and watched the cars go by. People intent on getting to work. Old people, young people, all normal. Cars of good-looking young men. Laughing, talking. Never giving her a second glance. Never knowing the yearnings that trembled, shrunken somewhere, in the back of her heart.

In all her life she had seldom had a second glance from a man unless he looked again to make sure he had seen what he thought he had seen—a dwarfed hunchback with a face so ugly it made you sick to your stomach.

Was it really that way, or did she only feel it was? Sometimes a faint surge of hope made her wonder.

She didn't care. She hated men anyway. Only in her most private dreams did she not hate them. Only when she was someone else and could be desired by them.

A thick strand of hair blew across her mouth, and she spit it away, but her eyes caught the glimmer of old gold, of silken heaviness. For a moment she saw it was beautiful hair and she remembered something from out of her past. Someone's hand had once tangled gently in her hair. She jerked away even then, startled, immediately on the defensive. "*What are you doing?*" She looked up into dark brown eyes, familiar eyes that belonged to a boy with whom she had gone through school. Familiar eyes, familiar face. But a stranger as they all were.

"It's such perfect hair," he'd said. "Gladys, would you be my girl? Would you let me touch your hair, hold your hand? Gladys?"

She backed away from him. Horrified, trembling. She had thought him as normal as the rest. But if he wanted to date *her*, there had to be something wrong with him. Without answering his question she hurried away. At the end of the block she looked back and the expression on his face revealed his hurt.

Years later she heard he was married and had two children. And now she hardly ever thought of him.

The bus came and she had to stand up all the way, hanging on to the back of a seat because she wasn't tall enough to comfortably reach the strap. A man with pity in his eyes reluctantly half rose and said, "Would you like to—"

"No, thank you." She turned her back, saving him the trouble of finishing what he had started to say; telling herself not to fall in love with a stranger who had pity in his eyes, who had only been trying to give a handicapped person a place to sit.

Other people crowded in at the next stop and she was lost from sight among them. For miles then she stared at the bottom button on a woman's coat.

At the factory she clocked in, moving slowly forward in the long row of workers and again she felt as if she might suddenly vomit. But this time it wasn't the hatred of the face in her mirror. It was the old, old fear of being away from home and the security she sought there. But then the feeling passed and her hands stopped trembling when she reached her table on the production line. The racket of the machines drowned out everything, locked her away from the people around her.

A bolt here, and a bolt there. A bolt here, and a bolt there. All day, all year. And all the rest of her life until she was sixty-five.

She counted. One, two. One, two. Thirty-three from sixty-five leaves thirty-two. Thirty-two years to put one bolt here, and another there. Thirty-two years.

What then? Sit all day in the tavern under her house and drink beers in the back booth? Read the novels she hid under her mattress?

At noon she ate. Among hundreds of women who didn't know her because they were wrapped up in their own worlds. She didn't know them either. Only faces. Average faces. Not bad faces.

At three-thirty a whistle blew and she fell into the long line of workers headed for home. In front of her a man walked. He had a nice build, and although she couldn't see his face she knew he was young. She wanted to touch him, to feel, for once in her life, the ribs of a male under her fingers. Someone behind her moved forward, shoving, and she was knocked against the young man, but only her shoulder touched him. For one moment he glanced back, and he smiled and started to say something, but she quickly lowered her face.

After that she was careful to keep more distance between them. When he reached up to slip his card into the clock-out machine she noticed he wore a wedding ring. She could imagine him going home, shoving the door shut with his foot and taking his bride in his arms right there in the hall. Taking her down on the floor. Taking off her clothes, and his, and—

"Hurry up, will you? You asleep or something?" the woman behind her said sharply.

Nervously Gladys grabbed her card and shoved it into the slot and pushed it down. Her hand trembled when she returned the card to the place where it had been for so many years.

She hurried out then, her face down against the cold and against the people. The bar—all she wanted now was the privacy of the back booth in the bar, where she could drink her beers and read the novel in her purse.

The bus stopped one block from the tavern which was under the apartment house where she had lived all her life. The wind blew straight down the street bringing with it needles of hard snow and ice. It struck her face, stung and melted and wet her scarf. She hurried as fast as she could, knocked about by taller people who didn't see her in time to avoid her. For protection she walked as close to the line of buildings as she could get.

The door into the tavern brought her first sense of security since she had left home that morning. First the darkness that kept out the reality of daylight and life, then the warmth that caused her to shiver under her coat as she began to relax.

"Good evening, Gladys," the bartender said as she went by.

She nodded, but she didn't speak. Eyes that belonged to people sitting at the nearly vacant bar followed her, and she wished she had the nerve to tell the bartender to stop speaking to her please, to leave her alone, not draw attention to her.

The back booth was empty as always except for the bartender's few papers. Sometimes she suspected he kept them there only to reserve it for her, but she would never ask. She only knew that he brought her beer and gathered up the papers when she sat down. He didn't have to ask what she wanted. He knew. He would talk a little, always about the weather, but he never paused in his work. He left the beer, took her change, and went back to his more talkative customers. When she finished the beer she pushed the bottle out where he could see it. That was the signal for another beer. Drunk quickly and in silence, her tired head resting against the high back of the ancient booth, her aching eyes closed.

Too tired to read the novel tonight. Later, when she was in bed with her door closed against her parents. Later.

She thought of the man who was in line ahead of her when they clocked out. She had never seen him before. It didn't matter. His wife —what would his wife look like? Would they be making love now, having sex, rubbing naked belly against soft breasts, teasing, getting ready before he penetrated her? A lovely girl she must be, slender and desirable. So desirable that he would want her naked all evening. So desirable they wouldn't even eat. Not until much, much later, after the fourth or fifth time.

Then tomorrow after her husband was gone she would be wearing a robe and nothing else, when the man came to check the meter she would walk ahead of him. He wouldn't be able to resist the movement of her hips and he would take her clothes off too, and his own, and they would spend an hour or more on the floor. Doing it over and over again.

Just like her favorite novels.

He would ask her name and she would tell him it was Gladys...

yes, Gladys. In a low and sexy voice. He would ask her if she had a lot of men and she would have to say yes, because all men desired Gladys.

All men.

"Another beer?" the voice said.

Gladys jumped, coming awake. She saw the bartender above her and shook her head.

"You must be extra tired this evening," he said and took her empty glass, wiping up the rings of moisture with a wrinkled towel.

She nodded her answer and began sliding out of the booth.

Out again into the cold, this time going through the back door so convenient to the booth, so close to the steep stairs that hung crookedly from the back of the building and reached upward toward the falling snow.

Her gloved hand clung in desperate fear to the handrail that had splinters. And icicles. She couldn't remember the day she had taken the fall down those long stairs, that had turned her from a quite pretty baby into a mass of broken bones. Only the fear remained now, not the memory. But a terrible anger inside her cried *why didn't you watch me, Mama?* And a deeper, even more terrible fear answered, *how did you get out to the top of the open stairway at the age of six months, how did it happen at all...*

It was a question she was afraid to answer. Perhaps her mother had hoped for something different from the fall.

No, that wasn't true! Her mother had loved her once. Before she became a burden. She had to believe that. She had to repeat it until she believed it. Her mother had loved her. She had loved her. She loved her.

"Hello, Mama," she said when she entered the kitchen and her mama grunted but didn't look at her.

Dinner as usual. Hamburgers tonight, with a mother and a father who were to weary to talk, had nothing to talk about. How was your day, they finally asked. Same as always.

A woman shoved me into a man. People stared at me on the sidewalk. No comment.

After supper, the television. But thinking that later, when she would be alone in her room, a new paperback novel about sex. Smuggled in under her coat like illegal pornography. Another paperback she had picked up by accident, by impulse really, was something about occult power. About making your dreams come true. But she would only glance at it tonight and lay it aside, because it was the sex novel she wanted to read. The one that would say again and again, they all did, that men had big things and women soft things to put them in. That men desired all women and took anyone who spread her legs.

What would the bartender do if one day as he brought her beer to the secluded back booth, she should open her coat, spread her legs and say here, here it is soft and wanting, wanting, wanting...

The books lied, she knew; men didn't desire all women. And men loved very few.

Then something unusual broke into the television commercial. A knock on the door, then Marian, the eldest of the three daughters, came in bringing a snowflake in her dark hair. She was tall, self-confident. Gladys envied her almost as much as she hated herself.

Mama's eyes were glowing now with pride in her first-born, with happiness that Marian had come over.

Marian was always laughing, it seemed, even when she was scolding. "Come on, get your coats on. Don't you remember this is the dress review of the 4-H girls? It starts at seven."

"Oh yes!" Mama hurried to get her coat, but Gladys didn't move.

She was tired to the depths of her existence. They didn't want her. She would only slow them down, humiliate them because strangers stared. She wished only to hide in her room and read. Even the presence of Marian made her uncomfortable and self-conscious. Too much aware of the difference between them, of her deformation, of Marian's perfection.

Marian wouldn't let her rest. "Come on, Gladys. Cinthy will be hurt if you don't come too. Only Grandpa is excused because this is a girl thing." She went to the closet and brought Gladys's coat. "Come on now, we can't be late. Cinthy went over with Mrs. Johnson."

"I'm not going, I'm tired," Gladys said. Why go watch Cinthy parade around? Slender, straight.

Hell with it. She knew from experience that her presence humiliated Cinthy. The girl didn't want anyone to know Gladys was her aunt.

"Come on. I drove forty miles to bring you."

"It's snowing."

"Only a little. Not enough to hurt you. The roads are safe, and I'm a good night driver."

Mama paused, the fun gone out of her face. "She does have a head cold, Marian, and she has to get up early. Maybe she ought to stay home."

Gladys could see Mama didn't want her, and she began to change her mind against her own will. A childish thing inside her said, *Take me too, Mama. Want me too, don't leave me behind. Include me in the family.*

"The car is warm," Marian answered. "I won't take no for an answer."

Sometimes there was no winning with Marian, anyway. So Gladys got up and allowed herself to be dressed to go out with coat and scarf, and gloves and overshoes. All the while Marian chatted, telling of her day running her four bedroom split-level at the edge of a suburb in the valley. Of getting her husband and two rowdy sons settled before she could take off to pick up her mother and sister.

Gladys hated hearing it, hated the envy that rose in her. Marian always tried to make it sound as if it weren't so great being so all-American normal.

Gladys envied her with a passion. And she envied her other sister, Clarissa, even more; she, with her executive secretary's job, and her handsome husband, and her apartment and new car. And the way Mama's eyes lighted when she came home looking like something out of a glamour magazine.

Gladys didn't want to go to the dress review and watch a bunch of 4-H girls show off things they had made. The drive out to Marian's suburban community was too long. The falling snow bothered her, reflecting lights from too many other cars, too much traffic. And she felt so out of place and unwanted sitting alone in the back seat of Marian's big car, with Marian and Mama chatting so happily in the front seat, never including her. Not ever really including her. Why did Marian insist she come along? Well, Marian prided herself on being a

Christian, a good member of the church. That was the only answer Gladys could find. Then, getting into the big, barny building was a nuisance. Not for someone tall, perhaps; as tall as Marian and Mama.

They went ahead of her, talking, never glancing back; never knowing the effort short, twisted legs required to keep up. Nor the sick thud of her heart when people looked at her.

Finally though, Gladys could sink onto a hard, metal chair near the platform that ran out into the middle of the large building.

Marian leaned forward and looked around Mama at Gladys. "Are you comfortable? Can you see? We were lucky to go so close."

She didn't wait for an answer, so Gladys didn't bother to think of one. That was the way it had always been—as if she weren't really a part of anything.

She only half looked at the girls as they began to appear. Cinthy came out wearing a pantsuit that Mama nearly cried over. "And to think she made it herself!"

Gladys couldn't see anything so great about it.

Marian was whispering loudly, "Of course they've done it all themselves. Cinthy is becoming a very good seamstress. The 4-H clubs are such a good thing."

Why shouldn't she be a good seamstress? No fitting problem, Gladys muttered under her breath. She envied Cinthy too. They were all so much alike, those girls, those teenagers, with young waistlines and lovely legs. Long hair, smiling lips. Cinthy smiled at her mother and her grandmother, but her glance passed over Gladys as if she didn't know her. She walked on, turning and passing like someone competing for Miss America, around the long platform.

Suddenly then Gladys' eyes found, like a star among planets, a face that made her stare. Eyes dark and shining lashes so long and thick they were clearly seen even when the girl was still at the far end of the platform, a perfect skin that contrasted softly with the long, nearly black hair. Every feature shaped and arranged so that the effect was breathtaking, put together in a way that made Gladys think swiftly, oh God, she's so beautiful. And then the body, young, slender but seductively curved, clothed in a short plain dress with a flippy skirt that bounced against her firm bottom as she walked. Of course, every movement as graceful as a young wild thing facing a fresh, clean wind. Gladys stared at her, watching her come closer.

Oh God, to be like her...

She felt Mama lean toward Marian and then heard her say, "What a pretty girl!"

Marian ceased her constant jabbering to snort daintily. Gladys wondered what the snort could mean. Was it contempt or jealousy?

"Why shouldn't she be?" Marian hissed in a loud whisper. "Her daddy's the richest farmer in this *and* the next county." Then she went on, her tone normal, giving information about other girls.

So it was jealousy, Gladys thought with a secret smile. So Marian wasn't immune after all. Good. It was good to know that about Marian. It was good to know that other people at times felt inadequate and awkward and ugly. But what had the girl's daddy's money to do with the perfect, natural beauty of the girl? Gladys felt like laughing. At least, now, she didn't feel that her own emotions were as strange and out of proportion as her body.

She watched the girl pivot at the end of the platform, never faltering as others did, never losing her poise, her grace, the natural perfection of herself. She was so superior to the others; yet her actions, her smile, her eyes showed her to be sweetly unaware of the effect she had on everyone.

Was she unaware of her extraordinary beauty?

Cinthy moving near her on the other side of the platform, looked pimply and too pink. Drab. As they all suddenly did.

Gladys watched the girl dreamily, seeing Marian's point. It would be lovely to be both beautiful and rich. Yes, lovely.

The dress review ended sometime during Gladys's wistful daydreaming, and the crowded building became an ant hill of activity as people moved about to leave. Gladys rose to stand close to her mother and sister, to make sure she didn't get lost in the crowd.

A girl came shoving through, and Gladys recognized the voice before she saw the face. Cinthy. Crying eagerly for attention from her mother.

"Mom, hey Mom! You'll never guess! We're invited to go along with the 4-H girls to a country club the O'Brions belong to."

Marian seemed inordinately awed. "The O'Brions? They invited us?"

"Come on, hurry, so we can follow the other cars. The O'Brions are entertaining all the 4-H girls and their families. Isn't that grand?"

Gladys lost the rest of the exchange in her concentration to keep up, to hurry along with the others, out the door and around to the car.

Cinthy rode with them on the way to the club, as full of jabbers as her mother. She sat forward on the back seat, her arms on the top of the front seat behind Marian's head. Names flew. Who won ribbons, and who didn't, and why.

Gladys spoke up, loudly, to get attention. So hard to do in her family.

"What did the rich girl get for her dress? It was cute."

A moment of silence then as Cinthy turned her head and glared at Gladys. Then with a snort not so dainty as Marian's had been, "You mean Peri Lee O'Brion? And don't say O-bry-on either; it's O'bree- on. With the accent on the *on*!"

Such contempt in the voice, Gladys thought with a wicked little chuckle bubbling inside her; such envy behind the contempt. So no one was immune. What of Peri Lee O'Brion herself? Of course she would be. You couldn't envy something that didn't exist, a beauty greater than her own.

Mama spoke, meekly. For Mama. "She's a pretty girl."

"Her daddy's rich," Cinthy snapped, jerking her head forward. "So of course *she'd* win a blue ribbon!"

But Gladys said, rubbing it in, enjoying for a moment that other people might feel inferior as well as she, "Not pretty. Beautiful. I've never seen a picture to compare with her. And it doesn't have anything to do with how much money her daddy's got."

She expected, and wanted, a dispute; but got none. The car moved through the night in silence, part of a long line of other cars with the same destination. Marian began to talk again.

But not about Peri Lee O'Brion.

They drove into a paved parking lot and stopped beneath the drooping branches of a Colorado Blue Spruce. The center portion of the club was brightly lighted; the doorway wide, arched, and welcoming. The room they entered was almost as large as the auditorium where the dress review had been held, but the resemblance ended with size. From the cathedral ceiling hung chandeliers that dazzled Gladys. Long, white-clothed tables were filled with refreshments. Thickly carpeted floors muffled footsteps.

When Gladys paused, gaping at the luxuries of the club, she found herself surrounded by strangers; standing in groups, laughing, talking, eating tiny sandwiches and drinking cups of punch. Marian, Mama and Cinthy had disappeared somewhere in the crowded hall.

Gladys pushed and wound her way to the hall to stand beneath a painting of mountains and deer.

She kept her eye on the door through which they had entered to make sure she wouldn't be forgotten and left behind.

She didn't notice the girl until she spoke.

"Hello there. Wouldn't you like something to eat and drink? I've brought you a sandwich and a cup of punch. I saw you standing here all alone."

Gladys looked up into the eyes of Peri Lee O'Brion, and found herself speechless. The girl was even more striking at close range, utterly and totally perfect. Gladys took the offering and smiled her thanks.

"You must be one of the girls' sisters," Peri Lee O'Brion said.

"No, an aunt," Gladys answered, surprised at her own voice coming so naturally from her constricted throat. Then, in fear the girl might leave, she said, "Congratulations. Your dress was the prettiest."

"Oh how nice of you. I like to sew, sometimes," she laughed at herself. "I'm not terribly consistent with my activities. Do you sew?"

"No. I'm afraid I don't have anything to sew for." She surprised herself again by giving a significant glance down at her body. For the first time in her life she had drawn attention to herself. Was it because the girl had made her feel normal and natural?

"Oh, of course you do," Peri Lee said. "You should try dressmaking. It can be a wonderful hobby and—"

A young voice called insistently, "Peri Lee! Come, I want you to meet someone."

Peri Lee glanced over her shoulder, then she touched Gladys's arm gently. "Excuse me, please. I think I'd better move around a little. Perhaps I'll see you later."

Gladys returned the girl's small wave and her smile, then watched her until she was out of sight in the crowd.

She ate the sandwich, drank the punch, and placed the empty cup on a table.

"What are you standing here grinning about?" another voice inquired, breaking harshly into her feelings of pleasure; of strange, glowing, quiet happiness. She looked wordlessly up into the face of her sister. "We're ready to go, Gladys."

"So soon?'

"I have a long way to drive, you know. I went forty miles out of my way to get you and Mama. And I've been looking all over for you. Do come on, Gladys."

She turned and walked toward the door with quick, snobbish steps, reflecting the irritation which had been in her voice. Mama and Cinthy were already waiting in the car. Cinthy made room for Gladys in the back seat in silence.

Gladys looked out the window at the passing night scene but saw instead the face of the girl called Peri Lee, and the smile that now brought an aching to her heart. She forgot the others, forgot to needle them at their sore spot. For the first time in her life her thoughts centered on another person. Then moved so entirely to that other person that when at last she escaped Marian and Cinthy, and the third-floor apartment was quiet except for the movements of her mama getting ready for bed in the next room, when in her warm flannel gown she had crawled into the security of her own bed, she had lost all desire to open the new novel.

It, and the other new paperback, lay on the blanket beside her, untouched except for the golden spread of light from her bedside lamp. She stared at the wall not far from the foot of her bed, and saw the face of the girl in the vague tracings of old wallpaper designs.

Peri Lee O'Brion.

A beautiful name. Something about it as poetic and lovely and unearthly as the girl to whom it belonged. Pronounced right, it had a rhythm like soft music.

Unearthly.

Gladys glanced down at the unopened books on the bed beside her; a soft, yearning sigh moving out from the depths of all that she wished to be and never could. The title on the books blurred, shapeless, then suddenly one of them took form as if it came alive before her. YOUR OTHER SELVES.

Your other selves?

Gladys picked up the book and turned it over to read the smaller print on the back. *Know your powers, your many existences. Learn astral projection, have out-of-body experiences at your will. Learn that possession of another's body is possible. Learn that no one is confined to his physical existence.*

Just a gimmick to sell a book, that was all, reason told Gladys. She didn't believe in things like that. She didn't even know why she had bought the book.

Her hands turned the small paperback, not throwing it down, feeling it, yet not opening it. These things—another part of her mind asked—all these things—could they be possible? She had picked up the small, cheap book from the back of the store out of simple impulse. Something she had never done before. Now she was half afraid to read it, but read it she must, because it might hold the secret of being and not being. Perhaps somewhere, someone, whose name meant nothing to her had stumbled across the secret that was unknown in the daily world of hunting, searching, grubbing for the greedy gut and dissatisfied mind.

Her hands trembled slightly as she opened the book, her breath held against fear of disappointment, smothered under a heart that pounded for a mystical revelation of some kind— any kind.

The words of the first sentence struck her consciousness as if they had been thrown onto a lighted screen. *You can be anything or anyone you want to be.*

She placed one stubby hand flat on the opened book, covering it, closing her eyes and seeing again the face and figure of Peri Lee O'Brion. Softly she whispered, "If it were only true. Let it be true."

For a while she sat with her eyes closed, her hand on the book, then eagerly and impatiently she began to read.

After several quickly read pages she began to skip through, her hopes falling. It sounded like some kind of ancient foolishness to her. To bring about the love of someone, a man especially, one was supposed to boil a hummingbird's tongue in cat blood and a mixture of other stuff that began to make her sick. Gladys closed the book in disgust.

She looked at the wall and saw the ugly and faded paper. She had been to church a few times and found no comfort there. The great mystery and love of God that the preacher cried about seemed beyond her. She was too crushed by the lack of love of humanity.

Was there no way out?

She sighed and started to lay the book aside and go back to her dream world of stories, but found herself opening the book again, near the middle.

Astral body. *The astral body is capable of separating itself from the physical body and traveling about, passing through walls, ceilings and other solid obstructions. It is also said to survive death, when it leaves the physical body. It exists in what is called the astral plane, which includes the normal, everyday world but extends beyond it.*

She bent closer and began to read faster, her breath suspended for a moment.

It was possible to leave the body and travel free by lying still, by concentrating heavily, by extreme effort of will.

She read the chapter hastily and then returned to read it slowly, letting every word become absorbed by her mind. Other people had done it, so the book said; therefore, so could she.

She laid the book aside once again and made herself as comfortable as possible in the bed so that her mind would not be distracted by her body.

She closed her eyes then and followed the suggestions of total relaxation; then imagining herself rising from her own body to stand straight and tall on the floor at the foot of her bed. Once standing she could rise through any obstacle and immediately be where she wanted to be. Only of that goal was she positive: Peri Lee. She wanted to travel each night at the side of Peri Lee as she went through her dates.

Her men would be handsome. None other would have the courage to ask for a date. And they probably wouldn't go anywhere but to his apartment, where he would make love to her. He would be too jealous to take her out. But after a few dates with him Gladys, or Peri Lee, was bored. So there would have to be different men every night, and finally dancing, driving, eating out. Peri Lee would never have to worry about gaining weight and losing her figure, and then going home to make love. To his apartment. *Their* apartments. They would all be in love with her, how could they not be? From among them she would choose a husband...maybe. But not for a long time. She would still be beautiful in another ten years. Would she be twenty-seven then, or twenty-eight perhaps?

Ten years in which to be unforgettably perfect. And then to mature into a body ripe, rich and sexy.

How would she feel if she were Peri Lee O'Brion, living in a bedroom of rich colors and many square yards of soft carpet, rising from a great bed every morning to look at that face in the mirror? Perhaps then to shower in her private bath and then dress her perfect body in things smooth and soft.

When Gladys woke in the morning she felt oddly happy and elated. For a moment she couldn't remember why. Then with the same suddenness as before, she saw the face again.

Gladys grunted and laughed shortly. Her astral projection attempt had turned to a sound sleep. And then only a dream. A daydream, even. And she had felt happiness from it? From imagining that she was someone else?

She began to prepare for the day, and when she looked into her mirror to brush her hair she hardly saw herself.

At work it was the same. One, two. One, two. And her mind was free to go, to wander; to see Peri Lee O'Brion going through summer vacation, swimming, dancing, laughing her beautiful laugh, tossing her dark hair, never losing control of her ivory-tan complexion, never needing lipstick for the redness of her full, sharply cut lips. And boys everywhere.

Boys, boys, boys.

Men.

A kiss by a private pool, and laughter as she broke away...

That night again, and the next, Gladys attempted to leave her body by astral projection. On the third night she gave up and sat in her bed reading the book with her lips curled in contempt. If astral projection were possible at all she was not capable of it. Just as she had been denied capabilities in all other things, she was even denied such a harmless escape as that?

Her anger turned to a deep yearning sadness as she read, tears filled her eyes, and she leaned her head back against the bed post. Dear God, no escape, no escape at all.

She looked through the wavy prison of her tears at the book in which she had unaccountably put her hopes these past few nights. She was now ready to lay it aside forever, unfinished. What good would it be to finish reading it? As she had feared it was only ancient superstition. Other people's long dead hopes buried beneath years of trying to find magic in the hard world of reality.

Suicide...the word stood out on the page, brought to her by her own tears and narrowed vision. And then... *freedom by suicide if all else fails and there is a desire so strong that...* Gladys wiped her eyes on the back of one hand and bent closer to the book. She read quickly, skipping what didn't look important, receiving a gist of what the book said in two short paragraphs that looked as though they had been thrown in by accident.

Suicide that must not be suicide. *How?* Accidental death, because death is the ultimate freedom. Death releases the astral body to take any form, if so wished, in the possession of another body.

And that was all?

Gladys could have cried again, because that was all she could find. In italics the book said: *...the important thing about this is that the death must be accidental, must not seem like suicide...*

Hands shaking with anxiety she searched the book for a part about possession. Once one was free in death, how did possession take place?

Finally, she found it. *It is said that prior to possession, the one to be possessed must be kept constantly on the mind, concentrated upon; lived in, as it were, until the day that freedom is gained. Then the spirit may go to its destination and take its place in the mind of the possessed, at which time the possessed goes into a kind of comatose condition and the possessor has full control of the body and mind.*

Gladys dropped the book and stared at the wall in front of her. She murmured aloud, "Impossible. It can't be possible." But what if it were? *What had she to lose?*

She went to work the next morning thinking of it, and always she came back to the thought, what have I to lose? Life was nothing to her as it was. She had never been anything but lost, lonely, unhappy. She had never done anything but hide from the eyes of others, so that she was even afraid to go to the park where so many people gathered. She had nothing to look forward to anyway but release from the pain and drudgery of her life. But an accidental death? She was afraid.

Afraid of what? Either she would be free—or her life would be ended in an endless pool of blackness that would close out everything.

It was on a very cold day when the snow fell heavily, blowing hard against her face as she fought the drifts to find the bus stop on her way to work, that she finally decided to take possession of the body of Peri Lee. She decided on death that looked accidental, and began to prepare for it by concentrating on the face of Peri Lee. The other part, the death part, she pushed aside with a half-hope, half-fear that it would come with no help on her part.

There were many ways it could happen. The plant could blow up. But that would kill hundreds of people who didn't want to die. People who looked forward to paychecks so that they could feed and care for families they loved. People who looked forward to paid vacations, short though they were. No, the plant must not blow up.

The bus could be struck by a train as it crossed the tracks. But no, that would kill others too. Then she must go alone, on this private trip through death.

Gladys moved through the days, concentrating on Peri Lee, learning from Cinthy the approximate location of the rich farm that was Peri Lee's home. She was trying to live in Peri Lee, in her imagination. To become Peri Lee.

She looked through eyes dreamily shadowed by heavy, curled,

black lashes; and winter became spring and flowering trees began to bloom.

And instead of hiding in the back booth of the tavern to drink beer, Gladys began to take walks on her day off.

She went down the street, her head high, feeling the spring breeze and knowing there was no description better than soft for a breeze such as this one, because she was no longer Gladys. She was Peri Lee.

In her mind she went shopping with her. Buying dresses. Brief bikinis too, even though they were going out of style now. Tonight she would dress up and go dancing with another new date, and he would make love to her. His mouth would roam her body in his extreme desire and she would tease and pull away; but then she would have to give in to her own passion, her own need for his body.

Gladys turned to cross the street and someone yelled. She stopped just long enough to see that she was about to step in front of a huge truck whose brakes screamed and smoked in an attempt to stop. Then she remembered, and knew this was her chance. Finally, it had come, and she was ready.

She kept walking as if she hadn't heard the man shout for her to stop.

CHAPTER 2

Peri Lee sang as she crossed the alfalfa field, a soft crooning in a voice that was not great at all, but true in pitch. Dale liked it, he said. But then Dale would have said that even if she hadn't been able to carry a tune at all.

Ahead of her bounded her dog; a chunky little brown fellow with short legs, funny ears that looked like a collie's, and then dropped like a cocker spaniel's. His short, stubby legs suggested cocker spaniel blood too, but his long body definitely was dachshund. Peri Lee's daddy, Harry O'Brion, had brought him to her five years ago from the local animal shelter. A tiny, scared puppy with big sad eyes.

She laughed as the dog yelped with delight and took after a jack rabbit. He never caught one. He had never caught one in his life. But he would run until he was so hot and tired he would have to haul himself to the nearest irrigation ditch and fall in to cool off.

Beyond the field, and the row of tall and stately Lombardy poplars that separated her father's farm from Dale's farm, she saw a familiar blue and white pickup, and her laughter died to a smile. Soft and secret. She ceased to watch the dog.

She touched her fingers to her lips, and waited. Then she saw him wave, and drive into the narrow road that ran alongside the fence. A pocket of dust billowed out behind the pickup like a parachute.

She began to run, but by the time she reached the fence he had already gotten out of his truck, and vaulted the fence to meet her on the O'Brion land. Laughing, she held her arms high and he caught her around the waist. He lifted her so that her feet dangled above ground and her face was slightly above his own height of six-two. She looked down into his eyes, and neither of them spoke. Gently, though still holding her tightly against him, he lowered her until her toes touched the ground. His lips met hers lightly, and nuzzled, parting hers, and then his mouth took possession for a long and breathless moment.

The thrill had begun the moment she saw his truck. It had been that way, even back in the days when instead of a truck he rode a bicycle. Dale Larson. Always it had been Dale, and always it would be.

When he released her, holding her hand instead of her body, she looked back toward the house.

He read her thoughts. "He didn't see. I met him and your new hired man about thirty minutes ago. They were headed north."

He looked amused, but she felt a flush of embarrassment, and lowered her eyes.

Dale said, "He should know my intentions are honorable. I asked him once if he'd let you marry me, you know."

Her eyes opened wide in surprise. "No. When?"

"Well, that was the year you did that cute little dance in the Christmas play."

She laughed, tipping her head back to look at the sky. "Oh Dale. What was I? Eight?"

"The point was, I was already fourteen and I knew the girl I wanted to marry when she grew up. I considered myself pretty well grown."

She stopped laughing, and her eyes looked into his. He always halted and sobered whenever her eyes met his. "I love you, Dale," she whispered.

"Peri Lee." He bent to kiss her, lightly again, whispering against her lips. "I love you. What's really holding a formal announcement back? I want everyone to know you're my girl. And always will be."

"They know," she said. They began to walk, slowly, hands clasped and swinging between them. "When my birthday comes, maybe. At eighteen maybe I won't be considered so much a baby. A teenager. Or perhaps we should wait until Christmas, and let me go to college one year. To please the folks. Give Daddy another six months to get used to us, together."

"Speaking of birthdays," he said in a lighter tone, "what would you like most to do? That's next Tuesday, isn't it?"

"You've forgotten already!" she teased, smiling, knowing he had never forgotten, and never would forget. "What will you be like when we come to anniversaries?'

"I promise to write it down, for fifty years ahead so that I can keep it in mind."

She smiled up at him, and he stopped their walk to interrupt her with another kiss.

A shower of water struck them and they turned to see the dog, his eyes squeezed shut, shaking his soaked coat.

"Oh, Butchy!" Peri Lee cried. Laughing, they began to run again, through the field of green alfalfa, with the wet dog joyously at their heels.

They stopped at the fence, just across from the truck, and Butch stopped too. He squeezed shut his eyes and finished shaking the water from his cocker spaniel-collie-dachshund fur. When he had finished he laughed up at them in a silent, doggy laugh.

"See," said Dale. "Just as I thought. He did that all on purpose. Towels, that's what we are. Just canine towels."

"Love me, love my dog," Peri Lee replied lightly.

"I love him! I love him!" Dale held his hand up, swearing to it. He bent without touching her and kissed her cheek tenderly. Then, with one hand on a post, he vaulted the fence again and turned to look at her from across the wire. "When will I see you? Tonight?"

"Yes, if you want."

"If I want!" He went to his truck, and from there waved and said, "About seven?"

She nodded, and watched the truck leave and follow the long lane to the end of the field, then turn back west, toward the mountains, toward the cluster of trees and silos and barns where his home was. She couldn't see the house, shrouded by trees as it was, but she knew each square foot of it by heart, because it was there she would live. As soon as she thought her daddy could stand the thought of having his little girl get married, she would tell him that she really didn't want to go to college. She wanted to be Dale's wife, and have two children. Her mother would be more sensible about it, she was sure. Mother was allowing her to grow up, allowing her to make her own decisions even though she had stood carefully behind her to see that none of them were the wrong ones. It had all been done so subtly that Peri Lee hadn't even realized what her mother was doing, until recently. Now she knew she would bring up her own children the same way. With love.

She sat down in the alfalfa and put her arms around the neck of the dog. He licked her cheek, and she laughed and pushed his nose away.

"If you don't mind, Butchy, I'll live without your kisses. You just stand still and let me hug you." Then, feeling fourteen again, she got up to race him back across the field to her own house.

By the time she reached the driveway she was breathless, and feeling rather foolish. She slipped through the trees that lined the driveway, wondering if her mother or anyone had seen her running with Butch across the field, after standing by the fence letting Dale kiss her the way he had.

No one was in sight, so she sedately patted Butch's head, and they crossed the driveway side by side, walking. He stopped on the long, front porch and flattened out with his stomach against the floor, and she went into the house.

She went through the central hall and turned left into a room that jutted out from the rest of the house, surrounded on three sides by long windows and a patio door. It was her mother's favorite room and held comfortable, white wicker furniture, a virtual jungle of potted plants, and twelve tropical birds in large cages. They sang and chattered incessantly.

Her mother was not there. The needle work lay in her chair, recently put aside. Peri Lee went out onto the terrace beyond the patio doors, but instead of finding her mother she saw the men coming up from the graveled lot where the machine shop and parking space and buildings for farm trucks were located, among a dozen other buildings and barns.

She went to meet them. Her father and her older brother, Gene. Hamilton, who had been with them longer than she had and seemed like a dear old uncle; and the new hired man, Pete. She had noticed three things about the new man: He was short, dark, and bashful.

Pete's car, a souped-up, slick red thing with white racing stripes painted over the top length, was parked beside the bunkhouse, under a tree. When she came even with it her attention was suddenly drawn and held to a spot on its hood. A patch of red, about the size of a hand, on one of the white stripes.

She went over to look at it. Pete was so particular with his car he spent every free moment polishing and cleaning, or driving. To see a spot on it was like finding a spot on one of Bertha's plates at the table. Just not credible.

To her amazement it looked like blood. She touched the edge of it with a finger and saw that it was wet, and stained her finger red.

She stared at the blood and a feeling as if winter wind swept down from snow-shrouded mountains spread over her and into her mind and heart. All sunlight and happiness was blackened by the blanket of death. *Who had died?* Someone had died and she felt like running from the fear and despondency that it brought her. The fear grew and she held her hand away, staring at it but unable to find her voice to cry out against this strange emotion, this terror that was so new to her...

The men had reached her by then. Her brother, Gene, said, "What is it? What's wrong?"

She looked up and vaguely his face took familiar form above her. She looked at the others, seeing them staring at her, and gradually she came awake, back to reality. She looked around, saw the house, the buildings, the familiar. She pushed away the grip of unreality that had held her in its hands for a moment.

The blood on her finger was real. Something had dropped its life's blood on the car and the sorrow in her heart was the sorrow of sympathy, no longer of terror.

"I don't know. Pete, what's this on your car?"

Peri Lee stood back to let Pete and Gene look at it. The two older men looked over their shoulders.

"Looks like blood," Gene said.

Pete said nothing. Looking somewhat stunned, he merely peered down at it.

"That's what I thought," Peri Lee said. "But where did it come from? Is it a hand print?"

Gene looked up into the tree. "No. It looks as if it dripped down. Something up there is bleeding."

A touch of red on the ground, in the grass against the bunkhouse, caught Peri Lee's eyes. She rushed over to kneel and picked up in her hands a limp and dying cardinal redbird.

"Oh no," she murmured, pushing back tears she would have let flow freely ten years ago. "Gene, it's been shot! Who would do a thing like that?"

The bird gasped in her hands, limp, and she watched it as it died. She was hardly aware of the brief conversation that took place behind her.

"I thought I heard someone shooting," Hamilton said.

"Yeah," Harry agreed. "I saw the car. Out on the highway."

"Against the law to shoot from a car."

Gene said angrily, "Against the law to shoot song birds. But what the hell can you do about it when they shoot from the car and just keep on driving?"

Pete pulled a big handkerchief from his pocket and wiped away the blood on his car, then continued to rub the spot vigorously. "Some bastard out for kicks," he muttered, and then glanced sideways at Peri Lee.

But she paid him no attention. She sat on her heels, holding the dead bird in both hands and tried to hold back the tears. She didn't want to break down like a baby in front of everyone, but there was no room in her sheltered world for cruelty and death; those things she hadn't learned to face. She knew that she should search for and gain some kind of philosophy about the whole thing. The sight of a bird dying, shot by someone from a car just for the fun of shooting at a living, moving target, was too much. She felt her daddy's hand on the top of her head.

"Come on, Kitten, it's gone now. Bertha's got dinner on the table and she'll be yelling in a minute."

"I can't just leave him here," Peri Lee answered and looked up at her brother. "Gene?"

"Yeah," he said, understanding quickly her unspoken question. "You fellows go on. Peri Lee and I will bury the bird."

She looked at him gratefully. He had always helped her bury any dead pet, so that they had a virtual cemetery now, in a lovely little spot among a group of spruce trees at the back of the big lawn. Tiny grave markers listed each name and date of death, and, if possible, date of birth.

"What shall we name him?" she asked. "We can't just put him away with no name. A bird with no name."

"You choose his name, and I'll fix the cross tonight."

He still used the old wood burning set he had gotten for a Christmas when he was a small boy. While he went after the spade she looked at the bird. When he came back and they walked together to the pet cemetery she had made up her mind.

"He's a very young bird. And he's male. See his color? And he has a crest. Let's call him Timmy, because he's so young. Would that be too hard to carve?"

"No, it's good so far as I'm concerned, and I guess he won't care."

She lined the tiny grave with grass, made a bed for the body of the bird, and covered it with a layer of green grass. And then Gene carefully replaced the soil and patted the top smooth. "Done," he said. "Now we'd better go."

IT HAD TAKEN MUCH LONGER than it seemed and Peri Lee was surprised to see that Bertha and Rene, a school girl hired for the summer, were already clearing the table, leaving the food, served in bowls the old-style farm way for working men, and the two clean plates.

"Oh, Bertha, I'm sorry," Peri Lee said. "I didn't think we would be so long."

"That's all right," the cook-housekeeper answered. "Just set down there and eat before all the food is ice cold."

The men had gone again, to rest awhile in chairs on one of the terraces. Their voices came, faintly, through the open windows. But her mother was still at the table, sipping a glass of iced tea.

"Hello, darlings. I'm sorry to hear about the bird."

"I think," Gene said as he sat down, "that a gun should not only be registered, but the owner should have to pass a test on the proper use of one, plus a lesson in ecology."

The phone rang. Peri Lee got up to answer it, a yellow wall phone beside the door to the central hall. She talked for a moment, and then turned to her mother.

"It's about a bazaar at the church. They want to know if I would like to donate some clothes."

Her mother looked at her without answering, but a faint smile of amusement touched the corners of her lips and made her face even more beautiful.

Peri Lee filled in the pause. "Of course I could clean a lot of last year's things out of my closet. But then it would mean a new wardrobe."

"That's just what I was thinking. A shopping trip, sort of a two-way accomplishment, right?"

Peri Lee laughed. "Well. One *should* donate."

Her mother nodded her head, and Peri Lee turned back to the phone, her voice light again, happy with the anticipation of two things she enjoyed immensely: a church bazaar, and a shopping trip for new clothes.

They went to Denver for the clothes, an all-day shopping trip that included lunch at one of the best restaurants. They came home with the back seat of the car loaded. But the pleasure, the happiness Peri Lee had anticipated, was missing. She blamed her feelings on being tired from the trip, but it disturbed her so much on the way home that her mother noticed and asked, "Is something wrong, dear?"

"No, just tired," she said, and gave her mother a quick smile before she went back to gazing out the window at her side.

How could she tell her mother that the moment they entered the city limits of Denver she had suddenly been struck by the same coldness, the same fear and despondency, that she had felt for the first time in her life yesterday when she looked at the blood on her finger?

The blood! Of course, that was it.

She touched her forehead with her fingertips, sensing there was no logical reasoning to that at all. But it did have something to do with the blood obviously, because she had never felt that way before and hoped never to again. But she couldn't shake the feeling of oppression that was weighing her down, the sense of growing danger.

For the first time in her life she had not enjoyed a shopping trip. But she couldn't tell her mother that.

She was tired, that was all, just tired. All she needed was to go to bed earlier than usual. But she couldn't even remember if she had a date with Dale tonight, or any other appointment. She would have to check her appointment pad when she got home.

When she was alone in her room, surrounded by boxes of clothes that had to be put on hangers or in drawers, she sat down on the bed and looked at them.

Where was the enthusiasm that she usually felt for these things? She had a notion to call Rene to do the job for her, but she had never before done that. Rene would be busy now helping Bertha with the supper. Besides, she had always enjoyed taking care of her own room and her own clothes. Sometimes she sewed with more enthusiasm than she felt when shopping, but now she looked at the bulging paper bag of patterns, material, thread, zippers and buttons with a sigh that didn't seem to belong to her.

She looked up and saw her reflection in the long mirror that hung over the double dresser across the room and said aloud to it, "You're getting old. You just can't take it anymore." The laughter she attempted came out almost a sob and she flopped sideways onto the bed.

It would be good never to get up. To just lie here and rest forever. To close her eyes and sleep, sleep, sleep.

The door opened. A soft sound that brought her eyes open wide enough to see the black and grey lounging robe her mother was wearing. She tried to sit up, to be more natural so that her mother wouldn't start worrying about her, but gave it up and lay still.

The bed moved slightly as her mother sat down. Peri Lee felt the cool hand cover hers. It was a comforting touch. Filled with love and security.

"You *must* be tired," she said softly and a bit teasingly, "to leave your clothes in boxes while you rest."

Peri Lee smiled. "I have a right, you know. I'm almost eighteen now."

Her mother laughed. "Ah, old age is getting you?"

"I guess."

"Well, I have news for you dear. That part comes at eighty-eight, not eighteen."

"Oh. In that case I'd better get up and get things put away." She sat up as she talked, trying to hide the effort it took merely to push herself to a sitting position. "Is there anything to do at the church tonight for the bazaar?"

"There's always something to do, you know that. But I think we can beg off this time and go tomorrow night instead. I think they're just getting the booths set up and that's mostly men's work."

"But Dale would be expecting me to be there."

Her mother's hand squeezed hers gently, then released it. On her way to the door she said, "I intend to stay home this evening, because I *am* eighteen almost three times over and that gives me the right." She turned and smiled before she closed the door.

Peri Lee let herself sag again for a moment, then forced herself up to put the new dresses, robes, pantsuits, blouses and shorts on hangers. She hardly looked at them while putting them away, uncomfortably aware that her mind was dwelling on *itself*, as if part of her was standing back to observe the other part.

She looked at herself in the full-length mirror in her large walk-in dressing room closet. She removed her town dress and dropped it into the hamper and pulled a robe off a hanger. She could decide about tonight while she was eating supper. Maybe afterwards she'd feel like going and would wear one of the new pantsuits. Or the denim pants and jacket with the embroidered yoke. She really wanted to go—in a way. All of the kids would be there. And of course, Dale.

The thought of Dale heightened the sadness in her heart, the despondency in her mind. Instead of the usual happiness, the usual thrill, she felt suddenly that at all costs she must be with him. That she might never get another chance.

Oh Dear God—not a premonition of his death!

She had never experienced premonitions or prophetic dreams, but she knew a few people who had and knew they hadn't fabricated the stories. This strangeness she had been feeling—staring with the blood on her finger—and coming somehow to a peak with the thought of Dale, must in some way have something to do with him. But not his death. It couldn't be. She wouldn't allow herself to think that.

She threw the robe off, pulled off her slip, bra and pantyhose and ran into the bathroom to take a quick shower. Aloud she said firmly to herself, "I will not think of that. *Ever.*"

The shower was quickly over and she was back, running barefoot on the soft carpeting in her dressing-room to pull out the pantsuit that was Dale's favorite color. He had been on her mind when she bought it. But now she remembered that he hadn't been on her mind today as much as he usually was.

"Just a case of the blues," she said aloud, hurrying. She hardly looked at herself when she brushed her hair, and makeup was one thing she never bothered with, except sometimes mascara. And tonight she didn't take time for mascara.

When she passed the desk in her bedroom she paused long enough to read the note on the pad. Dale coming at seven. Bazaar fixing, etc.

Her notes were usually brief. She tore the sheet off, wadded it and tossed it into the basket. Then she glanced back at her room to make sure everything was neat again. The boxes had been put in the hall and she would carry them down as she went.

The room was neat. Good. She liked it that way.

She hurried out then, checking her wristwatch. Dale usually came right on time, unless he came early to talk to the men awhile. As Peri Lee ran down the stairs, she hoped this would be one of the nights when he was early.

The strange feeling had grown stronger and become one of near nausea in the center of her stomach, but she forced herself to eat a few bites of food so that she wouldn't be noticed by her family and worried over. She wouldn't be able to explain her anxiety concerning Dale. How could she explain a vague, gripping sense of fear and loss surrounding the man she loved?

After supper the family went onto the patio to sit, to watch the sunset beyond the mountains. Peri Lee watched the road for Dale and saw his car long before the others did. She got to her feet, said a quiet goodnight to her family and wandered out toward the driveway. Dale nearly always came in for awhile, but this evening she wanted to hurry him away so she could talk with him, be close to him. Hold him safely in her arms.

"What are you going to do?" her dad asked.

"We're going to the church to set up the booths for the bazaar. I see Dale's car coming down the highway so I thought I'd like to walk down and meet him. It's such a lovely evening."

"Oh. I forgot that bazaar business. Are you going, Gene?"

"Maybe later, but probably not if I can get out of it."

The mother said, "If all of them try to get out of it, who is there to do the work?"

Gene grunted lazily and Harry said, as he leaned back in his chair and laced his fingers behind his head comfortably, "You better go, Gene. Maybe I'll get in there later. Tomorrow night, maybe."

"Good idea," Gene said. "Tomorrow night."

"Not you, *me*," his dad answered, and Gene groaned.

Peri Lee smiled at the exchange, the arguing about who would go and who would not, but again felt as if the whole setting were unreal. That it was only a peaceful and pleasant dream that wouldn't be there the next time she looked.

She saw Dale's car turn into the driveway and she began to hurry to meet him; then she noticed she had company trotting at her side. She pointed an arm back toward the house. "Go back, Butchy, go back!"

The little dog stopped, drooping from tail to nose, and Peri Lee's feeling of loss went out to him also. She went down on her knees to hug him. And then she gave him a shove toward the house. "You go back and wait for me. Go now. Don't go chasing rabbits by the highway. Someone might take you for a midget coyote and shoot you, too. Go!" Then she got up and ran on, alone, to meet Dale.

He stopped the car, leaned over and pushed her door open. "Am I late?" he asked, clearly puzzled.

"No. I just felt like coming to meet you. Let's go someplace and talk awhile first, want to?"

"Want to," he answered, giving her a quick, light kiss before making a U-turn in the wide driveway and heading east toward town. He looked at her as she slid close. "Down by the river?"

She nodded, and after a minute said, "Dale, promise me you'll be careful on the farm machinery."

He laughed, slipped one arm around her and pulled her even closer.

"I'm serious," she said. "What about that man who got off his tractor, left it running and bent down to get something from beneath it, and it ran over him?"

"Now listen, this doesn't sound like you. What's wrong? You know I won't get run over by my tractor. I think it's sweet that you're concerned though. That you care."

She watched the river road take the place of the highway, as he turned the car toward the line of trees by the stream of mountain water which had generously been called a river, though it was hardly large enough to deserve the title.

"I care very much. I've been worried about losing you."

He stopped the car under the shelter of trees and turned to face her. "You're serious? Don't worry, Peri Lee. I promise to be careful."

She looked for a moment into the clear blue of his eyes, then with an urgency she had never felt before she pressed her body close to his and opened her lips for his kiss; her arms, over his shoulders, pulled his head fiercely toward her. He was there, he was warm and alive, and she knew she was losing him. And she couldn't lose him. She couldn't.

"Peri Lee," he whispered, "don't kiss me this way—you've got to remember I'm a man that wants you very much. Sometimes it takes too much out of me to wait—Peri Lee—"

She drew slight back. "I love you. Promise you won't leave me, Dale."

"Leave you? My God, Peri Lee—*leave you?*"

"Promise me," she pleaded.

"You know I won't leave you. Not for anything in heaven or on earth." He paused, then whispered against her ear, "I promise. Now, if you don't want yourself raped we'd better get on to the church—"

She turned her lips to his again, forcing his head around with her hands, pulling him tight and hard against her. "I want to be raped." Even as she said it she felt surprised that she had; she felt divided, as if another force had come alive in her mind, had wanted something different from the other, weakening that part of her mind that was familiar to her.

He pushed her away then and looked at her with eyes darkened. "Don't tease me, please. You wanted to wait, remember? Don't you want it that way anymore?"

Suddenly, as if a curtain of grey had risen from her mind, reality struck her. Dale was there, young, handsome, returning her love; not for just a night, but for a lifetime. Optimism rose once again in her heart and mind. She was glad she hadn't ruined that month toward which she dreamed—that month of honeymoon during the snowfall of winter when they would make love freely, play in the snow, ski—and go home to make love again—

"Oh yes," she said, drawing back, bringing her hands down from his shoulders. "I want it that way. I want very much to keep it that way." She turned and looked toward the clear waters of the small river. "What are we doing down here anyway? We're supposed to be on our way to work setting up booths."

He backed the car out and turned it toward the road, then he gave her a long, silent, and quizzical look. She returned it with a smile and felt the response in his hand as he reached to press her fingers in his.

CHAPTER 3

At first Gladys couldn't tell where she was. It was as if she had been deeply asleep for a long time, so that orienting herself was difficult.

But this was not her room. It was no ordinary room at all. Larger than a bedroom, larger even than a living room, with chairs like a theatre, and a quietness that seemed extreme. The people who came moving through the door at the far end of the room moved silently and solemnly. Somewhere, soft organ music played.

Only then did she notice the flowers, so many, many. And the thing they covered.

A coffin.

And she was standing behind it, of all places! Startled, she moved, thinking she must have come in the wrong door. Would they see her now? These people? See that she had come in the wrong door. Where was Mama?

She saw her then, in the little room to the side. She sat straight, her face stern as if it had been chipped from ice. Beside her, an arm around her shoulders, sat Marian.

Though Gladys knew she had stopped in full view of the people she remained where she was, confused, trying to remember. Had a member of her family died? Was that why she had wandered through the wrong door?

Who had died?

She spun around to look upon the coffin and the face she saw there was a waxy, colorless reproduction of her own. Someone had tried to make it look better by putting make-up on it, and had succeeded; so that in its stillness it was almost pretty.

It isn't possible, she cried, and found the silence unbroken. The lips in the coffin, unnatural with lipstick, didn't move. The big face lay cold and still. Gladys turned to look at her mother again, and all the relatives who had come to sit through the funeral service, and screamed at them, *I am not dead*! But they didn't look up. The silence was shattered only by a cough somewhere in the back of the house, and the low organ music that was piped in from somewhere else.

She remembered suddenly the last thing she had known. The truck. What had happened then was gone forever. Now she was aware again. *How?* How, she cried in her silent voice, how can it be? She looked down. She had to have a body, but there was nothing. The body lay bloodless and waxy and surrounded by flowers, its head resting in satin and lace. Her essence, all that she had been, her thoughts, her memories, had spun free to hang in the air. A tiny glob of nothing, nothing, nothing.

Suddenly another memory exploded into being, and it covered her life and her years of loneliness and heartaches, and the escape she had found in beer and novels; finally, the book on astral projection and the accidental death that was necessary for possession of another's body.

Peri Lee.

Beautiful, young, wealthy Peri Lee O'Brion.

Gladys paused, considering. Almost afraid to hope, but looking again at the casket, and the body that was gone forever. The prison from which she had escaped. She was afraid to go too near. Deathly afraid.

What if it somehow grabbed her again to imprison her forever in a still, locked casket underground? What hell beyond imagination that would be.

She whirled, frightened as the day she had fallen down the long,

long stairway to oblivion, and a life that would come in the form of a handicapped, crying out, wanting comfort. At once, she was beside her mother. She remained there, clinging without arms with which to cling, no fingers to touch her mother's cheek. In her soundless voice she cried into her mother's ear, but there was no answer.

Gladys edged away slightly, hurting yet beyond hurt; angry, yet beyond anger; hating her mother for years of rejection. For years of love unreturned.

She would leave this family. Leave as soon as she safely saw that body laid away. One more visit to each one, for one sign of caring, and then she would go.

And become Peri Lee O'Brion.

At the cemetery the small crowd gathered near the flower-banked coffin and listened in silence to the last prayer. The family turned away to go home. Gladys lingered behind a moment, seeing the closed coffin suspended and held on its ropes above the hole in the ground where it would rest. The body would be covered, gone forever. Gladys moved farther away, as if it would reach out and hold her prisoner again. She turned, leaving the coffin and the hole, and followed the others away from the cemetery, back to the waiting car and slowly home.

MAMA AND PAPA climbed the steep indoor stairway to the third-floor apartment with help from Marian and Clarissa, but there were no tears on their cheeks. Perhaps the tears had been shed, in those days during which Gladys was in limbo. Shed and forgotten. So soon? *So soon?*

Gladys followed slowly along behind the procession of her family, automatically choosing the height she would have walked in life, the last in line up the stairs, so low she could have grasped the coattails of Clarissa's husband Ralph.

The apartment looked dark and cramped, and had an unpleasant smell of old, dank wood. Mama went to her chair with a long sigh, Papa went to his. Marian, Clarissa and Ralph stood in the center of the small room, their presence making it look even smaller. Looking about, Gladys remembered that Marian's three children had left the cemetery in a car, with their father. They would be going home now, to take up the life that had been so briefly interrupted.

Gladys hovered near the door, and saw that Mama had begun to look contented.

"Out of her misery," Mama said. Papa nodded in silence.

"You must come home with us for a few days, dears," Clarissa said. "We have plenty of room for you, and no kids around to disturb you. This apartment will be too lonely for you without poor Gladys."

"Think of it this way," said Ralph as he walked about the confined space with his hands clasped behind his back. "She's really better off. What kind of life did she have? She never tried to do anything with herself, or make friends. I doubt if she had a friend in this world."

Mama nodded, agreeing to everything. "Out of her misery," she said again, so that Gladys felt like screaming at her to stop.

She felt as though she were a disembodied heart, a pulsing, hurting organism, with no voice in which to communicate; now, at last, could they not say something nice about her? Could not one of them say, *Gladys had lovely hair. Gladys looked so pretty in her casket.*

Could they not say, *I loved her!*

Marian and Clarissa rushed about to pack a small bag for Mama and Papa, then rushed them out the door. Mama glanced back once at the apartment, her eyes sweeping it in animation as though looking for something she might have forgotten. Close in a corner, Gladys cried in her silence, *here, Mama, I am here. Don't go. Don't leave me.*

But then she was left alone. The door was firmly closed and locked, and Gladys turned inward into herself to hide from the loneliness of the room. She huddled in fear, in lost silence; now, at last, afraid to move, to go on. Again, she remembered Peri Lee O'Brion, but the book hadn't explained beyond death. It hadn't told her how the possession of a new body occurred. What if she failed? My God, what then?

Others had died, where were they? But she drew swiftly into herself, not wanting to know, pushing with dread away from knowledge she couldn't face.

She trembled, inside herself, in that which was left of her.

And after long hours of night and loneliness and fear, after the sun rose again and made the world day, she began to move about, to search for herself, to make discoveries.

A thought was power, she decided. Movement, a mere thought. Faster than sound, faster than light, she moved across the room. Then, through the wall and into the tree. Birds there sang undisturbed. She was only a thought, and their thoughts were different from hers, still imprisoned in brains tiny and electric.

She thought of Marian's house, the big kitchen with the natural ash cabinets, and at once she was there. It was empty, no one had come down yet. She had wished once, briefly, to have Marian's kitchen. Now she could live there if she wished, she supposed, but there was a startled wonder that she had ever wanted to.

Footsteps slapped softly in the hall worn by someone who wore loose scuffs. She gasped in silent amazement when Marian appeared in the doorway. Marian, so neat and so proud and always so well dressed, in a sagging robe and old slippers? Yawning wide without bothering to cover her mouth. Her hairdo hidden beneath a nightcap made of satin and elastic, with the elastic pushing her eyebrows down and making her look so funny that Gladys let go the laughter that was building about her.

Goodbye Marian, she said in her silence. *I've come to tell you goodbye.*

Marian stopped suddenly, her yawn ending in midair, and sent her gaze warily from one end of the kitchen to the other. She shivered then, and pulled the robe together in front. Then she made the coffee while Gladys watched her.

The family came in one by one. The boys noisy, Cinthy irritable, their dad silent, and the morning progressed. There was no mourning in this house, Gladys saw. Not even her name was mentioned. She remained in a corner against the ceiling, looking down, absorbed in her feelings for them. They were more strangers than she had known. And all the time she had thought Marian was her favorite sister. At least less disliked than Clarissa.

One by one the family left until Marian was alone again. She sat at the table sipping coffee, and occasionally looking over her shoulder. At last she moved and reached for the phone on the snack bar and dialed a number.

"June? Are you busy? I was wondering if you could run over and have a drink with me. I feel—odd. As if someone were looking over my shoulder all the time. You know the feeling. I'd get out and go somewhere, except that Donald is expecting a phone call that I have to wait for—" She paused, listened, smiled. "Good. I'll run and get dressed and be looking for you."

Gladys, still in the darkest corner by the cabinets, watched her leave the room. She considered the conversation, and found a sense of pleasure in it. She was not entirely gone if she still had an effect on living people.

She moved away, out of the house, out of Marian's life.

Her least favorite sister lived in one of the new high-rise apartment buildings back in the city. She wouldn't have gone there at all if Mama hadn't been there, because the one time she had gone she had spoiled everyone's fun by getting sick when she looked out the window. The height was too extreme for her. They had to take her home. The elevator ride down seemed to last forever. "Why did you have to move so far up?", she asked Clarissa.

And her sophisticated sister had looked at her with her usual contempt and answered flatly, "We like it."

Now, Gladys's approach to the apartment house was slow and hesitant, and just slightly above the heads of people in the crowded sidewalk. None of them noticed her. They hurried their ways, like ants.

Gladys forgot she didn't need to use an elevator and crowded into one corner for the long ride up. Her mama and papa were sitting in the plush living room, looking at the large face of a color television. They were silent, absorbed in the picture. Gladys swept swiftly over and futilely tried to embrace her mother. One time; this was her goodbye. One time to put her arms around her mother. No arms, no hands, no way to touch, to say *Mama, I did love you.*

The woman moved, turned, and said to her husband, "It's so cold in here, would you get me my sweater?"

Gladys said *Yes* and began to dart in search of the sweater. Her papa got slowly to his feet and went to the closet door and got the sweater off a hanger.

Gladys hung helplessly in the air. For a moment she had forgotten.

She watched them, saddened. They seemed content without her. The weariness on her mother's face had already drifted away; when she smiled her thanks she looked far younger than Gladys remembered her.

Was she the burden that had caused her mother's anxiety? Gladys pressed into the corner, the essence of grief; lonely, frightened again. Then she screamed her helplessness in voiceless agony, on and on, because she could not find release in tears anymore.

THE ANSWER CAME from above and began to reach her in the soft sounds of strange music, a calling from far beyond. A rainbow of light surrounded her. The sounds of music beckoned her and she grew quiet, huddling, more afraid than ever. She was crying out inside herself no, no, no, please, *no... whatever you are go away. . .*

The music halted and began to withdraw, the light faded, receding into the mysteries beyond life.

GLADYS, pressed closely into the corner, relaxed with relief. She knew now. She didn't have to go until she was ready. And she would never be ready because she was afraid. If her own mother couldn't love her, ugly as she was ... She had to be beautiful and to be loved. She wanted first to live, fully. She wanted to suck dry all the pleasures of earth which she had missed.

She had to first become Peri Lee O'Brion. She let her being fill with the image of Peri Lee, the girl with the lovely skin and dark, contrasting hair. The girl of perfect beauty. Now that she was freed from her physical prison she would go to be with the girl, live her life with her. And finally to possess her.

Where had Cinthy said she lived? On a farm, one of the richest farms in the next county. It didn't matter the exact farm, if a thought could move her. Indeed, what was she now, but a thought? What more was she than that?

A force of something with frightening and promising power poured about her again, but she shrank away and hid the best she could and trembled and wept tearless tears, until it withdrew. She didn't want to go beyond what was familiar to her. What if, after all, the Christian Bible was right and there was a day of revelation where all people were judged? Who could love and accept her ugliness? God? Who was God? No. If the dogs and the whores were to be cast into hell, why not the ugly too? No. She didn't want to know more than she knew. She wanted only to live, to be, the only kind of being that seemed worthwhile. The young, the tender, and the beautiful. Peri Lee O'Brion.

She moved upward instantly, through the blue sky, through small white clouds, and came down over one of the richest agricultural counties in America. It lay on the eastern border of the great Rockies, a level, green terrain. Carefully chosen and planted trees lined white-graveled or paved driveways. Irrigation ditches of clear, cold water poured swiftly down from mountain streams to keep level fields green and lush, gardens rich, productive, colorful. The houses looked more like mansions than farm houses. Invisible though she was, Gladys approached the shaded lawn slowly, very slowly; as if someone would come out and remind her she didn't belong. Her place was not the clean cool air in the maple shade, but the dust-filled air of a city factory.

A dog lay on the long, white-pillared veranda, stretched out flat on its stomach, irrigation-wet belly pressed to cool concrete. He had just chased a rabbit across the alfalfa field. His eyes were closed but he panted, not yet asleep. Gladys had watched him. She approached him slowly now, wonder within her. Would he sense her presence? Weren't cats and dogs supposed to know ghosts? Wasn't that what she was now, a ghost?

The dog didn't move. His panting slowed, he licked his nose, swallowed, and drew a deep sigh. As she settled beside him he went to sleep. He didn't know she was there.

So all the stories and books had been wrong. The dog was not aware of her at all. But a cat? She left the porch, found one after a moment; a black cat was sitting on a walk that went from a rear door to a building behind the house. A mother cat, she had one leg stretched out and was giving it a good going over, removing burrs, stickers and whatever her cat's brain thought should be removed. Gladys approached swiftly, to scare it, but there was not so much as a breeze of her to stir the cat's long fur, and it kept licking it leg.

So the books were wrong.

Gladys hovered awhile near the cat, listening to the noises inside the back door. A woman's voice was giving orders to someone to get tomatoes from the garden, and also to get new onions and peppers and slice them for dinner.

Gladys remembered that here on the farm, dinner would be served at noon as well as in the evening.

A door opened and languid footsteps crossed a screened porch. The back screen door opened and slammed. A girl came out carrying a small basket with a handle. She was young, but very plain. A hired girl? She left the walk and crossed the grass to a white gate and went through it into a vegetable garden.

Gladys watched her. The cat got up and moved, her steps as languid as the girl's, never noticing that Gladys huddled within a paw's reach. Gladys chuckled to herself, to think of all the people in the world who had been so wrong about cats and ghosts and things.

She wondered about the girl. She wondered if there was anything at all she could cause to happen. Like the tomato in the girl's hand suddenly exploding. Gladys hollered and laughed to herself, imagining the girl's reaction to an exploding tomato. If she could do things like that, what fun she could have. At least for awhile.

The girl had stooped and was placing ripe tomatoes into the basket. Gladys moved beside her, the substance of herself near the hand with the tomato. The girl kept picking, her attention fixed. Unaware. Gladys tried to touch the basket, to jerk it from her hand, to squish the fruit, but there was nothing of her and she began to sense her helplessness again. She couldn't even have fun with the girl because she had no power over the physical. For a moment frustration and fear gathered about her; then she reminded herself that the power to do physical acts when she was not yet physical again was unimportant. The important thing was to discover as much as she could about this family that would be hers now: to discover how to make it so. How to bring about the act of possession. *That* was important. Scaring the girl, just for a bit of fun, by making the fruit explode in the basket was silly and childish.

She stayed by the girl until the vegetables were picked, then preceded her into the house.

The kitchen, was large, clean, colorful, and supervised by one very stern-faced woman. As cranky looking as her own mama.

"You'd better set the table," the woman said irritably to the girl. "As long as it took you to pick that stuff, I'd better get them ready. You set the table."

The girl put the basket down on the clean counter by the sinks and went to the long cloth-covered table at the end of the kitchen. The side windows overlooked a piece of green lawn, the white driveway, and rows of neat trees and white farm buildings. So dinner was to be in the kitchen, thought Gladys, and set for eight people.

She huddled against the ceiling, unmoving, between a tall china cabinet and the window curtains, and watched the drama of the noon meal unfold.

A pretty woman came in from the front of the house, and there was no mistaking her identity. Peri Lee's mother. Her dark hair glistened with slender threads of silver, and was pulled back into a neat coil that showed off the bones and features of a lovely face. Here was Peri Lee twenty-five years from now, thought Gladys. How lovely it would be to be Peri Lee, and know that over all those long, lovely years nothing bad would happen to her beauty.

Men began coming in from outside. One of them kissed Peri Lee's mother's cheek. He was tall, with strong arms, and a strong face, and had lost a good deal of his hair. Another called her Mom, and Gladys saw that he too was dark-haired and looked a mixture of both the man and the woman. He had to be a brother of Peri Lee's. A third, a man who looked tiny and wrinkled beside the others, old enough to retire, nodded and called the woman Mrs. O'Brion. A fourth stood rather shyly, near the door.

Gladys looked at him and gasped. He was all that her heart had ever longed for in a man. Young, strong, well-muscled, built like a boxer. Eyes sultry with concealed and repressed passions.

Mr. O'Brion said, "Come on, Pete, sit down. I think Bertha outdid herself today. Smells great."

The cranky cook smiled, and her face was no longer stern.

But the good-looking hired man glanced toward the door. The young O'Brion, who had called Peri Lee's mother "Mom", said, "Pete, haven't you found out we don't wait for the kid sister around here? She'll pop in before long."

Mrs. O'Brion was seated, already serving. The men joined her, then the hired girl. And finally the cook. In the clatter of talk, dishes against silverware, ice against glasses, the back screen door opened and Peri Lee ran in.

Her black hair was pulled back and tied with a ribbon. She wore a checked, loose shirt, and blue-jean shorts rolled high on brown, firm thighs. Her legs still dripped water, and she was barefoot.

"You've been in the irrigation ditch," her mother said. "I would have thought it would be too cold for wading yet."

"No, just refreshing. Sorry I'm late."

Her father said, as he ladled a great glob of mashed potatoes onto his plate, "You'll get cramps in your legs."

Mother continued, "I hope you washed the mud off your feet before you came in." She glanced at the young hired man. "I don't believe her eighteenth birthday made a bit of difference. For a young lady who can sometimes be very poised and proper, I sometimes wonder."

She obviously was teasing in a mild way, and Pete smiled politely. But then his eyes slid sideways as the girl took the chair beside him, lingered, and moved for a moment to where her thighs met. Gladys was the only one who saw.

"Eighteen's not very old," her dad said, his voice saying tenderly, between the lines, that eighteen was synonymous with eight so far as he was concerned. "Is it, Kitten?"

Peri Lee heaved a great and deliberate sigh and looked at her dad. But it was a look of patient love.

And it was her brother who spoke.

"Old enough to get married though. Dale was by awhile ago to see you, and where were you? Out wading irrigation ditches."

"So he's getting a talented wife," Peri Lee said. "A very good irrigation ditch wader."

This evidently was news for her mother. She paused and looked up, surprised. "Wife?"

"Well probably, Mother," Peri Lee said. "That dumb son of yours keeps trying to marry me off, so I might as well. Sometimes I think he'd like to get rid of me, don't you, Pete?" She reached over and poked Pete's muscled arm with her index finger. He gulped and nearly choked. But her attention had already gone back to her brother. "What you ought to do, darling, is stop worrying about me and do something about yourself. You're the one who should be getting married. At your age, yet. But then, who'd have you?"

She laughed, her eyes sparkling with this game they played. He pretended to be insulted.

"Me! Why I'm only twenty-two, I'm handsome, popular. I'm not worried about me. I'm perfect. No conceit, nothing. I could get married, anytime. I was just trying to keep you from becoming an old maid, so I told Dale you'd be ready to go about seven."

The dad spoke up. "Go where?"

"Oh, Harry," Mrs. O'Brion said with a touch of impatience, "To young people's meeting at the church, of course, just like every Wednesday night."

"Oh." He sounded relieved, nevertheless. But kept grumbling a little. "Seems to me she's never home at night. Gone every night for a week, with that bazaar business."

"Just three nights, Daddy." Peri Lee said. She slipped out of her chair, went around the table and kissed his cheek, then headed toward an interior door.

"Where are you going? You hardly ate."

"I ate all I wanted. I'm going to my room, and I might even take a nap. And get prepared for that wild date tonight."

The only one who watched her go was Pete, his smoldering eyes half hidden behind the glass he raised to his lips.

Gladys didn't move until Peri Lee was already running up the spiral staircase near the large entry door at the front of the house. She followed far behind, timid in the strange surroundings. The house surprised her. It was neither ornate nor elegant. It was large-roomed, large-windowed, furnished in a rather haphazard Early American with a bit of Mediterranean. It combined to give an atmosphere of comfort and hominess such as she had never seen. There was light and cheerfulness everywhere.

In the bedroom, third door back on the second floor hall, Peri Lee closed and locked her door; then to Gladys' sudden embarrassment she unzipped her shorts and let them fall to the floor, stripped off her lace bikini panties, her blouse and bra. Then, glowingly naked, she flopped down on her bed and closed her eyes. And drew a deep sigh of relaxation. Her round breasts reached firmly and whitely up, dark nippled.

Gladys's embarrassment eased. She had never seen anyone undress before. But as long as the girl didn't know she was being seen, it wasn't so uncomfortable a situation.

Gladys stayed by the door until Peri Lee was asleep. In sleep her face looked almost like the face of a baby, smooth, angelically innocent. Timidity still holding her, Gladys went closer and looked down at the face. At the body. The lovely, lovely body. Within the memory that hovered somehow within her a great longing came alive, and she remembered when she was ten years old. She had felt sure the doctors could help her to grow up into a beautiful young girl, like her sisters. Beauty, that was it. So important in this sexual world. So everything. How lucky Peri Lee was, and she didn't even know it. If only, Gladys yearned, *if only I could have looked like her in my own body—if only...*

Peri Lee's eyes opened suddenly, widely. Her breath stopped. She seemed to be listening, hard, for something that had disturbed her sleep.

Gladys drew back, behind her, settling against the wall at the head of the bed.

Peri Lee sat up, her wide gaze taking in the entire room, slowly, again and again. Then, moving silently, she eased off the bed, crossed her thick shag carpet and opened her door. Obviously remembering that she was nude, she turned back warily to her closet and came out with a robe. Then, slipping it on, she turned with a last frightened glance around her and ran from the room.

Gladys followed, edging along the corners of the ceiling and wall, watching Peri Lee stumble down the curved stairway, her glances thrown backward more often than forwards. She ran into the sunroom where her mother sat in a white wicker rocking chair surrounded by potted plants, several birds in large cages. Lighted windows looked out upon cool, green lawns where a water sprinkler threw a rainbow of colors into the air.

The woman was doing embroidery work, but let it fall into her lap when Peri Lee dropped to the floor at her knees.

"Why—dear—" She said slowly, her eyes taking in the bewildered frown on Peri Lee's face. "What is the matter?"

The girl shivered, and hugged the robe closer about her. "I don't know, Mother. When I woke up I had this most awful feeling."

"What feeling, dear?"

"That I was being watched." Her voice lowered and she spoke softly. "By something horrible, Mother, really horrible. It scared me."

"It must have been a bad dream," her mother said in the same, calm, gentle voice. But her hand reached out immediately to touch the back of Peri Lee's head and pull her forward, so that she had only to lean down to press her lips to the smooth forehead. "You don't seem to have fever. But you may be taking a bit. Come on back upstairs and let mother take your temperature."

Gladys watched them go, amazed, and oddly perplexed. The girl, of all people, had felt her presence. But horrible? When they met at the country club, the girl had been friendly and sweet. She had not thought her horrible then. But now, invisible, dead, only a feeling, was she so horrible?

Gladys trembled, pressed into the corner, hating, hating; hating this self that made her horrible even now. Life was not fair. And neither was death. Nothing really changed. Not yet. But it would. It had to. When she became the force in Peri Lee, the horrible and repulsive part of her would be gone forever.

But couldn't Peri Lee understand she really meant her no harm? She wanted only to be accepted.

After several long minutes the mother came back, and passed

within inches of Gladys. But she passed by unconcerned, the worried look gone from her face.

On impulse Gladys followed, closer and closer, until she could have reached her flesh-less hands into the woman's hair and torn it from its hidden pins. But the women went on, humming faintly, into the kitchen.

The cook said, "Peri Lee not feeling good?"

"I'm sure she'll be fine. Her temperature is normal. She evidently had an unpleasant dream."

"Them things'll happen," said the cook.

There was something about the cook that Gladys suddenly feared and disliked. Her unpleasantness, even when she tried to be pleasant, it showed through. Like the unhappy women in the factory. The ones who hated something. Their jobs. Themselves. Their husbands. Something. Like her mama, who hated her own child. Gladys zipped across the room to the woman's heat-reddened face and attempted to wrap herself around the head, to make herself felt, to frighten the woman. But though the woman jerked to a halt and stood frowning for a moment, still and with breath abated, she then moved as if Gladys did not exist at all, even in spirit; or as if she had deliberately pushed her away, her mind occupied by something Gladys did not penetrate.

Gladys fell back, puzzled again, trying to understand. Only the girl seemed to sense her presence. Her sister had, a little. And her mother, a little. The cook might have just a bit, but most strongly it was felt by Peri Lee.

A sense of accomplishment and pleasure trembled in Gladys as she realized the implications of that. The mental suggestions of the past months, the preparation for actual possession of Peri Lee must have been effective. The girl's mind was receptive to her presence, was opening to her.

That was the answer Gladys had been seeking, wondering about and not finding. How her move into the other's body could be accomplished. It would be a mental thing. A move into her brain. When the girl was worn down, unresisting, it could be done.

What would happen to her then? To Peri Lee? The thought almost threw Gladys. She meant her no harm. She wanted only to live once, fully, completely; in beauty, youth and happiness, loved by many people as Peri Lee was. *She meant her no harm.*

Couldn't the girl understand that!

Maybe if she waited farther away for awhile, Peri Lee would begin to like her. Maybe too she would understand and even welcome her and they could live as one, with happiness for both.

No, that would not be possible. Instinct told Gladys the mind of Peri Lee must sleep unresisting. Forever.

Gladys went to the corner between china cabinet and kitchen windows and remained there until seven in the evening, after supper, when Peri Lee came into the room to be admired. Her father and mother were still at the table, and the girl, so beautiful Gladys felt lost, pirouetted near the table, showing off a red and white-checked dress and white sandals. Her mother smiled.

"It's lovely, dear."

But her father looked critically from sandals to skirt hem. "Little short, isn't it?"

Mrs. O'Brion glanced smiling at her husband. "You always say that, Harry. And I always answer the same thing. It's the style, dear, remember?"

"But for church?"

"Yes, Daddy," Peri Lee said. "You don't want me to look dowdy, do you?"

"Your mother doesn't wear her dresses above her knees and she doesn't look dowdy."

"But," Mrs. O'Brion said, "I'm not a teenager, Harry. Let her be young."

"You usually tell me I'm trying to keep her too young."

"And yet allow her to grow up. I'm sure you understand me."

A voice at the back door interrupted.

"Hello, Mrs. O'Brion, Mr. O'Brion."

He didn't speak to Peri Lee, he only looked. He was tall, large-boned with very broad, square shoulders; his hair blond, skin suntanned, eyes clear sky-blue. And, Gladys thought, he's crazy in love with Peri Lee. God, how he wants Peri Lee.

The girl smiled, and spoke in a voice that was revealingly different. Soft and submissive. "Hi, Dale."

Her slight arrogance seemed to have vanished, and she stood demurely still, her hands folded together in front of her. She was aware of Dale's desire, and seemed subdued and conquered by it, Gladys thought. Yet Peri Lee hadn't even been aware of the hired man's lust.

Foolish girl.

The men she could have, Gladys thought. *Ah, the men she could have. And all she can see is this one?*

"Ready?" asked Dale.

"Yes." She kissed the cheeks of both her parents and then, with another smile up at Dale, went ahead of him out the door.

Would they really go to church?, Gladys wondered, following. When they could park somewhere on a private road so he could make love to her?

Excitement thudded and gasped in Gladys. Here, at last, she could enjoy actual love-making, be a part of what he would do to her. The books said there were so many kinds of lovers, her own dreams fantasized many kinds—which kind was this man?

She followed closely, watching for a touch, for the moment when they would begin to come together. They sat within reach of each other in the bucket seats of his sports car, and after a moment his hand felt for and found hers. His fingers pressed tightly for a moment before they relaxed to hold her gently.

"Hi," he said.

And she answered. "Hi."

Then, silence. Gladys, in the back seat, waited for him to suggest skipping church, going off alone, but his conversation was casual. What did you do today? Nothing much. I came by to see you. I know, I was doing crazy things like wading water. Tomorrow let's go horseback riding, all right? All right, yes, I'd love to ride down to the creek. With you. With you, love, with you.

Gladys, disappointed, settled down and didn't even go into the church with them. Dull, dull, dull she thought. Why waste that beautiful body which all men wanted? When she had it she wouldn't waste it.

She realized she was pouting, childishly. It had gained her something once. Her mother's impatience, if nothing else. But now? How useless. Still, an old habit would be hard to break. Even now, evidently.

After a boring two hours Peri Lee and Dale came out of the church and got into the car. For a moment it looked as if he would kiss her, but the lights of other cars spotlighted them and he drove on.

Gladys moved forward, eagerly, to settle on the back of the front seat near Peri Lee's shoulder. She saw he was holding her hand, but that was all. They passed road after road where it would be safe to park. Peri Lee glanced back straight through Gladys into the darkness, and Gladys moved away into the corner of the back of the car. Still, Peri Lee kept glancing back toward the rear window, and became very quiet, hardly answering Dale when he talked.

"What's wrong?," he finally asked, his eyes on her more than on the road.

She turned straight toward the road, staring down it, her shoulders straight, her head up. "Nothing," she said.

"There's something. Did I do something?"

"No. No, not you, Dale."

The car slowed while he continued to look at her profile. After a few moments of silence he said, "Want to go somewhere for awhile? Want to go get a pizza at the Hut?"

"No, I just want to go home." Her voice was almost a sob.

He had nearly stopped the car by now, giving all his attention to Peri Lee. Her profile was outlined faintly against the lights of the dash and the headlights that shone in the black road. "Something's wrong, Peri Lee. Don't you think I can tell? It's been coming on, more and more, for several days. Is it something you can tell me?"

"No!" she cried in growing hysteria, as if his words had triggered something in her mind she couldn't face. "I mean it's nothing. I just want to go home, please." She cast one quick frightened glance over her shoulder into the darkness of the road behind. "Please, Dale, hurry and take me home."

His movements coordinated smoothly. He reached down and shifted his sports car into second gear, glanced back into the darkness, and pressed down on the accelerator. Gladys felt the thrill of sudden speed.

His hand moved from the shift knob to Peri Lee's shoulder. His fingers touched the back of her neck and pressed gently. "What was it? Something scared you."

"Nothing scared me," she denied, but her voice broke.

He swung the car into the driveway of her home and eased it slowly up the tree-lined lane to the house. Then he pulled her toward him suddenly and kissed her hard but quickly, on the mouth. After the kiss she had leaned toward him, and when he stopped her head was on his shoulder. His arms reached to pull her tenderly close. Everyone was tender with her, Gladys thought. Too tender: The hired hand, he wouldn't be tender. He hadn't a tender bone in his body. If she were Peri Lee...

"I don't know what's the matter with me, Dale", Peri Lee said softly against his collar. "Coming down the road back there I felt like something was right behind us, in the dark. Something awful, and scary, that wanted me. I don't know what's wrong with me, except maybe I'm going nuts."

"The only thing back there in the dark that wanted you was me. I'm awful, and I'm scary, so your feelings were justified, and you're not going nuts. You're just sweet, and bright, and beautiful, and intuitive, that's what you are."

She had begun to smile, and then to laugh. She drew back just far enough to look up into his eyes, midnight dark in the dim light from the car dash. "You? Awful and scary, Dale? Kiss me and let me see."

His lips came to meet hers slowly, as he savored the thoughts of the kiss, and the kiss was so soft and so gentle that Gladys felt like beating him with something. But Peri Lee didn't seem displeased. Dale's arms, around her, shook, and his voice was unsteady when he spoke.

"Peri Lee, Peri Lee. I love you so much. I could carry you away and never bring you back."

"I love you, Dale,"

"When can we pick out your ring?"

"Maybe Christmas? I don't think I should announce our engagement before I'm eighteen and a half. Daddy would die. He thinks I'm about two or three yet."

"He'll get used to it. He ought to be used to me by now."

"Yes, of course, but not as my husband. I haven't even told Mother that I want to get married next winter or spring, instead of going back to college. I think she knows, but I thought maybe we should ease Daddy into it. All right, Dale?"

"Whatever you want, Peri Lee, you know that. I guess I'd wait for you forever, if I had to."

"You won't have to, I promise. I want to be with you, too."

She instigated that kiss, with her hand reaching up to touch his cheek.

Gladys, hidden in shadows in the back seat, sighed in boredom. The novels she had read were more exciting than the real thing after all. Than this, anyway. Soft little kisses. Even long deep ones, as they were becoming. Yet he didn't even try to feel her full breast that barely touched his coat, or the dark curve of the nylon-covered knee that was pressed against his. He touched only her waist. His hand gently feeling the dip of its slenderness between the curve of rib-cage and the curve of hip.

Gladys watched the hand eagerly, wishing it would go in under the skirt and pull down the pantyhose to feel there between her legs. Feel the softness and the wetness of desire. No one would see if he pulled the hose below her knees and then got on top of her, opened his pants and pulled out the big, big lump that throbbed there and put it in her—*do it, you idiot,* she screamed in frustration at him, words filled with longing and silence. *She'll let you—don't you know she'll let you? I know. If she doesn't let you, then make her. Do it, you fool—make real, wild love to her—*

But the hand stayed at the waist, pressing, moving slightly toward one breast only to move back to the waist again. The kiss continued, and Gladys sulked in disgust with the whole thing. A kiss might be fun, but the other would be a lot more fun. It was plain to see that nothing was going to happen in this car, with this man.

Gladys left the car and went through the darkness toward the glow of a cigarette at the end of the bunkhouse. Pete stood there, his eyes narrowed as if it would help penetrate the darkness, watching the car. He watched until Dale had taken Peri Lee to the house, then returned to his car and drove away. Then Pete moved. But instead of going into the bunkhouse he crossed the lawn to the garden side of the house, and Gladys saw why. He had a full view of Peri Lee's lighted bedroom window.

Peri Lee didn't pull her blinds, but she undressed in her bathroom and came out into full view wearing a see-through shorty nightgown. For one brief moment her body was outlined in the window against the light.

Pete drew in his breath, and held it, long after Peri Lee had disappeared beyond the window.

Gladys watched his longing with a satisfaction not even the novels had given her. Watched it and laughed, and wondered if those thick, heavy hands would ever get what they wanted.

She followed and watched him strip off his clothes in the dark of the bunkhouse and saw he wore nothing underneath. No shorts, no undershirt.

No shorts.

She had never seen a naked man before, either, but she laughed to herself to see the misery he must be in with that huge, rather revolting, but fascinating, thing that had so many names. She laughed harder to think what he would do if he knew someone was watching when he put his thick, heavy hands on it and groaned and pulled. His face screwed into a mask of frustration, hatred of Dale Larson, and lust for the girl he couldn't hope to get.

No one else slept in the bunkhouse, and Gladys assumed the middle-aged man lived somewhere else and went home at night.

All lights in the house had been put out when Gladys returned to it. There was not even a night light, anywhere. The open window let in moonlight filtered by leaves and branches of shade trees.

Peri Lee slept on one side, one shapely leg thrown over her light blanket, one arm under her cheek.

Gladys looked at her for awhile, moving lightly over the bed, dropping down within inches of the girl. She wondered if Peri Lee could feel a touch from her, and was afraid she might. The girl must go on sleeping. Sleeping.

Gladys went to the dresser mirror where moonlight touched the glass. Not once had she looked to see if she might still be visible to herself, and her approach was filled with fear and dread. The prayer under her thoughts was automatic, with no real faith. *Please no, please God. Not that face, or that body, not ever again.* The mirror reflected the moonlight softly, and the dark headboard of Peri Lee's bed, with the pictures on the wall, the lamp on the table at the bedside, but nothing else. Relieved, but still searching, Gladys moved closer to the glass, staring, looking for an outline of what she had been; for the pale, whitish veil that ghosts were supposed to be, and saw nothing.

Then, she wondered, what had Peri Lee seen?

She had been so engrossed in looking for herself in the mirror that she hadn't seen Peri Lee sit up in the bed. But suddenly the face was there, reflected in the mirror, white against the mahogany of the high headboard. Her eyes dark in her white face, stared, wide, terror-filled, directly at the mirror.

Then she screamed, covered her face with her hands and bowed her head, and screamed and screamed, her cries of fear muffled by her hands.

The house became filled with sound. Running steps, doors opening and slamming. Calls crying Peri Lee's name. Many lights coming on in the room as people burst in.

The brother reached her first and took her in his arms. She clung to him with hands that shook uncontrollably and collapsed into sobs against his chest. The mother and the father came to hover over them. Even the housekeeper came to stand at the foot of the bed. Every face wore the same startled, worried expression.

Gladys searched for a spot of shadow in the light-filled room and finally found it beneath the dresser. As frightened as a mouse she scurried to the tiny, dusty, dark corner. She hadn't wanted to scare Peri Lee again. *No, no, no.* Peri Lee had to get used to her. She had to. Because Gladys wouldn't be leaving her, ever. The girl had to relax and sleep and become receptive. She must not fight her anymore. She must stop fighting.

Oh please make her stop fighting me, Gladys begged to nothing in particular.

The voices came out of their clamor of confusion and found a path of communication.

"A nightmare?" the brother said. "Did you have a nightmare?'

"No, no," Peri Lee sobbed. "I was awake. I woke up. I woke up. It was there, by the mirror. In the moonlight."

"What was there?' asked her father.

"It. I don't know. Oh, Daddy, it's so horrible It. . . wants me, Daddy."

"She's hysterical," said her mother. "Maybe we should call the doctor."

"A nightmare," the brother said, sounding stubborn, unsuccessfully covering an undertone of worry and concern, as if he were trying to appease a baby sister who had fallen and cut her knee. "Everybody has nightmares like that. I've done it myself. Woke up scared and not knowing why."

"No," she cried again, tears wetting her cheeks and running into the corners of her mouth. She brushed them away with the back of a trembling hand. "Don't you understand? Something was there? Something has come into my room! It's following me. Help me, oh please."

"She *is* hysterical," her mother said, in a tone much like her son's. "She hasn't felt well lately. You have to call the—"

Her father thundered out suddenly, interrupting, as if he weren't hearing all that was being said, "But why should she be hysterical? Go on and get the doctor. Two nightmares in one day are too much."

The housekeeper left in a hurry saying, "I'll call him." Then, back over her shoulder, a remark filled with anger. "But it looks to me like she *saw* something and I don't know what good that doctor's going to do. If she saw something, if something's after her, it is, and no doctor's pill is going to cure it. If it was me, I'd take a look around that room. I'd ask her *what* about it. I'd find out more, that's what I'd do—" Her mutters faded down the hall.

"Go ahead, honey," said Peri Lee's father, in as understanding a voice as he could muster, "Tell me about it. Is it because you're nervous about going away to college? Is that what is is?"

Peri Lee shook her head, saying no without words. After a moment she began to talk, her voice calmed and softened. "I don't know what it is, Daddy. I can't really see anything, but I just have these very strong feelings that something horrible is there."

"Where?"

"Uh—over by the mirror tonight. This afternoon here, close to me. And tonight, coming home from church, behind me, in the dark."

The brother made another try, hopefully. "She must have been reading something. Ghost stories?"

"No! I haven't opened a book since school was out. Mother, you know that."

"Yes, dear, I know."

"Television—" the brother persisted.

"Gene," Harry said, "why don't you go on back to bed?"

Their mother softened it by adding, "I know you mean well, dear, but there may be more involved than her imagination. She was terrified, Gene. She isn't putting it on.'

"I know that. But what the devil could it be but her imagination?"

He was grasping for a logical answer, and his fear for his sister seemed not apparent to the others. "She's talking like there's—there's something invisible, ready to take her away, and you know that can't be possible. In movies, on television—goddammit, there's no-such thing as—as—don't you see, it's got to be her imagination. A dream she couldn't remember. It's *got* to be."

"Gene, please. Will you calm down and lower your voice? Why don't you do as your dad suggested and go on to bed?"

He left without saying anymore. But there was an angry stomp to his barefooted steps.

"You can go too, Harry, if you wish. I'll stay with her."

"No. I'm waiting for the doctor. Would you rather go downstairs, Kitten? Out of this room?"

"I don't know. I'd be afraid there too. All at once I'm afraid everywhere."

"Do you want your mother to stay and sleep with you?"

"I don't know. I—yes. Mother, do you mind?"

"Of course I'll stay with you, darling, if you think it will help."

"I don't know. I don't understand what's going wrong with me."

The doctor came in rather quietly, and Gladys surmised he didn't live too far away, in the small town where the church was.

The situation was explained to him, and for awhile there were patches of silence. Then he began to talk, his voice soft, and obviously not worried.

"She seems all right. No fever. Sometimes fever will cause night terrors. Why don't you bring her in for a thorough examination tomorrow? Tonight one of these little pills won't hurt her, just give her a good night's sleep."

Gladys perked up with interest. She hadn't thought of sleeping pills, but that might be the answer. It would reduce Peri Lee's resistance to nearly nothing. But she must sleep and rest now because Gladys wasn't ready. The thought of the moment of entry kept her still and timid. Afraid. What if she failed?

She couldn't face failure. She would wait. Put it off awhile. Learn more about the home, the friends, and other boyfriends. Surely Dale wasn't the only one.

Yes, there were many reasons why it would be best to wait awhile before attempting entry into Peri Lee's brain.

Harry left the room with the doctor and Olivia O'Brion sat on the bed beside her daughter, the lights out again except for a lamp at the bedside. She held the girl's hand and gently stroked the smooth arm. Her face held a puzzled frown, and when Gladys slipped out of the dusty corner beneath the dresser she saw Olivia staring at the mirror. Wondering. Worried.

Peri Lee seemed to be sleeping, finally, and her fingers relaxed and fell out of her mother's hand.

Olivia stood up, removed her robe and draped it over the foot of the bed. She was wearing a long, filmy lavender nightgown, the prettiest gown Gladys had ever seen. Trying not to disturb the girl, her mother lay down on the bed facing her. But she didn't turn out the light and she didn't close her eyes. She kept watching the sleeping girl.

Gladys moved up into the light, but Olivia's eyes didn't turn toward her. She seemed totally unaware that Gladys was there. Gladys eased closer and closer to the faces that were so much alike. Peri Lee didn't stir. She slept deeply and breathed evenly. After a while her mother slept too. How could the girl get used to her, so that they could go on together for awhile? A girl and her shadow. Without fear.

How sweet to be possessor of that body. To look into the mirror and see that face. To feel the emotions she could feel when she was in the arms of many lovers.

When the dawn came bringing pinks, lavenders and golds to the eastern Sky and sounds of life began outside, Peri Lee moved restlessly and opened her eyes. Gladys was still on the pillow between the girl and the woman. She remained motionless and nearly thoughtless, in hopes Peri Lee didn't sense her presence. The girl sat up and looked down at her mother, then she raised both hands to her own face to push back her hair and smooth it.

At once she grew very tense and still.

And Gladys knew. Even before Peri Lee edged quickly off the bed, before her eyes grew wide again as they searched the pillows, the head of the bed, her mother's face. Gladys moved swiftly upwards, straight through the ceiling. A wish, a thought, put her free of the confines of the house. Away from Peri Lee.

She remained outside throughout the day. From near the barn she watched. Peri Lee came out to leave in the car with her mother. And Gladys watched them return hours later.

Peri Lee carried a dress box under her arm; she was laughing and talking again.

That was good. Peri Lee was happy.

Off guard.

CHAPTER 4

In the evening Dale came on horseback, and Hamilton, the old hired man, saddled a horse for Peri Lee. The two went down the driveway together, laughing, talking, saying things Gladys couldn't hear. Finally she moved again, and followed, keeping a long distance between them.

At the creek both riders dismounted, left their horses tied to a tree and walked away with hands linked, toward the mountain stream, cold and clear. Part of the water's noise came from a dam just upstream. The backed-up pool of water supplied the irrigation ditches of farms downstream, the Larson farm, the O'Brion farm, and others in their turn.

Gladys moved to the horses, and they didn't mind. Like most creatures, they didn't seem to know she was there.

The couple stopped, faced each other, and after talking earnestly for a moment, kissed just as earnestly. And just as briefly.

Gladys began to be aware that the light in Dale's eyes was a worshipping love, his tenderness and gentleness toward Peri Lee a result of that love.

She hadn't thought much about that kind of love.

It had seemed too far beyond her. As far out of her reach as the other unreachable parts of life, as far away as heaven. And now it had come near, as close as Peri Lee.

How would it feel to be loved by Dale? It was a thought in some way disturbing, and she tried not to dwell on it. In a way it seemed to threaten her concept of life and what she felt was fun in life. *And the lion shall lie down by the lamb—and the lamb is the light—and the beasts from the wild shall be led by a child—and I'll be changed, changed from this creature that I am...*

All at once Gladys was sobbing, sobbing sounds that were non-existent, tears that did not fall, that had no substance. Only the hurt was there, a nearly obscured cry from the depths of her being for something she had never dared dream of—the adoration, the love of a man who would stand beside her to face a harsh and unkind world.

Gladys started to leave them to their wandering little walk along the grassy bank of the swiftly moving water, but on childish impulse swept toward them instead. A game would liven things up, make her less sad and lonely. Less confused. Besides, there was something she wanted to know. How close could she come to Peri Lee without being felt? Or could she now, at this time, finish what she had come for?

They were bending forward, looking into the water, and Gladys caught a bit of conversation about a fish. She slowed, and moved down through the lower branches of the trees, closer and closer.

Peri Lee straightened, and turned, her eyes searching the tree behind them.

About ten feet away Gladys paused, hovering. Fear of failure was holding her still again. Peri Lee felt her presence, knew she was there, and Gladys knew the time had come. She must try even if she failed, because Peri Lee knew she was there. Slowly Gladys moved nearer, straight for the girl's face, pausing among the pine boughs. She remembered bitterly that Peri Lee had called her horrible, and she trembled with the memory. Would that cause the girl to reject her?

"What's wrong?" Dale too had straightened and turned, looking first at Peri Lee, then following with his eyes the path hers sought. "Did you see something?"

"I'm not sure. But it's getting dark here, Dale. Let's go, please."

"Sure, Peri Lee, if you want to."

They went without talking, back toward the horses. Peri Lee hurried ahead of him, pulling, her hand still in his. Gladys followed closely, feeling her power in the growing effect she had on Peri Lee.

Like an invisible bird in the growing dusk she flew silent circles over her head, faster and faster, wearing her down, down, down. Making her helpless, unable to stay in control of her own brain.

And now to enter—where? The most vulnerable, the most tender—the throat? Yes, the throat. Where the blood throbbed and pulsed visibly in the girl's fear and flight.

Peri Lee's dark eyes widened and darted in her helplessness, her chin trembled. She pressed for a moment against Dale, as though the contact would drive away the other thing. Dale's arms closed on her tense body.

"Peri Lee? Peri—"

She raised her hands to protect her face, pushing at the air around her. "Oh God," she cried in low-voiced terror. "Oh God, no!"

Dale's hands on her arms tightened, tried desperately to hold her.

"Peri Lee, please, what is it? Don't do this, don't pull away from me."

She did not hear him. There was only the force, the growing power of the other.

A low cry came from Peri Lee and she jerked loose from Dale's hand, ran to her horse and mounted, leaning low over the horse's neck to urge him faster. Dale's calls to her were lost in the sudden beat of hooves on the hard floor of the pasture.

Gladys stayed with her, closer and closer about her in the spinning flight, feeling the resistance of the girl's fear as if it were a psychic wall thrown out for protection. Gladys fought desperately against it, trying to edge through, while Peri Lee's hands dropped the reins and came out to claw at her. But the hands were helpless, of a different substance, and could only fling themselves uselessly at the air around them. Peri Lee swayed in the saddle, never quite falling, and the horse raced with his belly low as if he knew what was needed of him and exactly where he was to go. Gladys pushed at her power of mental resistance, that invisible something that was far more powerful than the hands. She finally began to melt through because her own desperation and need to live, to be beautiful and to be loved, was stronger than Peri Lee's fear of the unknown thing that was Gladys.

Both hands reached up to clutch her throat, pressing it free of Gladys, bringing with it added psychic resistance; the hooves of the horse left the pasture as he stretched long in a high jump over a white stockade fence. Peri Lee instinctively leaned forward again, and the jump was made with her still in the saddle. The horse turned up the driveway, hooves slinging white gravel behind it. He spun to a halt, circling, as if carefully keeping the swaying girl in her saddle. He stood panting, still at last, the race ended.

Peri Lee twisted out of the saddle and fell sideways onto the gravel and lay face down. Her hands still at her throat, she was sobbing, shaking, gravel cutting into the softness of her lower lip and bringing the blood.

The echoing, pounding hooves of the other horse were close behind. Then the horse slid to a stop and Dale jumped off and kneeled, gathering Peri Lee into his arms.

Gladys, defeated, drifted into a tree out of Peri Lee's sensitivity range and watched with a mixture of regret, loneliness, and sorrow; a deep ache of heart seemed to be in the air all around her, growing like a cold winter storm.

She didn't want to frighten or hurt Peri Lee, and wished she could tell her that, but she couldn't seem to convey any message to her at all. Only fear.

People came pouring out from various places. The only one missing was Pete, and Gladys saw his flashy red car with the wide white stripes was gone.

Peri Lee was sitting up now, sobbing to Dale and to her parents, "Something was after me. It flew down out of the—the trees—it—"

Dale, holding her, looking over her at the O'Brions, shook his head. "I didn't see what it was." But his voice shook too and his arms held her as if he was afraid to let her go.

"But it was dark!" the girl cried, putting anger into her voice. "It was there! It was too dark to see! Dale, help me! Don't any of you believe me? Dale, something wants me! Save me, please save me."

Olivia pulled her gently away from Dale and to her feet. "Come on into the house, darling. I'll stay with you."

No one said anything about the remaining light from a sinking sun that still cast shadows beneath the trees on the lawn, light that kept the dark away. No one said anything more. Silently, they filed along the concrete walk behind Olivia and Peri Lee. Only Hamilton remained standing in the driveway. After a moment, he took Peri Lee's horse by a dangling rein and clucked at it and led it toward the barn.

In the hall the others separated. Olivia took Peri Lee up the wide stairs to the second floor. The housekeeper and maid went their own ways toward the back of the house, with Bertha shaking her head and muttering dark words about evil spirits. Gene and Dale followed Harry into his private office.

Gladys entered the house too, gliding without sound along the ceiling. Once she thought to herself that it was strange that she knew she was against the ceiling, but the ceiling didn't know she was there any more than the family did. Stupid, insensitive family. They couldn't see a ghost when it was right in front of their eyes.

She went with the men, drawn by their faces. A decision was being made, she knew. One that would have an effect on her chance to live again.

They closed the door and sat down. Gene lighted a cigarette. After frowning at him in disapproval, Harry sighed, got up again and opened a cigar box. The paper was so old it crinkled with age when he broke it. The stink that filled the air when he lighted the cigar made him cough, but with a look of determination, as if he intended to conquer it or else, he brought it back to his mouth.

"I hoped we wouldn't have to do this," he said. "But I don't see any choice. The doctor said she needed a psychiatric examination if she had any more of these spells. She should be taken to a hospital for awhile."

Dale said quickly, "There might have been something in the trees that I didn't see. She was honestly scared."

"She's been scared too much of the time lately, Dale."

"I don't think she needs to go to a hospital. She's not crazy. I agree something has been bothering her for quite awhile, but she's not crazy!"

"No, we know that. That's not the reason. The doctor thinks a change might be the thing she needs. A couple of weeks, he said—"

Dale got up, shouting, interrupting. "Two weeks!" As if it were a lifetime. His hands made chopping motions in the air, helpless, but aggressive and angry. "All right, I'm telling you she saw something. Something *is* after her. Was. A bird, or a bat. I was keeping my eyes on her, so—well, maybe I saw it too. She's not sick!"

Gene said, as if all resistance had finally oozed out of him, "We don't want her to be sick, Dale. The quicker it's handled the quicker it will be cured. I felt just like you do. I wanted to hide my head in the sand about this—her change in behavior, from scared and nervous back to normal and happy again. But I saw that horse flying across the field and I saw Peri Lee about to fall, every step of the way, with her hands up like she was fighting something. And I saw there was nothing any bigger than a bumblebee. Whatever it is, it is in her mind, Dale. Let's take her—let doc send her—to that hospital. Anything to get her happy again. To get it cured."

Dale whirled to face him. "What? What will be cured? What will she do in a place like that by herself? A place with bars on the windows, just as if she were a criminal, just because she got scared of a bird that flew down out of the trees."

Harry said, "It won't be like that. It's only a hospital."

Dale's voice was still loud. "A *psychiatric* hospital! Did you ever see one? Well, I have. When I was in school I took that psych course. It's high security. No knobs on doors, and the kind of window screen that can't be broken. Might as well be bars, because there is constant supervision."

He looked from one face to the other and they looked back at him. Silent. Waiting for him to settle down and accept the fact that Peri Lee, his darling, his ideal girl, was mentally ill. Finally, the father spoke again.

"We love her too, Dale, and we wouldn't hurt her for anything in the world. But she can't go on this way. She needs help."

Dale sat down. He swallowed, something painful and lumpy in his throat, and said nothing more.

Gladys wished to be outside, where the air had grown cool and the shadows deepened. Where a kind of peaceful quiet had settled over the rich agricultural community. She rose up into the sky, above the trees of the driveway where her view of the three-section farm was nearly complete. The sun had dropped below the western mountains, leaving a rainbow of reflecting colors in the streaks of clouds that hung in the sky.

Gladys considered the conversation she had just heard.

In another few days, they would be thinking Peri Lee was going insane. They were already beginning to think it. If Gladys didn't do something fast, they would have the girl locked up behind doors with no knobs in some mental hospital. With a psychiatrist there for her to talk to, she might increase her resistance against the penetration of her brain. And if that happened there would be no hope for Gladys.

But she had failed in her attempt at possession a few minutes ago. What had she done wrong?

Instantly, from nowhere, she knew. She had gone to the throat when she should have gone directly to the brain. The temple was the only place of entry. And she must wait until Peri Lee slept. It would be easier then.

Gladys dropped back toward the house, back into Peri Lee's bedroom.

To her surprise, Peri Lee was not in her room. The lights had not been turned on, the bed was untouched. Suddenly, terribly anxious to find her, Gladys flew from room to room, and finally came to the guest room where Peri Lee lay sleeping in one of the twin beds. Two soft lights had been turned on, but Peri Lee had been left alone, with the door closed, her mother gone.

Gladys could tell by the way the girl was breathing that she had been given another sleeping pill. She was soundly, defenselessly asleep.

They had done exactly the one thing that made it easy for Gladys.

She moved toward Peri Lee, closer and closer, slowly; going down toward the vulnerable temples, pulsing and unprotected. Peri Lee didn't move. She breathed evenly and deeply, her mind at rest, with not even a dream to protect her against Gladys. Gladys knew with sudden trepidation that this was the time. The only time she might ever have. She didn't know what to do, only to go to the temple and try somehow to enter. She had to reach the brain. Reach it and take it as her own, in order to live again.

Peri Lee began to move restlessly when Gladys touched her, but it was a weak, helpless move.

GLADYS BECAME aware of a sensation of warmth and was amazed to realize she was feeling the touch of smooth, living flesh. She had not really noticed a lack of sensations since death, until now. Then, as she moved nearer to the brain, as she passed through the thicknesses of human skin, she became aware of another sensation: the electrical currents that moved constantly about her. But the pace of it began to change, its throbbings took on a different rhythm as she pressed slowly inward. For one brief moment, she saw something like a wide, endless blurred stairway, or far away layers of thought and mind depth. As she watched, for a moment held in abeyance by her astonishment at the heights and depths of worlds unknown to the living, the surprising sight began to fade as it moved toward the lower depths—*Peri Lee—the mind, the thoughts, the knowledge, the essence that was Peri Lee, was going to rest in the abyss of her subconscious mind.*

A great happiness enveloped Gladys. She wasn't destroying the girl after all, as part of her had feared. There would be no actual harm done, she assured herself. No harm at all. With a great surge, Gladys rushed inward. Then she was no longer aware of Peri Lee's feeble bodily movements.

THERE WAS FIRST the sound of the heartbeat, loud in her ears, like drums in the night. Then a sense of intense fear because a huge, shadowy vulture-beast had closed in on her face, its great wings flapping silently over the bed, its head burrowing into her temple. She fought to breathe, to push it away, but her hands went through it as if it didn't exist.

The great dark bird was gone, and with it the fear. She opened her eyes and saw where she was, and there was a moment of puzzled wonder; as if she had awakened from a dream to find herself in a strange world.

Then came the excitement.

Because the eyes through which she looked were the eyes of Peri Lee.

CHAPTER 5

Her brain was drugged with the sleeping capsule, yet she didn't dare waste a moment of this new person she had become. She was alive, and she had to rise and live.

She threw back the cover and got out of bed. An open door showed her a private bathroom, and she went toward it, but a mirror she passed stopped her. She stared. Pale blue pajamas, long and concealing, tonight. A pale, beautiful face, with eyes dark and deep and black hair that hung long and slightly tangled. Her mouth was open in wonder and astonishment, the lower lip full and softly moist. A very deep flesh red with a small mark where the gravel had cut her. In sudden, wild excitement she pushed down the bottom of the pajamas and stepped out of them to look at the legs in the full-length mirror. Long and straight, curved just enough to make them perfect. Her fingers tore at the buttons on the blouse, and one button ripped off and rolled onto the carpet. She threw the top aside and stared at her body. Then she began to touch it, with hands that were sensitive and smooth. The waist that curved in, the breasts that pushed out, firm and full enough to arouse envy in any girl years younger than she.

Years younger? She laughed aloud, then said to the reflection in the mirror, "Remember, you dumb fool; you're not thirty-three, you're eighteen." Her voice was the voice of Peri Lee, slightly hoarsened, a bit huskier than usual.

At that moment she saw in the mirror that Olivia had come silently into the room and was standing behind her, staring at her, a look of disbelief on her face. Gladys dropped her hands, and simply looked back into the mirror at the older woman.

Olivia visibly composed herself, but Gladys could see the astonishment still there, and with it a growing softness. It was as if she were reminding herself that Peri Lee was mentally ill and, under the circumstances, it was understandable that her young daughter would feel herself in so lascivious a manner. Gladys guessed to herself that Oliva O'Briion left the feeling of her own body up to Harry. The thought of it made her tremble inside, and she wished Olivia would go to bed with him so she could find someone for herself. She was long overdue a man now.

"What are you doing out of bed, dear?" Olivia asked, coming over and stooping to pick up the pajamas. She held the top for Gladys to put her arms in. "You'll catch cold. Let Mother get you back to bed."

She was supposed to be asleep, Gladys remembered, and there would be no getting rid of the woman until she was. Besides, she had to remember that she wasn't Gladys anymore, she was Peri Lee O'Brion. She had to behave as such when her parents were around, or they would stick her away so fast and permanently she would never get out.

Maybe, if she didn't say anymore, her mother would think she had been sleepwalking.

Obediently she put her arms into the long sleeves of the pajama top, and then let them fall to her sides while Olivia buttoned her up. Then she stepped into the bottoms, and allowed herself to be guided back to the bed and tucked in. Olivia bent down and kissed her forehead.

For the first time in her memory someone had kissed her, was putting her into her bed with love. For the first time, she knew what it was to have a nearly dead yearning awakened and touched briefly. But she was no child, she was a mature woman, and she couldn't respond to the mother's love. The yearning was replaced by regret that it was too late for her to accept parental love. It brought back unhappy memories and a sudden, deep feeling of homesickness. She wanted the love of her own mama—not the love of Peri Lee's mother.

She closed her eyes quickly so that she wouldn't have to talk to Olivia, to push away the homesickness and found she was sleepy after all. The drug stirred in her brain, rocking her gently out of reality.

When she awoke her first vague thought was that another day had come, that she would have to get out of bed and drag herself down to the factory. Her mama must have forgotten to call her and her alarm hadn't gone off and be damned if she wouldn't be late and the foreman would bawl her out... Then she remembered and opened her eyes.

It was not her ugly room in the old apartment house; it was the lovely guest room in Peri Lee's house. The draperies had been drawn over the window and the room was softly shadowed against daylight. She turned onto her side and saw that the door was closed, the other bed smoothly made.

She was alone.

She was no longer twisted, crippled and ugly. She touched herself, her lovely, lovely body. Slipping her hands under the pajamas she examined every inch of the body that was now hers. No more standing in front of the mirror in an unlocked room. She pushed the cover back and looked down at herself; she wondered how long it would be before she could get to Pete. Because that was where she was going, the first chance she got.

She lay still and thought about it. How would he do it? And where? In his bunk? In the hay in the barn loft? She laughed. Yes, the hay. Wasn't that usually where farm girls were supposed to get screwed the first time? She laughed aloud, harder, at her own little joke. Then she heard a voice somewhere in the lower part of the house and sobered quickly. She had to remember not to act like a goof.

She got out of bed and stood, wondering what Peri Lee would do now. Get the robe off the foot of the bed and go downstairs, probably.

She went down the stairs barefoot, slowly, her hand touching the white bannister, feeling its smoothness. Olivia was in the sunroom again, and she was talking to someone. Probably the cook-housekeeper.

"I don't believe they need water today, Bertha. You'll have all you can do with the house and meals, because I have to go soon and wake Peri Lee. We have an appointment to see the doctor at—" Gladys's entry into the room caused her to drop the sentence. She smiled. "Well good morning, darling. How are you feeling?'

"Okay," Gladys answered, and remembered that she must call her mother. "I don't want to go to the doctor, Mother. There's nothing wrong with me."

The woman's smile languished and almost died; a tiny frown flitted for an instant, the shadow of a thought. "It's only a visit. To talk to him."

"But I'm fine now. Really I am."

Hope brightened the woman's eyes. "You do look better."

The housekeeper spoke up in a voice unusually gentle for her, Gladys thought. "Maybe some breakfast is all she needs. A good, warm breakfast. What would you like the best, Peri Lee?"

The two women were looking at her, anticipating an answer which they knew better than Gladys did.

Frantically Gladys wondered what Peri Lee's favorite breakfast was. The only thing she could remember was that the girl hadn't eaten much. "Oh—orange juice and toast."

Immediately she saw the answer was wrong. Both of them said, at the same time, "Orange juice?" Gladys instantly surmised that Peri Lee hadn't liked orange juice. Then the woman explained.

"Darling, you know orange juice gives you a rash. Whatever makes you think you'd like orange juice?"

"Well," muttered Gladys, knowing she was on dangerous ground, "It's been so long, I thought maybe I could drink it now. But," she added hurriedly, remembering she had seen Peri Lee drink milk, "milk will do as well."

"Weller, I'd say," the cook said, in a more normal tone of voice. She was already headed out of the room, and Gladys turned to follow her.

Olivia joined her at the table by the windows and drank a cup of tea while Gladys munched slowly through the toast, buttered, without jam. She had remembered that Peri Lee turned down jam once when Pete offered it to her.

She didn't attempt to carry on much of a conversation. When Olivia said something Gladys smiled and listened, then ate her toast. But she kept wishing the woman would go away and just let her look out the window and enjoy being alive.

She wondered about Pete and tried to catch a glimpse of him somewhere. If she leaned back a bit she could see the barn through the poplar trees that lined the driveway. The first chance she got, she thought, she would sneak down there and see. But then, why sneak? No one would think anything about Peri Lee going to the barn. Or anywhere on the farm.

"I think," she said, finally, when the toast was gone, "I'll go wading. Okay, Mama?"

Olivia looked up quickly, and Gladys knew why too late. The *mama* had been spontaneous.

Gladys laughed and attempted to straighten it out. "Now I'm beginning to sound like Gene, with that dumb name 'mom'."

Olivia smiled, but she didn't say anything.

"Okay?" Gladys repeated. Peri Lee would have asked permission, she thought, especially on this day. "We don't really have to go to see the doctor, do we?"

"I think we should, Peri Lee. We do have an appointment. You can go wading when we get back." She glanced at her watch. "We have to be there at eleven, so I think you'd only have time to dress. Why don't you wear your blue dress?"

"The blue dress?"

Olivia hesitated, and said gently, "Yes, dear. The one you like so well. I think this would be a nice day for it, don't you?"

"Uh—sure, I guess so."

Hurriedly she got up and dashed out of the room. She ran up the stairs, delighting in her ability to do so. In the novels she had read about girls running up and down stairs, and she wondered how they could, or if they really did. But now she knew all it took was youth and strong legs. Then she thought about the blue dress. And hoped fervently that Peri Lee had only one blue dress that would be nice to wear today. But what the hell had Olivia meant about that?

As she had deeply suspected, the closet was large; a walk-in deal that had a three-way mirror against the back wall, lights overhead, a satin-covered bench, shoe racks that looked like book cases against the wall, and apparently miles of hanging clothes at both ends. She stood helplessly in the center of it, hardly aware of the plush yellow carpet under her feet, not at all aware of the reflection in the mirror. All she began to see was blue, scattered among all the other colors.

All shades of blue, too. "Holy macaroni," she said under her breath.

She began to pull out dresses. They were all suitable, as far as she could see. But Olivia had been speaking of a certain dress, and Peri Lee would know which dress that was. All Gladys could do was grab one and try to fake it.

She began to be taken up by the sheer joy of having a lot of things she had never had before. Everything was expensive and looked great to her. She finally settled on a decidedly springy affair with ruffles.

She chose shoes the same color, and a bag to match. Then she went to the make-up mirror to do something great with her face. When she looked at it she remembered that Peri Lee hadn't worn makeup, and the drawers in the make-up table didn't reveal much beyond lotions, perfumes, and a couple of tubes of very pale lipstick. One tube of mascara, but no eye shadow; nothing to have fun with. Gladys wondered why. Most teenaged girls loved making up once in a while. Oh well.

She chose a bracelet from among clutters of jewelry. It was a charm bracelet of white gold, loaded with interesting little things that she would have to look at some time.

When she went downstairs she walked slowly and with dread: knowing deep down that she had dressed wrongly. She was wondering how to carry it off. Otherwise Olivia would be thinking her darling Peri Lee had lost her memory. Nothing could be worse right now.

She stopped on the stairs, wondering about Peri Lee. Would any of her thoughts return, or had she gone so deeply into the world of the inner mind that she could never exist on this plane? Or what if she gathered strength and knowledge, then returned to force Gladys out again? She pushed the uncomfortable thought aside and went on, determined never to think about her again.

Olivia was in the sunroom again and had added to her costume a pair of white gloves and a white handbag. When she looked up at the girl she stopped adjusting a glove and stared.

Gladys took a deep breath and stood straighter. "I couldn't find it," she said quickly. "I thought I'd wear this one instead." She didn't dare say anymore and to her astonishment, Olivia's eyes grew wider.

"But dear," she said, "that is the dress I meant. The one you made. I was only admiring you, you look so lovely."

Gladys closed her eyes. "Oh, holy macaroni," she said without thinking. Of all those damned dresses she had picked the right one after all, then had to open her big mouth!

"What?' Olivia said, surprised.

"Nothing—uh—Mother. Thank you. For the compliment. Are you ready to go?"

The car, Gladys saw when they went outside, was a black Cadillac. It was nicer than any car she had ever ridden in. But she was very careful to say nothing about it. She stared out at the passing landscape, silent, until Olivia interrupted her own spotty conversation to ask her a question.

"Why are you so quiet? Don't you feel well again today?"

"I'm okay. I just was thinking about the doctor, and dreading it. I really don't need to go. Couldn't we just go shopping instead, then go home?'

"It won't take long to see Doctor Jim."

To persist would probably the wrong thing, Gladys thought, so she kept quiet.

Doctor Jim, she soon saw, was the same doctor who had come to Peri Lee's room that night. He looked at her expectantly. Gladys forced herself to relax, to be composed and dignified, as was Olivia. Even as she listened to Olivia explain about the night before.

"She was terrified. I had to give her another sleeping capsule."

Doctor Jim asked the girl, "What was it you saw?"

Gladys wished for the magic words that would straighten it all out, explain it to satisfy both of them. After a moment she said, "I thought I saw this bird, but I've been thinking, and now I'm not scared anymore. You see, there was this book I read, in school. About the vampires. And

I saw a bunch of movies. Anyway, I'm all right now. Really I am." She looked the doctor directly in the eyes and smiled sweetly, aware that Olivia was staring at her profile. She had a feeling the woman was remembering the little things since, such as coming into the room find her standing naked in front of the mirror, feeling her body.

But Olivia said nothing.

The doctor sat back in his chair. "Are you sure?'

"Yes, I'm sure," Gladys answered, relieved, eager to get out of the office and go back to the farm. "I feel fine. I won't be afraid anymore. Ever again." She wished Olivia would stop staring at her.

The doctor tapped his fingertips together silently and Olivia said, "May I speak to you alone, doctor?' To Gladys, "Would you mind waiting for me, dear?"

He got up and opened the door and Gladys went out. But when the door closed she stopped and stood there in the hall, where for the moment she was alone. Farther down, in another room, a nurse was talking to a patient, but their voices didn't interfere with the voices beyond the door behind her.

Olivia was saying, "It just isn't that simple, doctor. There are too many things. She seems to be losing touch somehow—she's forgetting, on the verge of losing her memory I'm afraid."

"Can you give me a specific incident?' he asked.

"Just small things—like the dress this morning. She has an old favorite and had forgotten what it was. There are other changes— vague—I can't quite put my finger on anything—it's more a feeling"

"But she does seem improved today, and her explanation was logical and entirely possible. Mrs. O'Brion, why don't you keep a close watch on her and report to me anything you feel important. But remember, it could have been just a phase, a nervous reaction from the book she read. Literature, and movies, can have powerful effects on anyone, no matter what the age. So let's wait a while before we consider taking her for a psychiatric exam. She may come out of this and be quite herself. You know too, don't you, that she has reached the age of rebellion, and young people sometimes do things that parents simply aren't prepared for. They usually manage to grow up, mature mentally, and come out of it in a few years—"

The voices were near the door and Gladys knew the doctor and Olivia were coming out. She hurried down the hall a ways, pretending to be walking slowly to the waiting room.

When they left the office, with instructions from the doctor to call him if they needed him, Olivia was very quiet. Gladys wondered why, what she had done wrong this time, then attempted to see the whole thing from an objective point of view. The change in her had been sudden, she supposed. Yesterday Peri Lee had been trying to convince everyone that something was there, and today... Oh well, Olivia would get used to it. Give her a few days. Meantime, try to stay away from her as much as possible so that she wouldn't have anything to report to the doctor.

After a lunch in a cafeteria and a short trip through a supermarket they drove home, and Gladys went immediately to her room. She carefully hung the dress back in the closet, and dressed in shorts and matching top. She thought of Pete then, and her mission for the afternoon, and removed her shorts so that she could pull off the panties underneath. Even though they were lacy bikini, they were too much. She pulled the shorts back on over a naked bottom, and left the dressing room giggling softly to herself.

She tiptoed down the stairs, listening for Olivia's voice and hoping to avoid her. When she reached the hall she heard her, back in the kitchen, talking to the cook. About dinner, or supper, as it was called.

The tall grandfather clock in the hall was about to strike one-thirty when Gladys slipped noiselessly out the front door. She crossed the open, graveled drive running, and went down on her belly to crawl under the bordering trees. Hoping she was out of sight, concealed from the house by the trees, she made her way toward the barn. At the lot she had to climb a board fence, and she paused to sit on the top board a moment and breathe deeply of her new freedom. It was going to be great, she thought, to be rich and beautiful, and really live. *Really* alive. As Gladys Swartz she hadn't even been alive. Never kissed a boy or man, to say nothing of going to bed.

The thought urged her on, and she jumped down from the fence to cross the barn lot.

In a lot on the other side cattle were eating hay, and it was being thrown down by someone in the barn loft. She was in luck, after all.

She entered the first small door she came to, and stepped into the dimly lit interior of the barn.

The smell of it stopped her. A mixture of odors she had never smelled before, slightly musty, slightly sweet, mixed with the dark in a way that stimulated and excited her. She closed the door quietly and leaned against it, waiting for her eyes to adjust to the dimness. Overhead was the sound of movement, someone in the hay loft, getting hay over to the big doors at the far end, to pitch down to the cattle in the pen below.

Pete. Of the sultry eyes and the virile body.

She walked slowly along the windowless room, searching for a way into the loft, and almost missed it. Like a ladder it hung against the wall, tucked into a dark corner where spiders lived undisturbed among their webs. On second glance she saw there was a hole in the ceiling at its top, and that it was no ladder at all but a wall-hugging stairway of sorts.

Old harness hung on the wall, and she grabbed a short strip of leather with a buckle on one end and holes in the other. Using it, she tore away the spider's web that was a bit too close to the ladder to suit her. And then she climbed.

She came out on a wood floor where loose hay was scattered, dropped from the bales dragged by. Light came in through the open doors, and the man outlined against the light was not Pete at all.

The disappointment she felt became a sharp cousin to anger. The old man, Hamilton. He was bending over a bale of hay, dragging it along toward the doors. He glanced her way, and straightened.

"Well. Hello, Peri Lee, how are you today?"

"Okay," she answered shortly, pouting.

He dragged a big blue handkerchief from his pocket and wiped his forehead. "Thought maybe you was bringing iced tea around. It's just about that kind of weather, ain't it?"

She didn't answer. Her heart beat heavily in disappointment. Her first chance for a man, and what did she find? She turned to leave, and stopped. And turned back to look at Hamilton. She hadn't really thought of it before, but he was a man.

She went nearer to him, staying out of the light of the door, keeping the stacked bales of hay between her and the light. When she was a few feet away from Hamilton she stopped. His eyes were a grey-blue, she saw, and set in skin wrinkled and brown. His thin hair had long since gone grey. It amused her to think what he would do to Peri Lee if he had a chance.

She unzipped her shorts and let them fall to her ankles.

Waves of color splashed across Hamilton's face as his eyes followed the shorts and came swiftly back up her bare legs. He raised his eyes quickly and looked into hers, locked them there as if he were afraid to let them move down again.

"You'd better get them back on, Peri Lee," he dried, hoarsely, pointing at her feet. "You'll take sick. You'll take your death of pneumonia." His hand shook as he pointed.

She laughed. "Death of pneumonia! Just because my bottom is naked? That's wild! Look at me, Hamilton, don't you like to look at me?"

"Peri Lee," he said, misery in his voice, "you'd better go back to the house before your daddy sees you."

"Where is my daddy, Ham?"

"He's—he's—I don't know."

"I know. He's gone somewhere on the farm, and you're here all alone, with me. Don't you want to look closely at me, Ham? I'll let you." She began unbuttoning her blouse, delighting in the way his eyes refused to move from hers, in the way he was beginning to shake all over.

"Peri Lee, I've knowed you all my life. Why—why I used to take you horseback riding. I learned you how to ride, I held you on my lap!"

She tossed her blouse and bra aside, and said softly, "I've come to pay you back. Now I'll hold you on my lap. Look at my pretty body, Ham."

He didn't answer, and he didn't look. His chin had begun to tremble, too, like the hand that still reached toward her. She went down on the floor, lay back and spread her legs wide. She waited, watching him, hoping suddenly that he wouldn't refuse her, that he wouldn't tell her to get out of there and then go tell Harry O'Brion what she had done. Her needs increased to near panic. She couldn't be told 'no,' and she had to have him come down on her to relieve the sexual tension that was building like layers of a tornado storm. Was the beauty of her body not enough? What would she have to do to make him forget who he was, and who she was?

She couldn't speak again, but her unsteady hands reached down to spread her own legs farther apart. She moved her hips up and down and saw his staring eyes glaze, saliva dripping from one corner of his opened mouth. It was working and she knew a moment of exalted anticipation as she watched him unbuckle his overalls and let them fall. Her eyes lowered from his face to the penis that stood out from his body—as large, as erect as Pete's had been. His age didn't matter then. Not at all. He wasn't impotent. He came at her groaning low in his throat, and his body was surprisingly heavy on hers, and wet and cold as he stretched flat on her stomach. His hands struggled with the rest of his clothing until he was free of it and his belly sweating wet against hers. His hands became rough then on her thighs and hips, and for a moment she hurt. Then she began to pull at him, helping him, her fingers digging into his flat buttocks.

She forgot that she had ever considered him old. It didn't matter. Finally, she had a man, and he wanted her so much that he had forgotten everything. Everything but her, and the act with which nothing in human experience could compare.

When he was through with her he cried. She stared at him silently, not understanding. He sat all hunched in the spilled hay, his thin white body shaking with sobs, his face lowered into his brown, dried-up hands. "My God, oh my God." His voice was low and private, only for himself and his God, and the brutal sting of his conscience. "My God, what have I done? What have I done?"

She stood up and pulled her clothes on, then stood a moment watching him, waiting for the awful sobbing to stop. In a way now, he was revolting; his neck and arms dark brown and making of his body something white and slimy looking that might have crawled out of a shell. In a way too he seemed pitiful, though she didn't know why. Hadn't she just given him what every man wanted most?

"Ham? Ham, it's all right. It was great. I liked it so much that I'll come every day if you want me to." She touched him lightly on the shoulder and he jerked sideways, away from her.

The rejection confounded her. "To hell with you, then," she said, hardly loud enough for him to hear. But then it hadn't really been for his ears.

She turned and left the barn loft, going down the ladder, and on out into the sunshine. A feeling of intense joy possessed her suddenly. She felt like running, straight into the wind, across the alfalfa field to the irrigating ditch. It had to be there, somewhere.

It was. About four feet wide and two feet deep, the water rushing cold and clear to its destination. She leaped into the middle of it, shorts and all, and sat down. Laughing aloud as the cold water swirled at her chin, she swept the ends of her hair downstream. She undressed in the water and threw her clothes up onto the bank. The bottom of the water-filled ditch was hard and slick, almost impossible to stand in, the soil packed into a mud that held the water as securely as rock. The swiftness of the water swept her feet from under her and she fell, laughing. She let it carry her along for a while, then she crawled out and walked back up out of the ditch in search of her clothes.

When she found them she had to wring the water out the best she could, then put them on wet and slightly muddy. If she dared, she would go without them, because she wasn't ashamed of this body. But if Olivia saw her... Well.

She wrung the water from her hair too, but still it dripped onto her back and breasts, and water from the shorts kept trickling down her legs. She ran back across the alfalfa field, jumping occasionally like the jack rabbits that were frightened out of her way, and the air began to dry her.

SHE SAW the group standing in the driveway the moment she passed the trees, and knew something was wrong. They stood in a small circle, looking at an object Gene was holding. Olivia, Harry, the cook, the maid, and even Pete. Everyone but Hamilton. And all eyes turned toward her.

No one spoke. Nor even smiled. She wondered what was up, and looked from one to the next. Then she saw what Gene was holding. The dog. It's body was limp in death.

Gene said softly, "He chased a rabbit in front of a car last night I guess. I found him just now, beside the highway."

Gladys went forward and stared at it. Curious, she thought, how small it looked now that it was dead.

They kept watching her, still not speaking, and the silence began to get on her nerves. Somewhere in the barnyard a rooster crowed, and tractors whined in a field far away. Gladys realized she didn't even know the dog's name.

Looking into their faces, she guessed they expected more emotion from her. This ratty looking little dog had probably been very important to Peri Lee—he had been an irrigation wader too, or swimmer, as his legs were so short. Gladys managed a deep breath, but that was all. She couldn't bring forth a tear. How long was it since she had really cried? Messy wet tears. She almost laughed, wondering what these people would do if they actually knew.

Gene saved her by saying in a very tender, brotherly voice, "I'll bury him beside old Ring, all right? And Timmy." Gladys nodded her head, wondering who Timmy was. Or what. Old Ring no doubt was another dog, but Timmy?

Gene went walking away, toward a group of tall spruce and pine trees at the back of the yard. Beneath them lower, varied evergreens screened whatever lay beyond. A pet cemetery, Gladys thought, and pulled away from Olivia when the woman tried to take her arm. She followed Gene, lagging several yards behind. She only wanted to see approximately where he was going so that she could investigate later. She wanted to know who, and what, Timmy was. For some reason it was going to bug her, she knew, until she found out.

Gene stopped in a small open space well concealed by evergreen trees and shrubs on all sides, and lay the dog on the grass. He turned away toward the garden shed, to get a spade Gladys supposed. She decided to go ahead and investigate now, while he was gone.

She slipped past the shrubbery and found herself in a strange little cemetery. A lot of things had been buried here, and every grave was marked by small crosses made of redwood. Each one had a name carved into the wood. The dog lay to one side on an unused portion of the cemetery. Gladys didn't know whether to laugh or snort. How dumb, she thought, to bury things as people were buried. The thought of it gave her chills, and she bent to read names to get her mind off it.

John Boy. Old Ring. Laddie. She didn't pause to read any dates. Where the hell was Timmy? And what was he? Or it. She had never thought about things—animals—having souls, or even names, until now. She had never been allowed to have a pet to love. She remembered wanting a kitten once that was homeless in the alley behind the bar, but her mama had said a flat, no-way no. So she had never known how it felt to give her affection to a pet. But Peri Lee probably had, so where the hell was Timmy?

She went down on her hands and knees and moved along, her face at the level of the grave markers.

"What are you doing?" Gene asked, behind her.

She jumped and straightened up, aware of what he had seen and how odd it must have struck him—his sister on her hands and knees reaching each little marker. She got up, brushed stuff off her knees and dusted her hands.

"I was just—well—looking. Bye." She left hastily, knowing he was watching her.

"Bye," he answered, automatically.

She went back to the driveway, but everyone had gone. Even Pete. After a moment of looking around for him she went into the house through the patio doors of the sunroom. She could hear the sounds of cooking from the kitchen, or the setting of the table in the dining room, but no voices. Quietly, she moved along the hall and saw that Mr. O'Brion's office door was closed. She pressed her right ear against it.

They were in there, Olivia and her husband Harry, and they were talking. She could barely hear them.

"It might have been a kind of shock," Olivia said. "After all, she is growing up. We can't expect her to behave the way she did when she was twelve and old Ring died."

"There's something about her that's not right," Harry said, and he sounded glum and stubborn. "Something about her eyes didn't look right. I tell you, Olly, and I hate to say it; something has happened to Peri Lee. I think she ought to go back to the doctor. I swear she was closer to laughing than crying."

"Harry!" Olivia cried softly. "What a horrible thing to say!"

"I know. I said I hated to say it. But that's the way it looked to me."

"Well, you were mistaken. The sun was shining in your eyes. You surely *are* mistaken." But her lowered voice sounded as if she were trying to convince herself, too.

"You mean to tell me, Olivia, honestly, that you don't notice a change in the girl?"

Silence. A silence that sent nervous chills down Gladys's arms. Then Olivia answered him, her voice as stubborn as his had been earlier.

"She's growing up. You have to expect a change, Harry. She can't stay a baby forever, as you apparently would like."

"Oh hell. I want her to be a normal girl, to grow into a normal woman."

"When? Ten years from now?"

"I let her go out with that Dale character, don't I?"

"Dale is not a *character*, and you know it. You liked him before he started dating Peri Lee."

"Well, he's too old for her. First thing you know he'll be wanting to get married. What is he? Twenty-four? Twenty-Five?"

"I don't really know which. He's been out of college for about a year." She had calmed down, gone nearly out of hearing range. "Good Lord, Harry, he's lived next door nearly all his life. And you've known him all that time."

"Yeah, you can say that again," he said with a grunt. "I heard about that little tramp in town."

"You mean to sit judgment on him, Harry? Can you say that you never dated a tramp before you married me?"

Another silence.

Then Olivia was speaking again. "Harry, it's hard to admit seeing a change in someone you love so much. But of course I have. I've been too close to my daughter for too many years not to see. But Doctor Jim said to not worry yet. To wait and keep an eye on her before we do anything definite about a psychiatrist."

"Do you think something is bothering her? Worrying her?"

"Doctor Jim thinks it's a growing-up phase—a growing away from us—"

Angrily, Harry interrupted, "I don't buy that! Besides, I said what do you think? You're the one who's with her all the time."

"Not as much as you might think. I keep feeling she's going to be all right. She has to, Harry. I can't bear to think of her becoming mentally ill."

Soft sobs ended her words, and heavy footsteps crossed the room.

"There, there, darling." Harry's voice had gotten low and very soft. Gladys could hardly hear him. "Whatever it is, we'll stand by her. Don't worry, sweetheart, I shouldn't have—"

There was silence then and Gladys hurriedly tiptoed away. The danger was there, just beyond the closed door, in the silence. Man and wife standing together, to watch over and protect their daughter. Of all things Gladys didn't need it was that. How long could she carry off the role of Peri Lee O'Brion?

Gladys went upstairs to her room, locked the door and began to look around. She found the private bathroom was larger than her old room at home had been and she stood admiring it for awhile. All blue and gold, with mirrors everywhere, it reflected her beauty satisfyingly. She poured a handful of bubble grains into the tub and ran it full of lukewarm water. She left her discarded clothes in the middle of the floor, deliberately, enjoying the feeling of superiority it gave her to know that the maid would have to pick them up.

Bathed in perfume, she did as Peri Lee had done and stretched out nude, full length on the bed. Then she did something that Peri Lee had not done. She felt the body, with hands that relished each curve.

Drowsy, halfway into sleep, thoughts came to her mind. Was the personality of Peri Lee as deeply buried as her own body? Would this last? Would she be able to keep this lovely body for herself? Would the folks accept the change in her eventually, so that she could be free and happy here?

She turned over, pushing the thoughts away. She had promised herself that she would forget all the negative thoughts. Forever. Of course it would last. She was desperate that it should last. She had to remember that she was no longer Gladys Swartz, the ugly one. If the kids who had teased her could see her now! She hated them, all of them.

She had to remember she was Peri Lee O'Brion, eighteen years old.

But in her dreams she was Gladys Swartz again, shapeless and ugly, and she was back in the factory and Ham was there. She followed him behind boxes in the corner, pulled down her panties again and lay down. She played with herself to make him hot, but he wouldn't touch her. He backed away, sneering, and called her horrible.

She woke cringing. Someone was knocking on her door.

"Peri Lee?'

Olivia's voice.

Gladys slid off the bed and ran to the closet. She pulled out a robe and put it on, then went to the door.

"Are you all right, dear?" Olivia was asking.

Gladys unlocked the door, and faced the woman. "Hello—Ma—Mother." At least she had remembered and changed it to mother, instead of the mama she was used to saying. There must be some improvement in her attempt to change her personality.

"What's the matter, Peri Lee?" Olivia asked, her lovely eyes looking worried.

Gladys groped for an answer, and came up with a memory of the dog. "I just lost my dog, Mother." The unfamiliar word felt strange on her tongue, but it was something she would have to get used to. She might even grow to like it and be as close to Olivia as Peri Lee had been. The thought brought a new warmth, a feeling she could define only as one of security and knowledge that she was loved. But that time had not come yet.

Olivia put out her arms and Gladys hesitantly went into them, but she turned her face away. She couldn't recall ever being hugged before, by anyone. This woman's proximity gave her a vague and undefinable uneasiness, as though to be near would let her know the truth about Peri Lee.

The tense moment passed and Olivia gently pushed her away.

"Now get dressed, it's time to eat. The men will be coming in soon."

The moment Olivia was gone, Gladys closed the door and pressed the button lock slowly. There was no telltale click. It locked smoothly and without sound.

She went into the dressing room and looked for short shorts, and a tight blouse. Pete would be sitting next to her, she hoped, as he had sat next to Peri Lee. She wanted him to suffer a little. She found shorts which had been cast into the back of the drawer. They were so tight she could hardly button them. The buttons were big and red, and went down the front from waist to crotch. Attention getters. Her round buttocks pushed the seat out seductively. Pete would love that. Give his imagination a good start. But she couldn't find a tight blouse, or top of any kind. Peri Lee had been a square, she thought angrily, tossing clothes out of drawers.

She gave up and bent to pick the clothes up, then remembered that the maid, whatever her name was, would do it. She smiled and stepped over them, deciding to use a couple of scarves and crisscross her bare breasts with them.

The effect pleased her. Everything showed just the way she wanted. The brown nipples protruded, visible both in color and substance. She practiced walking in front of the mirror. A bit less queenliness, and a bit more swing to the rear than Peri Lee. Especially when Pete was looking. *Not* in front of Olivia, however.

They were all at the table when she entered the kitchen, talking, passing a plate of meat. Pete's eyes found her first. They widened slightly, then narrowed, and stared. She returned his stare without blinking the long eyelashes that were strangely visible all the time, like small awnings. She noticed then that Pete sat alone on his side of the table, the chairs on both sides of him empty. One was hers, the other Hamilton's. But she noticed the emptiness of Hamilton's chair without really thinking about it.

Harry had turned, at his end of the table, and was looking over his shoulder through the windows at his back. He didn't see Gladys. He said, "I don't know why Ham hasn't shown up. Do you suppose he forgot what time it is?"

His wife, at the other end of the table, leaned back and put her hands into her lap. "Why don't we wait until someone goes and calls him? Gene?"

Harry turned back to face the table, and saw Gladys. His eyes moved quickly down and up her costume, and the words he had started to say ended in a wordless grunt. His stare made everyone else look at the girl.

All silence. And surprise on every face.

Gladys moved, seeing she had shocked the whole family, wishing she could laugh, yet not daring to go that far. Her eyes downcast, she went quickly around to her chair and slid in close to the table. Harry O'Brion cleared his throat.

"You going for a midnight swim or something?" he asked gruffly, disapproval plainly in his voice.

"Well, maybe," Gladys said.

"Isn't it a little cold for that, dear?" Olivia asked.

Gladys shrugged, and attempted to change the subject. "Where's Ham?"

Gene got up and mumbled, "I'll go get him."

All of a sudden everyone stopped looking at her, and for the first time she felt comfortably ignored by all but the maid across the table, and Pete at her side. The maid kept glancing up at her, then dropping her glance quickly. Pete's attention was silent and sneaky. He leaned back in his chair and dropped his left hand to his thigh. Gladys moved her own leg over so that his fingers touched her.

She heard the sudden difficulty in his breathing, and felt the urgent response in her own body. She wished she could say poof and turn all the others into dust, so she could get Pete down on the floor under the table cloth. His fingers raised and brushed her thigh, caressing. And then pressing down, digging into her flesh. Excitement thundered in her heart. This was better than any dream Gladys Swartz had ever had, she thought to herself, any sex she had ever read. Better than anything. Even better than Ham. She had to get to him, tonight, somehow.

Footsteps pounded on the back walk, and across the screened porch, then Gene stood panting in the kitchen doorway. Gladys turned in her chair to look at him and saw his face nearly as white as the shirt he wore. Pete's hand jerked away from her.

"Dad—" Gene said, "Pete—come help me. Hurry."

He ran out again, and both Pete and Harry moved to follow him. But before Harry went out the door he paused and glared down at Gladys.

"Get upstairs and put some clothes on."

The sternness in his face caused Gladys to instantly obey, but under her breath she said, "Bear!"

Behind her Gene's shout floated back. "Mom, call the doctor!"

Gladys hurried too. She didn't know what was up, but whatever it was she didn't want to miss it. Ham must have gotten sick. Had the tumble in the hay been too much for him? She ran up the stairs, down the hall to her room, and threw off the scarves and the shorts. Hoping to eliminate the disapproval of the man who unfortunately had control over her, she chose blue jeans and a loose shirt. She didn't even notice the colors. She zipped and buttoned up as she ran back down the stairs.

Olivia was just hanging up the telephone in the kitchen. She hardly glanced at Gladys as she crossed the kitchen to go outside and join the hired girl and the cook. Gladys followed closely behind her. In a small, silent group they stood on the walk and looked, and waited.

Gene came running back from the barn and passed them without speaking. But his mother called after him.

"Gene! What is it?"

"I have to call an ambulance and the sheriff," he answered. "Ham has hanged himself."

"Hanged himself!" Olivia whispered loudly. Her teeth bit into her lower lip, and she turned back to stare at the barn.

Gladys didn't move. Silence descended around them, until Gene came running back by. Then Olivia spoke softly, to herself, or to anyone who could answer.

"But why?'

The silence came back again. No one answered her. They all seemed to be holding their breath.

A car spun in to the driveway and roared to a stop, and Harry came running to meet it so that Olivia didn't have to speak to the doctor at all. Harry took his arm and wrenched him toward the barn. A moment later the siren of the ambulance rose faintly into the air, becoming louder and louder along the highway. The driver didn't shut it off until he had pulled to a stop, down by the white corral fences of the barn lots. The sheriff's car was right behind it.

It seemed ages before the stretcher, loaded with a rounded form and draped completely in white, emerged from the barn door. It was a picture in slow motion, a silent moving group of men, with the shrouded stretcher carried between two of them.

Two furious, guilt-ridden words slipped from Gladys' mouth. "The fool!"

Olivia, Bertha, and the hired girl all turned and stared at her. Gladys looked from one face to the other, but she didn't attempt to say anymore. After a moment their attentions went back to the silent picture near the barn, and Gladys was left with the pressure of her thoughts. He had hanged himself because of her? Why? Had he hated what they had done so much that he would die before he would be tempted again? Had he hated her so much—or was there another reason?

Whatever it was, he was dead now. And that meant he was capable of coming to make her suffer, if he so wished.

Goosebumps rose to cover her arms and she rubbed them and looked up into the sky. Had he gone on, or had he chosen to remain, as she had?

"Peri Lee."

For a moment the name meant nothing to Gladys, then she remembered and jumped nervously, answering with a hasty, "Huh?"

"Maybe you ought to go in." It was Bertha, the cook, talking to her.

Gladys simply, wordlessly shook her head and continued to wait with the women. Ham hadn't stayed, she silently reassured herself. She would know by now if he had. When he had chosen death it was because he wished to be freed from the burden he carried. He would not have remained here. She drew a long sigh of relief and began to relax a bit.

The ambulance left, and the doctor. But the sheriff remained and the group of men continued to stand near the barn, talking, their voices too low and far away to be heard.

Olivia turned first, shivering. "Let's go in. It's getting cold out here."

They went into the kitchen and sat at the table again, but no one noticed the food.

"I can't imagine," Olivia said, "*Why?*"

"I wonder if his wife knows," Bertha said.

Gladys felt a surge of surprise. Ham had a wife? Before she thought, she asked, "Did he live with her?"

Olivia glanced sharply at Gladys. "Of course."

"Then why did he always eat with you?"

"Peri Lee," Olivia said, "You surely knew. Mrs. Hamilton has worked the evening shift in a restaurant for years. He has always had his evening meal with us. Don't you remember meeting his grand-daughter? He used to bring her out to play with you. Don't you remember that at all?"

Gladys dropped her gaze, thinking hard. She was going to get herself in real trouble if she didn't watch her stupid mouth. "I guess that terrible thing he did made me forget. I'm sorry, Mother."

Bertha said, "That's easy to understand. Something like this would make anybody forget."

Olivia sighed deeply. "Yes, I guess so. Poor man. And poor woman. But I can't imagine why."

Gladys wished she would quit saying that. She gazed down at the meat someone had put in her plate and saw that it was baked pork ribs, brown and juicy, the meat thick on the bones. Ordinarily, it would have looked so good that her stomach would have ached pleadingly. But her appetite was gone. She kept seeing Ham writhing naked, and she kept hearing the terrible sobs of his guilt. Now she knew why. He'd had a granddaughter like Peri Lee, and a wife who undoubtedly trusted him. But mostly, it was probably the association of Peri Lee with his own daughter and granddaughters. Why in hell had she gone to the barn anyway? Why hadn't she waited for Pete? Pete wouldn't hang himself over it, not Pete. No. He'd come begging for more. She moved instinctively and put her hands on the plate. She started, then thought better of it.

"May I eat?" she asked. She wasn't hungry, but if she sat still another minute doing nothing she'd start screaming. She had to get her mind off Ham.

After a pause Olivia said, "Yes, of course. You too, Bertha, and Rene. There's no point in not eating, I guess."

Gladys hadn't waited for them. She picked the ribs up and tore them apart with her fingers. She gnawed her way long the bones, stopping only to lick each trembling finger thoroughly.

"Peri Lee," Olivia said in soft reproval, "Have you forgotten your manners also?"

Gladys lay the meat on her plate and wiped her hands on her napkin. Then she carefully wiped the grease from her face. The men coming in saved her from Olivia's watchful eye.

Only Pete seemed to have any appetite. Harry drank coffee, but all Gene did was sit in a wooden rocking chair near the windows. Leaning forward, his elbows were on his knees and eyes on clasped hands.

Olivia asked, "Shouldn't we go tell Mrs. Hamilton?"

"The sheriff will do that."

"Why did he do it, Harry?"

Harry shook his head. "Only God knows." He cleared his throat after a moment of dead silence in the room. He said, "If he had any troubles I didn't know about it. He didn't tell me. He seemed in good humor the last time I saw him. At noon."

Another moment of silence, and then Olivia said, "Do you think we should go to be with Mrs. Hamilton for awhile?"

Harry looked at his daughter, and Gladys knew he wanted to ask whether they should leave her alone now. Instead he quietly said, "We can go tomorrow. She'll have her family with her tonight, I'm sure."

The telephone rang, and no one moved to answer it. On its third ring, after looking over at Gladys, Bertha went to the phone.

"Like I figured," she said, holding it away from her, "it's for you."

Gladys, surprised, forgot for a moment that she was not Peri Lee. She said aloud, "But who could it be?"

Everyone looked at her then, even Gene. But no remarks were made.

The voice on the phone was Dale's. "Hi, Peri Lee. How are you?"

"Okay."

"Would you like to go out for awhile? To a movie or something?"

"Oh sure." Anything to get away, to get her mind on something else. She remembered she would probably have to ask, and said into the phone, "Just a minute." To the family she said, "Dale wants to take me to a movie."

"A movie!" Harry answered "Tonight? That's not showing very much respect for Hamilton, Peri Lee."

Olivia said, "Dale can't be expected to know—what has happened to Hamilton."

For the first time Gene spoke up. "Why didn't you tell him, Peri Lee?"

There was no use arguing, Gladys could see. She would be expected to go into a period of mourning, black rig and all probably, when she really didn't even know the man. Into the phone she mumbled, "I can't go, Dale. Something awful has happened to Hamilton. He hanged himself in the barn this afternoon."

The phone was quiet while Dale apparently absorbed what she had said. It seemed a long time before he answered her.

"Do you want me to come over?"

"Do I want him to come over?" she asked the family.

Harry said, "I don't know anything he can do."

So Gladys told him, not too unhappily because she saw Pete's dark, steady gaze growing darker by each moment, "I guess not tonight, Dale."

"Well, I'll see you Saturday night then, all right?"

"Yeah."

She hung up the phone, wondering where they were supposed to go Saturday night. Surely the dear old daddy bear, Harry, wouldn't keep her from dating then.

"I think I'll go upstairs," she said. The gloom in the kitchen was growing on her, getting her down. Not even Pete's presence helped that much. Maybe upstairs she could think of something happier.

Olivia asked, "Are you sure you'll be all right?"

"Yes, I'll be all right."

An idea occurred to her as she went up the stairs. If any of them couldn't accept the sudden change in Peri Lee, like her sudden freedom from night terrors, she would simply say that she suspected she had been having premonitions of Ham's suicide. They might not accept that either, but at least it would be an excuse. Meantime she was determined not to worry about it. Nothing was going to keep her from enjoying herself if she could help it. Not even Ham's death. Perhaps he had been thinking of suicide anyway. She, in her own life, had thought of it and no one had known.

In Peri Lee's room she found a record player and hundreds of records, but every title she looked at was a stranger to her. After trying a couple she found it was the music of the young, all right, too modern for her tastes. It only added to her sense of burden and growing depression, and brought Ham too clearly to her mind. She felt like pulling her hair in anguish. Softly aloud she whispered words that had a familiar sound, "He's better off. Out of his misery."

She bit her lip. That was what they had said about her. And they had been right.

Gladys raised her face, looked at the ceiling and thought of the endless universe far beyond and the lovely, lovely music that reached down to gently lift away the tired and the weary, the souls of all those freed in death. The mystery was still there, and her fear of it. But Ham wouldn't have been afraid.

She turned, a quick physical movement to bring herself back to what she had so deeply desired. At all costs she must live. Nothing, *nothing* must stop her now.

In disgust she left the records and turned on the radio to a station that played country-western. Then, dressed in a lovely peignoir and matching gown she had found in the closet, she lay down on the bed, forgetting that she hadn't locked the door.

She was making plans. Tonight she would go to Pete. She knew exactly where his bunk was. She knew too that he would be looking toward her window before he went to bed. She'd give him a show he wouldn't forget.

The slightest tap of a knock was followed immediately by the door opening. Gladys leaped up, startled, as if the intrusion had been into her thoughts. Seeing Olivia looking at her brought a flush of angry guilt, and she knew, too late, that she had frowned. Quickly she smoothed it away.

"Oh, hi, Mother. You surprised me."

Olivia seemed hesitant for the first time. She remained at the door. "I didn't wait for an answer to my knock because I was afraid a second knock would disturb you, if you had gone to sleep. Are you all right?"

"Sure, Mother." Just hurry and get out, Gladys thought to herself. For Christ's sake, even a loving mother could sometimes be a nuisance. Though another time she might need her terribly, she didn't now. She needed Pete.

Olivia looked at the radio, and listened a moment. She smiled. "That's rather lively music to fall asleep to, isn't it? Do you want me to stay with you tonight?"

"No, I'm okay."

Olivia kept looking at her, the smile gone, her deep-set, grey-black eyes revealing a kind of puzzled thought that began to disturb Gladys. She knew something was wrong again, but she didn't know what it was. She ground her teeth together furiously. She couldn't go on forever acting like Peri Lee. It was too much of a strain. Why couldn't they accept her as changed because she was no longer a child? The old Peri Lee had gone. Why couldn't Olivia see that and accept it? Or maybe that was the trouble now. She could see it, and it bothered her. Well, sure, Gladys could see that it would.

She didn't want to leave and go back to the city, but she might have to. At least then she could go back to being herself. With a difference.

Heavy steps came along the hall and Harry looked over Olivia's shoulder. "Hi, Kitten," he said.

Gladys smiled. "Hi." He wasn't so old, she noticed suddenly. In fact, he was a darned good-looking man. And he looked as if he could squeeze a woman in two.

"How're you doing?" he asked.

Olivia answered, "She wants to be alone."

"Alone! No, not after all she's been through. You'd better let your mother sleep with you again tonight, Kitten."

I'd rather sleep with you, Gladys thought to herself. Aloud she said, "I'm okay."

Harry said to his wife, "What did she say?"

And Olivia answered softly and slowly, her puzzled gaze fastened steadily to Gladys, "She said she was *okay*."

"Okay?" he said. "I thought you said that was one word you always thought was ugly, Kitten." He pushed past Olivia and came into the middle of the room.

So it was a simple word that was causing trouble now. Gladys sighed. "Well, I just changed my mind." She couldn't seem to do anything right. Just one damned little word was enough to make Olivia wonder about her mind.

"You must have changed your mind about music too," he said. "But that's one change for the better, in my opinion. Isn't that what you say, Olly?"

But Olivia was still withdrawn, and she began to move away from the room. Her eyes drifted from the girl on the bed to her husband. "Come on, Harry. Let her rest."

"No," he said in the deep voice that never could be very soft. It came out in a kind of thunder, no matter how tender he tried to be. "I don't want her left alone. Get off that bed, Kitten. Go sleep in the guest room again tonight, so you mother can be with you."

She'd be trapped then, Gladys thought. How would Peri Lee try to get out of it? "Daddy," she said, rather liking the word, the way it felt on her tongue. She had always called her own father Papa, on the rare occasions she called him at all. He had never liked her, either. "Daddy, I'd rather stay here. I'm not afraid anymore, honestly I'm not. You know what I think it was, Daddy? I think it was a premonition about poor Hamilton. I think that's what it was, because suddenly I'm not afraid to be alone."

Olivia was still backing into the hall, slowly, step by step. Gladys knew her attempt to sound like Peri Lee had come out an ugly whine. But Harry didn't seem to notice. He sat down on the bed beside her, and put his hand on her shoulder. The warmth from it spread through her like fingers of electricity. She had to kiss him. She sat up and put her arms around his neck, and for a moment his arms were around her, hugging her tightly. It felt good. She turned her lips toward his.

He kissed her, lightly. She let her breath out, her body going limp with passion; she pushed her mouth into his, her tongue caressing his lips. Instantly, she felt him recoil and pull back from her. When he stood up he kept his face turned away.

"Get up," he said again, gruffly. "Go sleep with your mother." This time it was a fierce order.

He went out without looking back. Nor did he look at Olivia when he passed her.

The kiss, the first Gladys had experienced, still tingled on her mouth and through her trembling body. It had been a fatherly kiss, until she pressed closer. Her heart pounded with regret, partly because she knew it would be her last kiss from Harry O'Brion. If she tried to get closer to him, they would institutionalize her so securely she would never get out.

Oh well. There was still Pete. And, as far as that went, there was even Gene.

This is Gladys Swartz? she thought to herself, smiling, as she got off the bed. *I thought I hated men, and here all of a sudden I'm a man-crazy fool. But I like it.*

She went ahead of Olivia to the guest room, got into the bed and turned her back toward the other bed. She hoped Olivia wouldn't try to kiss her goodnight, and she didn't. Her mother was unusually quiet, and Gladys knew it was a bad sign.

She began to wish she had controlled herself when Harry kissed her. Because of her own actions, she was driving herself out of the security, comfort and love that was in this home with the O'Brion family. But her desires were growing toward total physical freedom, where she could do just as she pleased.

There was no chance to get out of the room without being seen, so Gladys gave up and went to sleep.

The house was quiet when she woke, and the room was warmed by sunlight through the east windows. Olivia's bed was smoothly made, and the clock on the dresser said nearly ten. Good Lord, Gladys thought, throwing back the covers. What am I trying to do, sleep my life away?

She went to her own room, showered and dressed in shorts and shirt. She brushed the long, shining hair and let it fall naturally. She didn't waste any more time then. Her new face did not need makeup anyway.

Feeling great, she ran down the stairs and through the hall to the kitchen. To her surprise, she saw Olivia sitting at the table drinking coffee with Dale.

She had forgotten Dale existed.

"Well, did you finally wake up?" he asked.

She answered shortly. "No, I'm still asleep." She went to the refrigerator to pour a glass of milk. Why did he have to come over? She didn't want to see him. She wanted to see Pete.

Everybody in the room was watching her, and she felt a little uncomfortable. She wasn't used to being watched like that. Peri Lee was used to it, but she wasn't. Then she remembered again, she wasn't ugly anymore.

"I'm glad to see you're feeling better," Dale said.

She went to the table to drink her milk. "I feel great."

"I came to see if you'd like to spend the whole day with me. We'll take a drive up into the mountains, and eat at our favorite restaurant. Want to?"

She hesitated. It certainly wasn't what she had hoped to do today, but she guessed Pete would have to wait. "Okay."

Dale said, "Your mother has given you permission."

Gladys ignored Olivia. "Will you take me as I am, or do I have to wear something more decent?"

His laugh was short and embarrassed, but he answered her quickly, "I'll take you as you are."

Olivia said, "You'd better get hiking shoes on instead of open sandals, though, hadn't you, dear? The rocks in the mountains might cut your feet."

"These are okay. I'll be careful." Gladys answered, pushing her milk and chair aside as she got up. Now that she had thought of it, getting out of Olivia's sight was something not to be treated lightly. The faster she got out, the better. "Let's go," she said on her way to the door.

CHAPTER 6

S he hoped he would drive the car fast, give her a thrill, but he didn't. He turned right at the highway and headed away from town, at a speed that made her want to push forward. She was indestructible. She was young, alive, and she wanted to fly, not crawl.

He pushed buttons and music joined the hum of the tires on pavement. She sighed, leaned back in her seat and looked out her window. The hand closed over hers, just as it had over Peri Lee's, and the pressure of his fingers was so gentle that she sighed in boredom. If that was an example of what the day would be, she thought, then she might as well have kept on sleeping.

"I sure was glad to hear you're not scared anymore, Peri Lee. It was terrible seeing you change from a happy girl to a frightened one."

For a moment she couldn't think of what he was talking about. Then she recalled her story about the premonition. It had gone over okay, then, and made the rounds of the family. "Me too," she said.

"You had me worried, did you know that?"

"Did I?"

His hand squeezed down on hers, but the pressure was brief. "I thought maybe you'd like to forget it, and that's one reason we're out today. I just wanted you to know I'm glad it's all over for you. I'm sorry about Butchy, I really am."

She looked sharply toward him. "Sorry about whom?"

"Butch."

"Butch, who's that?"

He looked at her, a straight, hard stare. "Butch," he repeated after a long pause. "Your dog."

"Oh!" She bit her lower lip, mentally called herself a fool. She looked down the road ahead, avoided his eyes.

But she could him watching her, glancing occasionally back to see that he was keeping the car on the road. He didn't say anymore. After a few minutes he leaned away from her, his left arm resting on the door, his right hand on the wheel.

The car speeded up and began to climb smoothly towards the mountains. The farms were left behind, a patchwork of varied greens and browns in the valley. The highway, a secondary road, was nearly deserted, and through the window Gladys saw the secluded pale green of a meadow and a grove of slender, white-barked trees. Their leaves danced lightly and sparkled in the sun.

"Let's stop here," she said. "I want to walk over there."

He reacted instantly, and pulled onto the shoulder of the road.

She had never liked to ride anyway, come to think of it. It reminded her of the long bus rides to work and back. And a few Sunday drives with Marian. Just ride and ride all day, what was great about that? She bounded out of the car, and looked back at him.

"We can make love here."

She laughed at the flush of surprise that crossed his face, and ran away from him towards the sparkling-leaf aspens.

The freedom of being safely away from Olivia's concerned watch got to her as she ran. She held her arms up to the sky and the cool air and shouted in pleasure. She whirled and danced, and turned to see if Dale had followed.

He caught up, and she flattened her body against his for a moment as his arms went around her. But she saw over his shoulder when he lifted her that the road was still in sight, and pulled away. She ran on into the shelter of trees and new, tall grass.

Laughing, she went down on her stomach, safe and hidden in the grass. He sat down beside her. She rolled over and looked up at him, and he returned her gaze without moving or touching her. She stretched her arms above her head, pushed her breasts up, and spread her legs in silent invitation. He didn't even seem to notice.

Just as she had figured. She laughed aloud again, thinking of Harry being worried about his daughter dating this guy. He was about as dangerous as a wooden statue.

"Ham had more life than you," she said softly.

He frowned. "What?"

"Take them off," she said. "They zip in the front."

His glance flickered to his shorts and back to her face. His frown came and went, mixed with the attempt of a smile. "Take what off?"

"Oh you know. Come on, don't tell me you never have."

He didn't answer immediately. With gentle fingers he touched her forehead and smoothed the hair back from her face. He sounded sad and faraway: "What is it, Peri Lee, that has changed you? Sometimes —" He paused as though saying this was the most difficult thing he had ever done. "Sometimes I don't feel I really know you anymore."

Gladys answered impulsively, and emphatically. Her body was dictating the need to her thoughts, making her half-afraid that he, like Ham, might refuse her; and that he, unlike Ham, would simply get up and walk away from her. "Once you've done it, you have to go on. You *have* done it, haven't you? I'll bet you have, plenty of times. Then why not with me?" She bit her lip hard, too late, wondering if he once had gotten into Peri Lee's pants. He would know there was something out of whack with her—if she couldn't remember *that*.

His face stopped playing with the frowns and the smile. "Have *you* ever?" he asked. "Funny thing, it never even occurred to me before that you ever might have. All at once now, I wonder."

"Ah," she giggled nervously, the moment of danger past. In all the years he obviously had dated Peri Lee, he hadn't gone beyond kisses and a few caresses. Didn't the man have any sex drive? Maybe he was impotent and didn't want anyone to know it. Well, she wanted to know. "Why don't you find out? You'd be able to tell, you know. If I'm a virgin I'll bleed, maybe. Just a little, or maybe a whole lot."

He moved back. "Come on, Peri Lee, stop talking this way. Get up. Let's get out of this God-forsaken place."

She raised just enough to reach him. Her hand grasped his shirt, pulled him down and pulled his mouth to hers. She reached her tongue in to touch his, sucking at him. He didn't resist the kisses after the first try, but she had to unzip the shorts herself. She pushed them off and pulled her blouse up, then with her hand she moved his between her legs. He left it there, trembling, feeling her gently as if afraid he would injure her. She unzipped his pants, reached into his shorts and felt the hard penis. She brought it out, freed from his clothes, and moved both hands down to massage it the way Pete had done his. Dale gradually moved closer to her, continuing the kisses, deeper, closer, harder, without encouragement from her. She felt pushed into the ground as he kissed her, his reservations gone, his extreme gentleness leaving and being replaced by sexual urgency, by passion for her no longer repressed.

It didn't last as long as it had with Ham. One moment he was getting on top of her, pushing deeply into her, and then he was pulling off. She urged him back again, moving her hips up, wrapping her legs around his. He slipped into her again and for a brief few seconds moved against her. He breathed the other girl's name against her neck.

"Peri Lee. Peri Lee. What are you doing to me? To us? I promised you I'd wait. You wanted to wait. What happened to change your mind?"

"Everybody does it," she muttered thickly, hating the interruption. "Come on, don't stop now."

"But we wanted to—" He gave in to her kiss for a moment. "To wait. You'll have to marry me now."

"Why?'

"Because. After this, do you think I can leave you alone?"

"I don't want you to. You can do it anytime. Like right now. Keep going, don't quit yet, I haven't come."

He didn't answer. His mouth grew limp against hers, and unresponsive. She felt him begin to pull away, and she was filled suddenly with fury.

"What the hell—are you impotent or something?" She knew he

wasn't, but she knew that it was the best way to get back at a man. She knew that from reading about a man's ego where sex was concerned.

"I don't get this. What has happened to you?" he said, no longer tender and gentle with her.

She flopped onto her stomach, propped her chin up with her hands and grumbled aloud, "I'd like to know where the hell those twelve-times-a-day guys are that you read about all the time. Ham was better than this. At least he stayed on long enough for me to come."

In a voice dropped icy cold, he said, "That's the second time you've mentioned Hamilton. You surely don't mean it. You couldn't have done it with him. He was old enough to be your grandfather, and more. In fact, you used to say he seemed like a grandfather."

"Ha!"

"I want to know what the hell you meant about Ham." He took her arm, not gently, and shook her. Disgust colored his face and the tone of his voice.

"You and Ham—did he do it to you? Why? For God's sake, why would you let him? After handing me that bullshit about wanting to wait. What are you turning out to be, anyway?"

She jerked away, feeling his fury and his disgust with a mixture of emotions. He loved her, didn't he? She wanted him to love her. Now she was afraid she had caused him to hate her instead. She got to her feet and pulled her shorts on. She glanced at him and saw that his whole face, and the light in his eyes, had grown hard and cold too. She told herself she didn't care. The world was full of men. But she wanted suddenly to hurt him. Hurt him for loving Peri Lee, instead of her.

"I'll bet Pete could do it twice in a row."

"Yeah," he answered, "I'll bet. But has it ever occurred to you that you might get pregnant? You wouldn't even know who was responsible—me, or Pete, or Hamilton. Old Ham. Poor old devil. Why don't I just take you home now."

"Okay by me," she answered with a throbbing anger that matched his.

He walked ahead of her to the car, and didn't pause to open her door the way he always had for Peri Lee. She glared her disapproval at him, but he ignored her.

The car spun a fast U-turn in the road, and the speed it picked up gave her more thrills than the tumble in the grass. Some lover he was, she thought. Peri Lee was lucky to be rid of him.

Her anger and feeling of rejection turned to fear, as she realized that her own mind accepted the fact that Peri Lee would one day return strongly from the depths of the inner world; to push away the intrusion of another, push out into the lonely, lonely thing she had been. *No, no, no.* Thinking of it might make it happen, might in some mysterious manner open the way for her to return. *Whatever she did, she must not think about Peri Lee.* She, Gladys Swartz, was the one who existed now, not Peri Lee O'Brion. Maybe that was the only way she could exist. Go back to being Gladys Swartz, in a beautiful new body. She should never think of Peri Lee O'Brion, or these things, these lovely clothes, the love of these people, as belonging now to her.

The conflict surged, strongly, pulling her away, yet holding her back with a reluctance to leave.

He didn't speak once. The speedometer needle flicked its red tongue toward the one hundred and ten mark, and she decided to enjoy the speed. She laughed in delight and said, "You think you're going to kill me or something? Sorry to disappoint you, darling. You see, I'm indestructible. I guess you could say that in a way I'm already dead." She thought about that, about her body, and added, "But you could cripple me. My body would be broken and crushed like—like a fall down a long, steep stairway." The speed got to her and her body tensed. The memory of what broken bones could do was too real.

The red needle dropped back. He didn't look at her, but she saw the tightness of white pain on his face. But it was pain for Peri Lee, not for her. Not ever for her.

The despondency that settled over her was surprising in its intensity. "Just let me out at the road," she said. "I'll walk up the drive."

He stopped the car as she had suggested, on the highway. She let herself out of the car and crossed the road to the graveled driveway. It was a while before the car moved on, and she felt he had been watching her, but she didn't look back.

It was Peri Lee he had loved, not her. So why should she look back?

She walked slowly along the drive, deep in her own sadness. His semen was wet and sticky between her legs, dampening her shorts.

No one had ever loved her in all her life.

She had never known before how complete sadness could be. It followed her, a little black ghost at her heels, twisted and shapeless, the shadow of her real self.

She forgot about Olivia until the woman's voice was heard from a rose garden at the edge of the lawn.

"What on earth is wrong, Peri Lee? I thought you were—"

Gladys whirled and saw the face beneath the floppy brim of a bright straw hat.

"Why don't you just leave me alone!" she cried. Thinking, *Bitch*, wishing she dared say it. Her own tongue stopped her just in time, but the words kept tumbling. "All you do is spy, spy, spy! Now leave me alone!" She ran across the lawn to the front door and upstairs to her room.

After she had cleaned up, dressed and calmed down, she considered what she had done and wondered how Olivia would react to it. She dreaded facing her, dreaded going downstairs for the noon meal, but knew it had to be done. Everything she did was wrong. She couldn't seem to help herself. Words, actions, poured out without thought. She had to think before she blurted out something.

Right now, before anything else, she had to apologize to Olivia.

She went downstairs quietly and looked outside, but Olivia was no longer in the rose garden. Gladys turned back to the house to try to find her. She looked into the sunroom and saw the hat on a chair. That meant Olivia was somewhere in the house.

Gladys looked into the living room and listened at the closed kitchen door, then she went back along the hall to the door of Harry's office. They were there, in low-voiced conversation. Instinct told Gladys it was serious. It always was when Olivia went to Harry's office. She stepped close so that she could hear.

"—it could be Ham's death," Harry was saying.

"Harry," Olivia's voice was so low, so filled with hurt that much of her words were lost. She ended with a brief "I just can't understand. I feel I somehow have been blinded—"

"Anyway, let's wait until after the funeral and see the doctor then. If it has to be done, it has to be done."

"Oh dear God, Harry."

"Ollie, please. Ollie—"

Gladys left, going back up to her room. It was too late to apologize. Too late to straighten out her mistakes. Everything was going wrong. They were going to take her to the hospital in a few days, and she was terrified of that. The only solution she could see was to get out of the house and away as soon as she could.

But how?

She waited until she heard the men come in to eat, then she went quietly down the stairs and took her place at the table. Her glances at Olivia got no response. The woman was ignoring her, she saw, Olivia's feelings had been so deeply hurt that she was making a careful effort not to look at her daughter at all.

Gladys thought the smart thing now would be to stick to her room for the afternoon. She didn't dare chance running into a mother-daughter talk if she could help it. She didn't want to antagonize Olivia any more than she already had.

She spent the afternoon trapped in Peri Lee's room, wondering how to get away. Money, she needed desperately. Once in the city she knew she could make money on her looks. Go-go dancing or something. She pulled the blinds, stripped, and practiced in front of the mirror. Or men would pay her. She stopped, stared at her body, and touched it with her hands. Why not? The body wasn't really hers. She could always think of that if she got to feeling guilty or something. Well, why not? But it took money to get to the city.

With sudden eagerness she began to go through the purses in Peri Lee's closet, but when she had all the change on the bed it amounted to only four dollars and a few pennies over. She called it the dirtiest name she could think of and swept it all onto the floor.

Let the maid clean it up. The little sneak would probably keep it and not say a word about it to anyone.

That night, for the first time, she was left alone. When it finally dawned on her that Olivia was leaving her strictly alone, the excitement made her tremble with impatience for the hours to pass, for the rest of household to go to bed.

She remembered that Pete liked to watch Peri Lee's windows at night, and she went to stand there. She looked down toward the place where his cigarette would glow softly in the dark, hardly larger than the fireflies that were beginning to dot the stillness of night. Slowly she began to undress. She threw her blouse over her shoulder, let her shorts drop. Then she waited a moment before she removed her bra and panties. A pulse thudded in her abdomen as she visualized Pete, throwing away his cigarette and reaching down to handle himself— She stepped out of sight quickly, a new thought striking her. What if Pete was a once-a-night guy. If he jerked off now, there wouldn't be anything left for her.

The second hand on the clock moved slowly. How long would she have to wait before she dared leave her room?

She dressed in a pair of baby-doll pajamas, then waited in the dark, her door open. A long, silent hour passed and the old grandfather clock in the hall downstairs struck a deep-toned half hour. At last Gladys slipped barefoot into the hall, and went down the back way.

Pete was in bed in the bunkhouse, sleeping. There was no night-light. *Good*, Gladys murmured to herself, *I like the dark*. And he snored. A light sound that guided her through the long, black bunkhouse.

She stood by his bunk for a while, anticipating his reaction at finding her in bed with him. He would think he was dreaming, proba-bly, and have a wet one before she could get on it. Laughing softly under her breaths she pulled off her pajamas and dropped them, then gently and slowly raised his blanket. He stirred, snorted, and went on sleeping. She slipped in beside him and let her body touch his. He was sleeping nude again, and her own reaction to the touch of his bare skin almost took her mind away from the entertainment of his reaction. She put her hand on his belly and felt downward. Surprise struck her. That huge thing she had seen the other time had dwindled to a soft little floppy dinky. But then it began swelling, enlarging, as if she were blowing air into one end of it. She laughed aloud.

One last snort, and he was suddenly very still. His breath caught somewhere and held. "What the hell—" he said softly.

Against his ear, she replied, "You're dreaming. You've been watching me from the window, haven't you? Before you jerked off and went to bed."

He turned on his side and one hand closed on her bottom and pressed her to him. "Now how did you know that!"

She smiled in the dark, whispering, "Secret. You'll never know."

"There's a lot of things about you I'll never know. When I first came here, I thought you didn't have an eye for anybody but *him*. You're a surprise package, babe, the kind of surprise I like."

She bit his lower lip, kissed him, and whispered, "Shut up and get to work. I want to see if you're a twelve-times-a-night guy."

"*Twelve,*" he answered in contempt, rolling her over onto her back. Panting, voice breathless, contemptuous of her estimation, he bragged. "*Twelve.* Babe, you ain't lived yet." Like an animal leaping on its prey he grabbed her, his hands rough and hard, his mouth sucking and bruising. She bent backwards, groaning in ecstasy, and her body went limp, helpless and pulsing.

Pete didn't talk much, and there seemed to be no end to his lust for her. Only perceptibly did he slow down as the night spun away fast, like the blood in her head. She found he hadn't been bragging after all.

When the black of the night receded to leave shadows of grey in the building, Gladys slipped out of his bed, pulled on her pajamas, and ran. *Too late, too late, these people are already getting up,* she whispered frantically. How could she get upstairs without being seen?

Through the sunroom, maybe. The patio doors had been opened, and Gladys tiptoed through. And met Olivia face to face in the hallway. They stopped and stared at each other. Gladys became aware that her hair had been tangled and messed by his hands, that her face and neck burned from the kisses and scratches of her wild night. She gave the old, old answer that came automatically to her tongue, "I'm sick, Mama."

Olivia's sudden concern wiped out any surprise she might have felt at being called mama, or the state of her daughter's appearance. Gladys instantly regretted saying she was sick. This mother cared. Deeply. But not for her, not really for her, only for Peri Lee. Gladys suddenly hated Peri Lee.

Olivia's arms were around her. "What on earth has happened to you, darling?" Her soft hand brushed the hair way from the girl's face, and her fingers touched red blotches on cheeks and neck. "What do you mean, you're sick? Did you drink orange juice after all?"

"Yes," Gladys mumbled. "I almost vomited."

"Why on earth didn't you just go to the bathroom? You'll catch cold going outside. You vomited?"

"No. I didn't really. I'm over it now. I just want to go back to bed."

"Fine. I'll help you—"

"No," Gladys said swiftly. She had to get away from Olivia. "Why don't you bring me a glass of milk, Mother? Up to my room. I want to go back to bed."

"All right, dear."

Olivia disappeared toward the kitchen and Gladys hurried up the stairs, and into her bathroom. She washed herself, cleaning off the stink of Pete. She changed to a pair of pajamas the same color as the others, and got into bed. When she heard footsteps in the hall outside she closed her eyes and pretended to be asleep.

Olivia came to stand by her bed. For a moment she remained there, then her hands touched Gladys's forehead lightly and moved away. Gladys heard the glass being placed on the bedside table, and footsteps crossed the room. The door closed softly. Gladys didn't bother to open her eyes. The exhausted body begged for sleep and rest.

The house was as quiet when she woke as if it had been deserted. She sat up rubbing her eyes, then began to listen. Was she alone? Curiosity brought her out of bed. The clock on the dresser said it was a few minutes after four. She had slept the day away. Good, she thought, stretching and smiling. That brought the night that much closer again.

But where was everyone? Something was going on. She could feel it. They were sneaking around, bringing a doctor and a strait jacket, or whatever they brought when they put people away. She had better get out in a hurry.

She took a quick shower, dressed, and went downstairs. A faint noise, a clink came from the direction of the kitchen. Someone was there, then. She slipped quietly to the door and looked in.

Bertha was at the table, and the clink was a pitcher of iced tea against a glass. The cook smiled slightly when she saw Gladys.

"Well. I was beginning to think you'd never wake up." Gladys came into the room and looked around. But it seemed as though Bertha had been alone all the time.

"Where are they? Where have they gone?" Gladys asked sharply.

"You mean your folks? Well, they went to the funeral. Hamilton's funeral. Even Rene went. I stayed here to be with you because they didn't want to leave you alone."

"Oh." Gladys sat down at the: table. "I'd like some of that please."

"Some breakfast too, probably. Want an egg cooked?"

"No, I'll just eat—" She saw on the cabinet a three-layer chocolate cake. It was dark, rich brown, her favorite. "Let me have a big piece of that cake."

Bertha stared at her. "I thought you'd didn't like to ruin that pretty complexion. Say, what's wrong with it anyway?"

"With what?'

"Your skin. You got a big red streak on your neck."

Gladys pulled up the collar of her blouse impatiently. "I scratched it, that's all. Just give me some cake, will you?"

"*Tea* and *cake*?"

Gladys glared at the cook's ugly face. "Yes!" The face was almost as ugly as her own had been. Especially now that the frown of surprise and disapproval was there.

"Well?" Gladys said angrily at the staring, scowling Bertha. "I could have you fired, you know!"

Bertha placed her hands on her hips and in that stance of impenetrability, demanded abruptly, "When's your birthday?"

Gladys opened her mouth, but couldn't think. The hard eyes of the cook bored into her. "Huh?"

"How old are you? Speak! Answer me, *now*!"

"Thir—" Gladys stopped. She began to feel choked by her speeding heart. She had almost said thirty-three. Angrily she answered, "You know how old I am! Now will you please get me what I want?"

"Whatever was after Peri Lee got her, I say," she said fiercely, turning away. Bertha tightened her mouth, as if she were determined to say no more, and brought the cake.

Gladys ate it greedily and silently. She was sick of this whole thing, always having to be so careful about her behavior, always having people stare at her; just because she didn't want the same things Peri Lee had wanted. Just because the tone of her voice was different. How the hell was she to know what Peri Lee had wanted? What Peri Lee had done? Or when her birthday was. She was beginning to think that Peri Lee was a stupid, sugary type that never demanded anything. Or raised her voice, or even ate a piece of cake. *Crap.*

Now Bertha was after her; and worse, Bertha suspected the truth. The only good thing about it was she probably wouldn't tell, or if she did no one would believe her. Maybe.

They came in from the funeral then, and Gladys saw that even Pete had gone. He was wearing a black suit that made him look like a crow in a coat. Reminded her of pictures she had seen when she was a sickly brat. His face had a serious and thoughtful look that struck her as a put-on mask of some kind. Or else his tie was too tight. He met her eyes full on, but it didn't change his smug mask.

The whole family, Olivia, Harry, and Gene, were asking her questions. They all amounted to the same thing. "How are you, dear?"

The dear made her sick. She wasn't used to the silly name and she didn't like it. It was sticky, like honey, and she felt like a bee clogged down in its own honeycomb. Especially when she saw Bertha's sharp, hostile eyes watching her, listening for her every word. She answered the questions sweetly and demurely as she thought Peri Lee would. When the family's attention and conversation turned to other topics, Gladys returned Bertha's hard glare for a brief moment before she set about to ignore her.

After a while she began to study Pete, trying to decide what he was up to.

All through dinner the smug look as still on his face. No sideways glances from him, no feeling her legs under the table. Instead, he hung onto every word the parents said as if they were treasures. He talked a lot. Farm talk. An idea he'd had about a certain field and how its production might be increased. Both Harry and Gene were interested,

Gladys saw, and the smug look increased on Pete's face. And it wasn't caused by his tie.

It occurred to her finally, when the meal was over and the men remained to talk awhile, that Pete was different in another way. He was satisfied, he was excited and barely concealing it; and he was happy.

The whole thing made Gladys very uneasy.

When she felt she could safely get by with it, she excused herself and went to her room. The evening promised to be long and boring, so to entertain herself she went into the dressing room and tried on clothes.

Most of them were too immature to suit her. Nothing really sexy. The dresses fit loosely, and were mostly high at the neck. One long dress she pulled out and slipped on had a teal blue velvet bodice that buttoned to a small round collar, long sleeves with tailored cuffs, and a gathered skirt of quilted material that was lustrous and silky, but a very casual plaid. Gladys didn't know whether it was intended to be a formal of some kind for some special party or if it was simply a hostess dress or run-about robe. She took it off and hung it up and chose from the racks a red print that was long. It could have been Peri Lee's great-grandmother's dress Gladys thought as she looked at it in the mirror. Empire waist, princess lines, long sleeves. She took it off and hung it away again. Winter clothes, maybe.

She turned to the other end of the closet where the casuals were. Jackets, mostly waist length, with matching skirts, pants, blouses or sweaters, and almost all in plaids. Peri Lee had liked plaids, obviously, and her favorite color must be teal blue. Gladys didn't try any of the casuals on because she preferred sexy, slinky things. All she found that was sexy or slinky were the many drawers of bikini pajamas. Just a strip of something for the panty and a wisp of something else for the top.

Gladys smiled to herself. So Peri Lee liked to sleep light.

The dresses were young and demure, but at least part of them were the short style of teenagers and showed off plenty of shapely leg. Gladys liked that, except they made her feel about thirteen years old.

She stood back and viewed the racks of clothes. She wondered if

Olivia would take her shopping and let her buy a few more sophisticated things. At least she could ask. Olivia would probably not refuse her.

When she heard voices in the hall she put on a robe and went out to say goodnight. She thought about asking if they could go shopping tomorrow, but decided to wait until Harry wasn't around. She told Gene goodnight, and had a small-talk conversation with Harry and Olivia. She made it as short as she could, for her own protection, and even forced herself to do as she had seen Peri Lee do. She kissed the cheeks of both of them. The rewards came instantly. They were relieved, and they went away happy.

Gladys stepped into her room, leaned against the locked door, and drew a deep breath. She had carried it off well enough to suit them, evidently. Probably because she had kept away from them all evening and then had practically kept her mouth shut. And then the kisses. Little, sugary, Peri Lee kisses.

Gladys laughed and settled down to wait awhile. Tonight she wasn't changing to pajamas, because she didn't want to wait until everyone was in bed. If someone caught her this time she could at least say she'd been out for a walk.

She changed her mind about waiting. The light out, and the door closed behind her so they might think she had gone to bed, she slipped into the dimly lighted hallway and went quietly toward the back stairs. Within minutes she was outside, breathing the fresh cool air that was sweeping down from snow-peaked mountains.

A light was still on in the bunkhouse. Showing in a thin crack at the bottom of the door and through two unshaded windows. She slipped in quickly, and closed the door behind her.

Pete lay on his bunk, a magazine in his hands. Gladys noticed he had changed back to work clothes and had one boot sole flat on the blanket. The other foot hung toward the floor.

"Hey!" he said, jumping up. "You oughten to come here like this."

She gave him what she hoped was a bedroom look. "Why not? You didn't object last night."

"Well—this is too early, for Christ's sake. Why didn't you wait until everybody's asleep? If your old man caught you here with me he'd make it so hot for us the whole place would go to hell." He got off the bunk and came to meet her; his hands caught her at the waist and squeezed. "Just one kiss, for now. Then you run along and go to bed like a good girl." The kiss was hard and sucking, and she held weakly to him. It was the kind of man-kiss she had dreamed about in all her daydreams. But then it ended and he was talking again. "I got this plan, see. I'll come up and ask to take you out, in a few nights. Then your old man won't care. He'll get used to it."

She stood away from him, and found to her surprise that she was tall enough to look him nearly straight in the eyes. "Get used to what?"

"You and me," he said, pointing at her chest with a finger and his chest with the thumb. "Together."

"I don't want him to get used to it, Pete. I want to leave. I want you to take me away from here before long. It's getting—uh—nearly impossible for me to stay here. Let's plan to run away. I'll let you know when."

His face fell apart like a rose at frost time. "Away? What the hell for? I had it in mind that you and me could get married."

"Oh you did! Oh sure you did! Now I see!" She snorted, mocking him. "You and me get married, yet. So that's what you got in your dirty little mind. Marry the boss's daughter."

"You came down here last night," he pointed out angrily, his face flushed. "You come in here hot-assed as a bitch in heat. And you've got it right now, too! You've been after me!"

"Not for marriage, you dope."

She started to turn away, furious. He grabbed her arm and jerked her back to face him.

"Then what the hell do you want? Is that all you want? All right, little girl, you can have it. Right up to your damned chin."

He threw her down on the cold linoleum floor, so hard it popped against the back of her head. The weight of his body flattened the small of her back against the floor. She knew the windows were not curtained at all, their blank eyes open to the night and all who passed, but she didn't care. If somebody wanted to look in, let them look.

"I'll fix you up," he muttered heavily. "I'll fix you up little girl so you'll have to get married."

Gladys didn't answer. She would have to do something about that, she thought, when she got away from here. It wasn't babies she wanted, it was fun. And freedom. But, since she hadn't been using a contraceptive, she could always get an abortion if she had to.

He didn't bother to unbutton her robe. His hand grasped it near her waist and jerked. The material tore, and buttons rolled, soft sounds under his furious mutters.

"Try to tease me, will you? Too good to marry me, huh? You just coming out here to use me for your stud and then go marry that rich sonofabitch next door, huh? Well, when your kid is borned it's going to look like me. Let's see how you like that, you rich-kid whore. That's all you are, a rich-kid whore. Parading in front of your window knowing I'm watching. You get your kicks playing with your old man's hired hands? Well, take this, sister." He was deliberately trying to hurt her. She gasped in silent pain and dug her fingers into his shoulders, but he didn't ease up. With one hard push he was buried in her and his hands pushed her legs painfully far apart, as if to hear the shatter of her bones would sadistically delight him.

She took his treatment without comment. Being wanted at all, in any way, was worth the pain that mixed with the pleasure.

He didn't say another word to her, and she left him sullenly pulling his pants up, and went back to the house. She was trying to figure her way out. Pete wouldn't help, she could see that. He wanted Peri Lee, all right, but he wanted Peri Lee's inheritance, too. He didn't love her, if he couldn't use her to worm his way into a permanent position in the O'Brion family.

In her bathroom, to forget and relax, she ran a full tub of hot water, piled it with bubble bath and soaked until she felt sleepy. All she did to the tub then was release the water. She crawled into her bed so water-soaked her toes had begun to shrivel. She pulled the light blanket up to her chin and went to sleep.

When she woke the first thing she thought of was Pete. She thought of him with mingled surprise, anger, and despondency. How could he not fall in love with Peri Lee? Wasn't beauty supposed automatically to command a man's love?

She brushed her teeth, washed her face, brushed her hair and dressed, all to the tune of lively country-western on the radio. She told the reflection in the mirror that Pete wasn't that important.

Still, even in Peri Lee's lovely body, she had in a way been rejected. She had thought she would have power over men when she had perfect beauty, so what had gone wrong?

Deep inside her raged a desire to get even, but balancing it was the old fear of inadequacy.

By the time she went downstairs to hunt up her old breakfast of toast and tea she was almost dragging her feet. She felt ugly and hunched, forced always to look up to other people.

She didn't even look at Rene or Bertha, and although she was aware they looked at her they said nothing. She silently made her own toast and her own cup of tea and took it to the table by the window. There she stared out at the white gravel in the driveway, poked the toast down as if she had to run in order to punch the clock at the factory, but then instead of two quick sips of her tea she sipped it slowly even though it grew cold.

The swinging door into the hallway opened and closed several times as Bertha and Rene both went in and out, doing their morning chores.

Then the door opened again and Olivia came in and sat down near Gladys. The moment Gladys looked at her she knew that Bertha had reported something to Olivia.

Olivia waited, obviously, for Gladys to say something. But Gladys took another sip of tea instead, carefully looking down into her cup in an attempt to withdraw from questions.

"Aren't you feeling well?" Olivia finally asked.

So that was what Bertha had told her, Gladys thought with glum satisfaction. They were plotting against her, always, it seemed. She had to be on her guard constantly, especially around Bertha. "I was just drinking my tea," Gladys said, trying to sound very happy and pleased about life. She pulled a smile from somewhere among the muscles of her face for Olivia's benefit. "Did Bertha tell you I wasn't?"

"She mentioned you seemed depressed. I was wondering if there is anything you would enjoy doing today."

Gladys remembered the clothes suddenly and her intention of

asking Olivia to take her shopping. "Could we go to town?' she asked eagerly. "Could I buy a couple of new dresses? Maybe I could find something new I like."

Olivia looked elated and pleased. "That's a marvelous idea. Why don't you call Jodie and ask her if she'd like to join us? You haven't seen her since she got back, have you?"

Jodie? Back from where! "Uh... no."

Olivia started toward the door, still smiling as if the sun had finally come out after days of dark winter. She paused near the door, waiting for Gladys to answer. Through Gladys's mind flicked several things at once: she had never heard of Jodie, didn't know where she had been, and most important didn't have any idea what her phone number was. So she said quickly, as she got up to follow Olivia, "Couldn't we just stop and pick her up?'

"But you should call her so that she'll be ready. I'll get my gloves and bag and be ready in a minute. Bertha can tell the men we won't be here for lunch."

She started out again and Gladys reached out and touched her arm. "Mother," she said, desperation giving her confidence, picking out of nothing some way to get by with this one. "Please, will you call Jodie? I'd like to change to a dress. You'll have more time than I."

"Of course I'll call for you," Olivia said. "Run along then and change."

Gladys glanced once at Bertha and saw her eyes wore a gleam of smugness, as if the conversation had confirmed something for her. Instinctively, or by pure guess, Gladys thought, as she ran down the hallway and up the stairs, Bertha had put Olivia up to the whole thing. The meddlesome cook had suggested to Olivia that maybe if Peri Lee called her friend Jodie she would feel better. Thereby, Bertha had found out Jodie was a stranger to her.

But there was no way Gladys could fight Bertha and get by with it. She could only stay out of her way as much as possible and not give her a chance to watch her so closely.

Jodie, Gladys discovered, lived at the edge of town in a large house set in beautifully landscaped grounds. Olivia drove the black Cadillac into the curving driveway and stopped near a porch where a tall, slender girl with long blonde hair was waiting.

Gladys moved over to make room for her and Jodie opened the door and slid in to sit beside her. She leaned forward smiling to speak to Olivia. "It's so nice to see you, Mrs. O'Brion. How are you?"

"Fine, Jodie, thank you. How was your trip?" Jodie settled back and smiled at Gladys. "Oh, great. You should have gone along, Peri Lee."

Gladys answered slowly, "I'm glad you enjoyed it, Jodie." She noted the girl's soft, easy way of talking, and the way she was dressed. Gladys was pleased that she had gone upstairs and changed from slacks to a dress, because Jodie even wore small, white gloves. Just as if she were going to church. Gladys was uncomfortably aware of her own bare hands. She had thought the glove business was just an old-fashioned habit of Olivia's but if Jodie wore them too, then it was the accepted thing around this community.

Gladys let Jodie and Olivia do the talking, and gathered facts: Peri Lee and Jodie had gone to school together, probably all their lives, had graduated from high school together, and were going to the same college in the fall. There, for a moment, Gladys lost contact with their words because the college was just one more obstacle in her life as Peri Lee. At the most, she gathered, she had about six weeks before enrollment. Six weeks to live as Peri Lee, six weeks to be loved and adored, the secure little rich girl.

To be sure she made no mistakes, Gladys let Jodie take the lead in the dress shops. Although she longed to ask Olivia to buy some of the things Jodie passed by, she didn't dare risk it now. If she wanted to dress in a sexy outfit in a size smaller she would have to wait until she was out on her own again. Which was going to happen whether she liked it or not, because otherwise she didn't know how to make it into college when she hadn't taken a college preparatory course in high school. There was no way she could pass those tests, though if she could, she would.

The daydream began to occupy her mind. A college girl. Life in a coed dorm, where so many guys lived too, would make years of fun available to her. If only she could dredge up the intelligence and knowledge that had been Peri Lee's. Or, if somehow she could study... that was it! Study. Peri Lee was bound to have school books left. She could solve several problems that way. When the family questioned her she could simply say she was getting in shape for college.

Jodie's voice came softly to her finally, and Gladys realized she had been trying to get her attention. "Is something wrong, Peri Lee?"

"Oh, no. No," Gladys answered quickly. "What were you saying?"

Olivia was leading the way into a lunch room, and they followed her to a table and sat down.

"I was just asking you why you don't come over and spend a couple of nights with me so that I can tell you all about my trip."

"I—" She had to get out of this one fast. Peri Lee's closest friend made her extremely uncomfortable. She didn't like the way Jodie was beginning to look at her, as if she were wondering something. "I would like to, but I have so much work to do. Thanks anyway."

Olivia said, "Work?"

Gladys looked down at the white cloth on the table and the place setting that was already there, waiting. "Yes. I thought I'd brush up on my school work to be sure I don't have any trouble." Let them get used to the idea she *might* have trouble, she thought in slight surprise as if she had found a gem by the roadside. Maybe, if she did study, she could really go to college and remain Peri Lee O'Brion all her life.

"But how can you?" Jodie said.

Gladys answered quickly, taking the words as having one possible meaning. "I'll study."

No one said anything and Gladys looked up to find them both staring at her. Jodie looked down.

To clear up the matter, Gladys said, "I always forget so much during the summer vacation, don't you?" She forced a light laugh. "I wanted to be sure that I passed the tests."

Jodie looked at her again and leaned forward slightly. "But, Peri Lee, you've already passed them, don't you remember?"

Gladys returned her stare then until she sat back and looked down again.

Olivia said gently, "Perhaps we'd better decide what we want." She took the menu the waitress handed her.

Gladys buried her nose in the menu, wishing fervently she hadn't even opened her dumb mouth.

To be on the safe side she ordered the same thing Jodie did, even though Jodie looked at her questioningly again. Gladys thought it might still have something to do with something said earlier. The college, the clothes. She felt like getting up and running because it was so hard to try to be someone she wasn't.

She looked at the other people in the restaurant and saw that the eyes of a man at the next table were fixed steadily on her with open admiration. The message was clear. He'd like to be with her, anytime, anywhere. She met his look without reservation, letting him know silently that it was fine with her, and she began to feel better. She sat up straighter, leaned back in her chair, raised one arm and draped it over the back of the chair so that the man would get a good look at her body that was clothed in a dress not tight enough to show it off. She crossed her legs too, and let her skirt slide up. When she saw his eyes roving, letting her know he liked what he saw and understood what she was doing, she smiled.

Then she saw that Jodie hadn't missed one movement, and the look on her friend's face had gone cool and withdrawn. Very polite, very superior, it seemed to Gladys. At least it made her feel cheap and inferior, and more than a little angry.

She forced her attention back to her companions and away from the man, though she was aware he kept watching her.

She was glad to get out of the restaurant and back to the shops. Once again she copied everything Jodie did. When Jodie bought pantyhose, Gladys bought pantyhose. When Jodie chose a new blouse, so did Gladys. And so it went until Gladys felt it would be a relief to run screaming into the street.

She decided to end the shopping trip, and said to Olivia, "Mom, I'm tired. Can we go home now?"

"Of course, dear."

Jodie heard and said, "You do look tired, Peri Lee." She was friendly again, her unspoken disapproval of the scene in the restaurant apparently overlooked now. "Why don't you call me when you're rested so we can talk?"

"I'll do that." She deliberately didn't tell Jodie to call. Being with this girl was even more a strain than being with the family. Gladys felt that in some ways Jodie probably knew Peri Lee better than anyone else did.

When Olivia drove into the curved driveway to let Jodie out, the blonde girl lingered long enough to say to Gladys, "It's not too late you know. We could at least go up to the lodge for a couple of weeks and just play around. Hike, swim, go boating, or just lie around and talk. You'd feel better. That's not so far away that Dale couldn't come up at times."

Gladys said defensively, "I feel all right. I don't need to go anywhere." Of all things not two weeks with Jodie whoever-she-was.

Jodie, smiling vaguely, backed away, her glance going to Olivia. "Thank you very much for asking me along. It was a lovely day. Have a safe drive home."

"Thank you, Jodie. We enjoyed your company." She paused slightly, and added, "Didn't we, Peri Lee?"

Gladys answered shortly, wishing they could just get out of there, "Sure we did. See you, Jodie."

Olivia drove away then and didn't talk much on the way home. When she did make a comment, it was something easily and quickly answered so that Gladys was able to begin to relax.

At home she took her packages and went slowly upstairs to her room, dumped them on the bed and stood back to look at the boxes. There wasn't a damned thing there she really had wanted.

She pulled off her pantyhose and shoes and walked barefoot to a chair and flopped in it, her arms dangling, her head leaned back. She felt every bit of thirty-three years old. She felt as if she had just come home from a long, hard day at the factory, home without even the comfort of a few beers to help her feel better.

"Oh hell," she said softly aloud. "I don't think I like you, Jodie whats-your-name." But someday she would have to call her, and in order to do that, she would have to find out her name and number.

She wondered what the rest of the family was doing now. Probably they had all gone down to supper, because it was about that time.

She pushed herself up out of the chair and went barefoot into the hall and down the stairs to the lower hall, just in time to see Gene go toward Harry's office.

The coldness of warning passed over her. If the three of them had congregated in the office, that meant something serious was going on. It might have something to do with the farm, or it might have something to do with her.

Gladys slipped silently along to listen at the closed door. The first voice she caught was Gene's. "Would you be going with her, Mom?"

"Yes. Your father has already reserved a room for me in a motel near the hospital."

Harry said, as if clueing Gene in on what had transpired, "She'll be there to see her as often as she can, but the doctor said they probably won't let her in more than two or three times a week. In cases like ours, it's better if the patient is away from the family during the examination."

"Has he already made the arrangements?"

"Yes," Olivia said, "I called him as soon as we returned from town. He said we would take her up to Denver next Monday; he said he would call tomorrow and tell them we're coming."

Gene said, "Isn't this rather sudden?"

"No, you know we've been considering it for some time."

"But today—"

"Yes. Well, today we went shopping, you know. We stopped and picked up Jodie. She had just returned from her trip to Spain yesterday. The whole shopping excursion made me realize how changed Peri Lee is. I just don't think we dare waste any more time. If we take her now, maybe she will be ready for college on time after all. Of course, we won't know the diagnosis until after all the tests are made and evaluated by the psychiatrists. Then we will know ... " Her voice dropped out of hearing range.

Monday... Gladys backed away from the door and ran back up to her room, her bare feet silent on the carpet. This was—what day was this? She looked at the calendar on the desk and decided it must be Thursday. She had to get out and away before Monday because she had read about tests that were given people in mental hospitals. She was afraid she would never be able to fool them. They would either keep her locked up, trying to change her back into Peri Lee; or they would give her the drug that was called the truth serum, sodium pentothal or sodium amytal, and get the truth out of her. If that happened they would never believe her. They would declare her too ill to leave the hospital. She would be trapped for life.

But to stall, to think her way out, she had to go down to supper and sit through it as if she didn't have a worry on her mind. She had to do it. So that no one would be watching her tonight.

In order to escape the family, as soon as she had eaten a few bites she excused herself and said goodnight. She hoped they would accept her plea that the shopping had tired her and she wanted to go to bed early.

One thing she had noticed while she was in Pete's room was a flashy, red-leather key case on the top of a chest of drawers. The keys to his car.

Now, all she needed was money.

When she was back in her room again with the door locked, she stood in the middle of the floor looking around. There had to be money available somewhere: These people were rich. Considered rich, anyway. So Peri Lee was bound to have more money than the four dollars in change.

She noticed for the first time that it had all been picked up from the floor. Now, even four dollars would buy gas enough to get her to the city. Or close to it. She didn't know much about gas or cars. There might be enough gas in it to get her there, as it was. But she still needed money.

Maybe Peri Lee had a piggy bank she hadn't found. A piggy bank? *Jesus!* Gladys murmured to herself softly. "Not a piggy bank, a real bank! A check book!" Of course. Peri Lee O'Brion was bound to have her own checking account. She had spent so much time looking at Peri Lee's clothes, and trying them on, that she hadn't even looked at anything else in the room. Like the desk.

There were seven drawers, three on each side and one in the middle. She started going through them, and found them all full. Her impatience fed her evil mood and she began to jerk things out and dump the contents on the floor. Who cared? She'd be gone by the time the maid came in tomorrow morning.

No check book, none at all. On her hands and knees in the midst of the floor, she flung papers, pencils, notes and letters. Finally, when she was beginning to swear in nervous anger under her breath, she ran across the small brown booklet. She had seen it before in her mad search, several times, but it was so small and so thin that she hadn't noticed the printing on the front. Savings Account Book. First Federal Savings and Loan.

With hands that trembled she opened it and read the name. Peri Lee O'Brion. She began to laugh, though she felt like shouting. Peri Lee didn't have a checking account, she had a savings account. The kind that could be withdrawn.

She turned the pages slowly, seeing the deposits adding to the total. Fourteen thousand and forty-seven dollars.

Gladys sat back among the scattered papers of the desk. That was more money than she had earned in over two years of work at the factory. Enough to take her to town in style.

She tucked the booklet into the front of her bra, with a bit of trouble. But at least it was safe there. She giggled, thinking of the old TV westerns that had given her the idea.

She looked around, wondering what to take with her. Well, nothing, she thought. Just me and my little brown book. And Pete's car.

She started out the door, and stopped. Ten-thirty at night? If she ran off with Pete's car now, even if she could get the keys, the whole countryside would be looking for her by breakfast time. The damned bank didn't even open until nine-thirty or ten o'clock. She didn't even know what time it opened.

So she'd have to wait patiently until morning, then try to get away without Olivia seeing her. Or anyone else. There was another problem too. She had never driven a car. But she had watched Marian drive, and it looked so easy she could do it too. She could at least get to the edge of town with it.

No matter how she looked at it, she saw problems. Especially if she wanted the money. And she did.

The night was the longest she had ever known. It was past three before she even went to sleep, and the sleep was so light that she woke again at five.

She dressed carefully then in clothes she felt would attract the least attention. Pants, vest and white blouse. And shoes comfortable for walking. In case she couldn't get Pete's car. But she thought it must be about seven miles to the small town where the bank was located, and she had never walked seven miles in her life. It would take too long to walk seven miles today, when she was trying to get away unseen and not missed.

She paced the floor for two hours, then went downstairs to spend two more hours acting the most natural way Peri Lee would act.

Olivia was in and out of the house, the driveway always in her view. Getting past her was impossible. Then, at ten o'clock Olivia put on her straw hat and filled a thermos jug with iced tea.

Gladys watched her. "What are you going to do with that?" She was almost afraid to hope what she was thinking.

"I thought we might take it out to the men. Would you like to walk through the fields?"

Gladys's heart pounded. Her hopes had been justified. "I have a couple of things I'd like to do instead. You go ahead. I'll go next time."

Olivia smiled and looked down at the thermos, carefully testing the lid as if to see whether she had gotten it on right. But Gladys knew what she was doing, knew her attention was not on the thermos at all.

"I'll be glad to wait for you if you'd like," Olivia said, "so that you can join me. What did you have planned?"

Gladys searched her memory frantically for something Peri Lee had enjoyed doing, something she would do alone, in her room. Not a nap at this time of day. The answer came to her suddenly. "Sewing. I think I'll work on one of the new—uh—patterns." *Was that how she'd say it?*

Olivia looked disappointed, and Gladys guessed she was used to having her daughter walk along with her. But she seemed to accept the excuse and said, "All right, dear. I'll see you later. I won't be gone long. Just a few minutes."

She went out, and Gladys was alone in the kitchen. She watched from the window as Olivia crossed into a field and disappeared among the trees along a fence row. Once she stopped and looked back, and Gladys spent a tense moment waiting for Olivia to decide to go on.

Gladys looked around, anxious and nervous with excitement. She had to hurry. Not one minute could be wasted. The cook and maid were both in the garden. They were out of sight, but she could hear their voices. Now was her chance, her only chance, and it all depended on her being able to drive Pete's car.

She slipped out the patio door and then ran along the edge of the grass, so that her steps wouldn't alert the cook. Pete's car was still parked beside the bunkhouse and his keys were on the chest of drawers, in the same place she had seen them. She grabbed them, ran out again and got into the car.

Thankfully it wasn't as sporty inside as Dale's and it had the kind of automatic shift that Marian's car had. If it had been a sports model with stick shift like Dale's, she would have been hopeless.

She closed the door softly, catching it on the first latch, then she inserted keys until she found one that fit. She held her breath and turned the ignition. To her amazement the car started. Suddenly she felt as if she had conquered the world. The car ran smoothly, no problem. She pulled the gear down to drive and felt the car begin to move forward. Her world collapsed then and she clung to the steering wheel in terror. The slightest touch sent it moving toward one side of the driveway or the other, or over toward the bunkhouse. "My God," she mumbled aloud. "My God, stay on the road!"

Slowly the car moved down the drive, gravel crunching under the tires and sounding to her ears like gun shots. But she kept going, and in pure desperation she kept the car within the limits of the driveway. At the edge of the highway she nearly panicked, and when she put on the brake almost threw herself into the windshield. But at least the car stopped.

She took a couple of deep breaths, hoped fervently that no cars would be coming along, and inched her way out into the highway and cut the steering wheel left.

The car responded sharply and she almost went into the ditch before she got it straightened out and over to the right side of the road.

From there on it was fairly easy because the road was a straight track of pavement that ran close beside an irrigation canal.

When she reached the wide streets of the little town she pulled to the side, then parked without a single mistake. By the time she was standing on the sidewalk she was feeling again as if she had conquered the world.

Nearly everyone she met spoke to her, and she smiled and answered. Finding the bank took longer than she wished to spend, but to stop a local person and ask where it was would be the most stupid thing she could do. Finally, she rounded the corner at a drugstore, and there it was. A new building, with landscaped lawns. A rich bank, no doubt, but small. A rich little bank in a rich little town. It would hardly miss the little amount of cash she would be drawing out. She wished for a moment she could in some way get hold of more of the O'Brion money. But how? No way. Not yet.

She entered, stopped at the windows of the only cashier and pushed the little book at her.

"I'd like to withdraw this money, please."

The woman looked at her and smiled. "Well good morning, Peri Lee. How are you?" She looked at the book.

Gladys smiled too and answered, "Good morning, I'm fine. Thank you."

"How are things at home? Mr. and Mrs. O'Brion and your brother Gene?"

"Uh—fine, thank you." Gladys's mouth had gone dry. Not once had it occurred to her that in a town this small everyone would know her, even the cashier at the bank. And probably the president, too.

The cashier was still looking at the book. "How much of it did you want to withdraw?"

Gladys had a feeling she'd be smarter not to take it all and risk unwanted attention, but greed, plus need, made her suddenly reckless. "All of it, please."

"All of it?" the woman repeated.

"Yes, please. You see, I'm going away to school soon—" She stopped. Why explain? She might only get herself in trouble if she tried to find excuses. Sure enough, the woman smiled again and answered, "My daughter is going away this fall too. Where are you going?"

"Well—I haven't really made up my mind. Could we hurry please? I have—a date waiting.

"Oh, of course. I'll have to have you sign a release form."

She hadn't thought of that. She had no idea what Peri Lee's signature looked like. Well, too late to worry about that. Anyway, perhaps her handwriting had changed with the body, so she would automatically sign Peri Lee's name correctly. It had to be correct, because if it weren't she might be in for questioning by the police. Then the O'Brions would be called in and she wouldn't have another chance to get away.

She almost turned and walked out then, but thought of the difficulty of getting anywhere without so much as a dime. She decided to try to bluff her way through.

She waited through slow-moving minutes for the cashier to run a sheet of paper into a typewriter and do some typing. Gladys's palms grew moist with the anxiety of waiting, knowing she was going to have to sign her name.

Finally, the woman pulled the typed form out and brought it back to the window. She smiled again. "Sign right here, please."

Gladys took the pen and the release form and, after a pause to gather courage, signed the name. At first she saw only that it was in her own handwriting, not very neat, not anything special. Then to her horror she noticed she had misspelled the name. Stupid mistake. To try to change it would make it the more noticeable. She held her breath, then pushed the paper toward the woman. Maybe she wouldn't notice the mistake.

The cashier took the paper and looked at it, then looked at it again. "Excuse me a minute please, Peri Lee. I have to get Mr. Summerton's approval." She took the paper with her and disappeared into a back office. The passing seconds became long minutes before the woman returned. Behind her came a man.

Gladys froze against the counter. She felt as guilty as if she had been holding a gun.

"Peri Lee," the man said, looking from her to the paper in his hand,

"I see your signature has changed. I'm not sure the computer will accept this..."

"Well," she said, "I've been practicing a new way of writing—since I fell off my horse and hurt my wrist. I hadn't thought about it being so different. It's hard for me to write yet without pain."

"Oh, I'm sorry about that. I hadn't heard."

"It wasn't serious. Just a slight sprain. Can't you just give it to me anyway? Does the computer have to know?" She longed to bite her nails, and almost raised one to her mouth before she stopped and held her hands clenched at her sides.

"Withdrawing so much—you see I had to be sure it was you. May I ask your reason. She searched her mind for an excuse he would accept, but all she could think of was the college bit. She forced a smile, sweet, sugary as she "It's really a surprise for my daddy. He doesn't know I've saved so much..." *Or did he?* Wrong words, but too late. Another chance she had to take now. "And I'm leaving for college soon and I want to surprise him with it. I'd like to help pay my own expenses."

He smiled and nodded at the woman, then turned back toward the office door. "Just a minute longer," he said. "I'll have to make a note of the reason your signature is different and make out your check."

Gladys waited and waited, wondering if they were really calling the police. Or Harry O'Brion.

But both the man and the woman came back, and he stood smiling near his door while the woman handed her a check. Gladys mumbled, "Thank you," took it and forced herself to walk away normally. Her mouth had gone so dry she could not swallow the lump of fear in her throat.

Now. Only one more thing. The check had to be cashed.

Oh my God. She stopped, looking stunned, even though she knew the cashier and bank manager were still watching her.

"Did you want cash?" the woman said, in a tone rising with incredulity. "I had thought you might want to deposit it somewhere into a checking account."

Gladys turned to face her, and looked at the name on the little nameplate because it was plain that Peri Lee should know this woman very well.

Mrs. Forey.

"Oh, would you please," Gladys said, and smiled. "Mrs. Forey, I thought it would be fun to give him cash, real money, don't you think?"

Mrs. Forey looked at the man and they laughed as though humoring a child.

The man said, "Cash it. I'm sure Harry would appreciate it more that way too. Especially from so pretty a daughter, who's this considerate and thoughtful."

Gladys attempted a laugh too, but ducked her head quickly, reached for the pen and endorsed the check in her own halting, irregular script.

"But do be careful, Peri Lee," the man said. "That's too much money to carry around."

"Yes, sir."

He was looking at her penetratingly, clearly puzzled, and it seemed to Gladys, with a good deal of suspicion. His steady gaze made her even more nervous, more anxious to escape.

The cash was in her hand after another few moments, in hundred dollar bills so that she would have no trouble later. Though it made a large bundle she clutched it damply and went toward the door, telling herself to not be a fool now and run.

The president's voice carried clearly to her ears. "Such a sweet young girl, wanting to surprise her dad like this. It will be an unusual surprise too." He laughed again, a rather forced sound.

The woman answered, "I think so. Fourteen thousand dollars cash for a man as rich as Harry O'Brion?"

"It's a very odd thing to do," he said. "Of course, it's her money. I couldn't very well refuse. But I wonder—"

"Well, it's the thought that counts. At least she thought of it—"

The conversation behind her faded as Gladys went through the door and hurried toward freedom. She didn't have to run now. She had carried it off successfully.

Unless the man continued to be disturbed, to consider it so unusual he would decide, after all, to call Harry O'Brion.

CHAPTER 7

The men came in from the wash room and took their places at the tables. Harry O'Brion looked at his wife and asked, "Where's Peri Lee?"

"I don't know," she answered. "She wasn't in her room when I came back. She might have decided to go walking after all, or perhaps to see a friend. I expect she'll be in soon."

"Was she all right this morning?"

Her hesitation was so slight he hardly noticed. He was busy filling his plate with an ample noon meal.

"Yes," Olivia said. "She seemed more like herself. But—"

Harry let out a gruff, "Yeah?" for encouragement. "But I think I'll call the doctor again this afternoon and see if he can't arrange for her to go in tomorrow, instead of next Monday."

"Do you think that's necessary?"

"It might be. Rene, will you bring another pitcher of cold milk please?"

Peri Lee's name wasn't mentioned again until dessert was being served. Pete had begun to look over his shoulder toward the back door, his face serious and thoughtful, as if he were listening for something, or thinking of something he didn't want to share with the others.

Olivia hadn't been eating much. Her small salad was hardly touched. She looked at the hired girl. "Rene, why don't you run up to Peri Lee's room now and see if she's there?"

Conversation at the table lagged while the girl was gone. When she came back all faces turned expectantly toward her.

"Ma'am," she said, standing straight as a broom near the door, "she's not in her room. And Ma'am— " the pause became lengthy, but finally she got it out. "And Ma'am, I hadn't told you, but when I went to clean up her room this morning I found all the papers had been thrown out of her desk onto the floor."

Olivia rose from the table, her face composed but pensive. 'Please go ahead and eat," she told the men and Bertha. "I'll be back in a minute. Rene, would you come with, please?"

"Yes, Ma'am."

They went up the stairs without talking, Olivia in the lead. Her walk was graceful and unhurried, and her head held high. It was the natural structure of her body that gave her, and the daughter to whom she had given life, the queenly bearing that seemed carefully practiced. She was not especially aware of the way she walked.

In Peri Lee's room she stood in the center of the study area in the corner and looked at the desk. The floor was neat and clean, the few items on the top of the desk carefully placed in their exact spots.

"You've cleaned it beautifully, Rene," she said. "Where were the papers when you came in?"

Rene approached the desk and motioned around. "Everywhere. Just scattered all over. Like someone had thrown them there, or gone through them in an awful hurry, you know?"

Olivia didn't answer. She pulled out each drawer of the desk and found a careful, stacked neatness that was unnatural for any drawer.

"Why would she throw things out?" she murmured, aloud but to herself. "Why? Peri Lee was never..." Her voice drifted away as her glance followed each neatly aligned stack of papers, letters and general assemblage of years past.

Rene answered quickly, "I don't now, Ma'am. She never did it before. It really appeared like she was looking for something because she had them scattered all over. Like she was in a hurry."

Olivia closed the desk drawers and backed away. She turned and looked about the room, but she didn't touch anything else. After a moment she said quietly, "You've cleaned it very well, Rene."

Rene twisted in embarrassment. "Well, I try. Thank you."

Olivia led the way out of the room, but she paused to close the door softly after Rene had passed her. In silence they went back down the stairs.

The men seemed to have been waiting, and when Olivia took her chair Harry watched her expectantly. Her eyes met his for a brief glance.

"Rene did a very good job of straightening the desk," she said simply and calmly. Harry stared at her, waiting for more, but she said nothing. She raised a glass to her lips and sipped tea.

When Harry spoke he sounded unsure of himself, in territory unfamiliar to him. "Isn't it unusual for her to do things like that? I mean, isn't Peri Lee pretty neat about her room usually?"

"Oh, yes sir," Rene answered. "At least, she used to be. Only lately has she been messy. I mean—I don't mean to criticize her."

Olivia said, "That's all right, Rene. You're right. She has become very messy lately. But that's because she is ill. We have to accept it, and try to help her."

From Pete, as he pushed his chair back from the table, came a muttered, "Excuse me. I've been thinking that I didn't see my car where it's supposed to be."

The door slammed behind him and Harry asked, "What did he say?"

Gene answered, "He said he didn't see his car."

"*What?*"

"Didn't see his—"

"I know what you said," Harry yelled, getting up from the table, and heading toward the door. "I just don't get the connection. Why shouldn't his car be where it belongs?"

They all got up to follow Harry from the kitchen. They met Pete coming back up the walk in a run, his face red with many unspoken and unspeakable thoughts.

"My car! It's gone!" He stopped just short of the cook and demanded, "Did she take my car?"

Bertha spread her hands, palms toward the sky. "How should I know who took your car?"

"Somebody took my car! You been here all morning, ain't you?"

"Well sure," Bertha yelled back at him. "But most of that time I was out in the garden, and I didn't see your car! And if I had, I wouldn't have thought anything about it. You go in and out in it yourself!"

"Just a minute," Harry said, his voice strong and calming. "Why should she take your car, Pete, when she's got one of her own?'

Pete looked as if he were about to cry. "Well, I don't know Mr. O'Brion. But it's gone, and she's gone, and I'll lay you two to one she took it."

"Now wait a minute!" Harry's face was turning red too, the color creeping up from his neck. "I said she's got her own car! It doesn't have five thousand miles on it yet. There's no reason why she should take your car." He turned his back on Pete and asked Olivia, "Did she say anything to you about going anywhere?'

"Maybe," Gene said, interrupting, "she couldn't get her own car started or something."

Olivia answered her husband softly, "No, she didn't."

Pete yelled, "Well, she did to me! She wanted to run away with me last night."

He suddenly had the attention of everyone. They moved, to see him better, and became a hostile line that faced him. He instinctively took a step backwards.

"Well she did!"

"That's a goddamned lie," Gene said. "She's engaged to Dale."

Harry forgot Pete. "Engaged! Since when?"

"Since—since—hell, I don't know when it happened. When she started going with him. Now look, Dad, you know she never would even go out with another guy. She's loved Dale from the start whether you like it or not. Since she was five or six years old."

Harry, oddly, began to look thoughtful. He didn't answer. But if he had attempted to answer, he would not have been heard under Pete's bellow of contemptuous laughter.

"Loved shit! She didn't love anyone but Peri Lee, you can bet your sweet life on that!"

Gene took a step nearer him. "And how would you know about that?"

"She's been crawling into my bed for the last week."

In one jerky movement Gene struck Pete's chin and Pete fell, flat on his back. He raised up just far enough to lean on an elbow, his black eyes snapping fury, one hand holding his chin.

"All right, man, you asked for it! I don't take being called a liar by anybody."

"Let it go!" Harry thundered in a voice that successfully distracted the two younger men. "What you're going to do is get up and get out of here. Gene, go write him a check for the pay he's got coming."

"I'm not leaving without my car! Hell, I can't leave without my car."

Olivia spoke up rather timidly. "Harry, there's something I haven't told you."

"Now what?" he replied with a deep breath.

"I think Peri Lee and Dale must have had a quarrel. When they went for a drive to the mountains they planned to stay all day. She was back within two hours, and he didn't even bring her up to the house. He let her out down at the highway."

"Well, that's some hell of a way to treat—"

"She's been acting very strange lately, Harry," Olivia said. "She just wasn't herself. You said so, yourself."

"Well, she's sick. That's already been established, hasn't it? If any of us had any doubts about it, we might as well forget them and face it. Where the hell is she? She could be in terrible trouble by now. We've got to find her. She could have amnesia," Harry said.

Bertha was standing not far from Pete, looking down at him, her arms folded large and muscled across her bosom. "It ain't amnesia she's got," she said bluntly. "That girl ain't even Peri Lee."

Pete was still busy nursing his chin, but Olivia and Harry stared astonished at Bertha and spoke simultaneously,"*What*?" The tone of their words carrying unspoken opinions of, *have you gone mad, Bertha?*

"I believe it," Bertha stated flatly, watching Pete with undisguised satisfaction. "Peri Lee said it herself—something wanted her, and she was scared out of her mind. Then, all of a sudden she wasn't scared anymore and she had changed. Peri Lee was gone. Somebody else was there in her place. She didn't even act the same anymore. I've read about possession by other souls and now I believe it."

Olivia said quickly and severely, "Bertha, please don't be ridiculous. That sort of thing went out with the last century. A change in personality is now called schizophrenia, and that's why we made arrangements to take her to a hospital."

"Then why did she run off?" Bertha replied just as severely, determined to stick to her own opinion. "I'll tell you. She knew she would have to go, and whoever lives in that body ain't intending to go to *any* hospital."

Olivia put her hands over her face for a touch, light and helpless. "Oh, Bertha!"

Harry merely swallowed noisily, as if trying to swallow his own tongue. "No more of that, Bertha. We've got enough to think about without some wild imagination entering in."

Pete got up muttering and brushing bits of damp sod and cut grass from his clothes. "I told you she wanted to run away with me. I told you. She begged me. We had a thing going. But she wanted to run away, and that's what she's done; and to get even with me for not going with her, she took my car. How am I supposed to get the hell out of here without my car? You get my car back and I'll go. Believe me —I'll go."

Harry looked at him blankly, then turned and walked into the house and to his office. Gene was just coming out with a check in his hand, but Harry brushed past without saying anything. He went straight to the telephone.

The voice that answered said, "The Larson residence."

"Is Dale around?"

"Yes sir, just a moment please."

When Dale answered the phone, Harry asked, without preliminaries, "Have you seen Peri Lee today?'

After a moment of utter silence, Dale said, "No, I haven't."

The line hummed and Harry began to frown. "You don't know where she might have gone today?"

"She's gone?'

"It seems that way. I've been hearing some things around here that I don't like. Would you know why she would want to run away from home? Has she ever said anything to you about not being happy at home?'

"Run away!" he answered softly. "I'll be right over."

Harry hung up the phone just as Pete came into the room. Behind him, like a warden, stalked Gene. "Was that the police you called?' Pete demanded.

"No, it wasn't."

"Well, call them."

"Let's just wait a while."

"Wait for what? I got to have my goddamned car! I want it reported stolen, and right now, mister."

Harry sighed. "Gene, why don't you take Pete to town and drive around a bit. See if you can find his car."

"No sir! I want it reported," Pete said. "I ain't leaving this damned place till I get my car."

Harry ignored him, and asked Gene, "What's your mother doing?'

"She's calling Peri Lee's girlfriends to see if any of them have seen her." Harry nodded.

"Call the police," Pete said. "If you don't I will."

Gene turned on him as if to give him another poke, but let it go with a loud, "Can't you just wait a few minutes, Pete?"

Pete shrugged and didn't say anything.

The minutes passed, silent except for the ticking of the clock on the mantle. Then the sound of a car in the driveway. All three men crowded to the window, and then fell back.

Pete said, "Oh. It's that son of a bitch. What's he coming here for?"

Nobody answered him, and within a minute Olivia appeared at the door with Dale behind her. They came in and Olivia closed the door. Dale's tan looked bleached out, and his mouth was a tight line; well-shaped lips that had thinned and turned bitter. His wide, straight shoulders were covered only by a thin work-shirt, the sleeves rolled high on tanned, muscled arms. He looked as if he had just come in from the fields.

"Harry," Olivia said softly, "None of them have seen her. Or even heard from her. They haven't heard from her for several days; a week or more in most cases. None of them have any idea where she could have gone. I even called the shops in town where her charge accounts are, and no one has seen her."

Pete looked with satisfaction at Dale as he spoke to the family. "I tell you I know where she went. Away. Just anywhere away. I told you she came to my bed last night and begged me to run away with her, and because I wouldn't she stole my car. A few nights before that she stayed all night in my bed."

Silence fell over the room, but Dale didn't move. His blues eyes stared unwaveringly at Pete. Knotted veins throbbed in his arms.

Pete laughed. "They didn't believe me, but you do, don't you fella? You believe every word I'm saying, because you know her better than any of them do."

Still, Dale said nothing. His stare narrowed, and Pete closed his mouth and glanced uneasily away.

"Well, why don't you tell them?" he said. "Tell them. Maybe then they'll call the goddamn police and get my car back for me, because I'm not leaving here until they do. She's not one bit crazy, fella. She knows exactly what she's doing. Amnesia shit."

Dale moved then, to the desk. He opened the check book lying there, took up the pen and crossed out Harry O'Brion's name, address and account number. He wrote in his own, and then wrote the check to Pete for seven thousand dollars.

"There," he said, tossing it to him. "That ought to cover your car."

Dale started out of the room, and Harry called to stop him.

"Dale! Is this stuff true he's been feeding us?"

Dale stopped, but he didn't look back. "I'll find her," he said. "I'll find her if it takes the rest of my life."

They didn't try to stop him then, but a silence fell as they waited. The car roared in the driveway, spun through the edge of the lawn in a U-turn and picked up speed toward the highway. The tires squealed on the pavement, then the sound faded as he shifted to a higher speed.

Olivia cried in a low voice, "Oh my God, he'll kill himself."

Harry sat down heavily at his desk. Pete smiled at the check and fingered it tenderly. Then his smile died. "Hey! Can he do that? Is it legal?"

Gene said angrily, "When you own sixty percent of the bank, believe me it's legal. Don't worry, you'll get your money."

"Okay, what am I supposed to do now, walk to town?"

Gene said as he sat down, "Far as I'm concerned."

Harry got up. "No, I'll drive you. There are some things I want to do there anyway. Gene, you get on the phone and see if you can hire some men for farm work."

Olivia followed Harry and Pete to the door, then watched wordlessly as they left in Harry's pickup truck. It had taken perhaps two minutes for Pete to throw his belongings into the suitcase he tossed into the rear of the truck. She turned then and went slowly up the stairs and into Peri Lee's room.

She closed the door behind her and leaned against it for a moment, thinking, remembering. They had decorated the room together, she and Peri Lee, two years ago. Peri Lee had loved it. She had loved Dale also; Olivia knew that and had known it for years. Even before Peri Lee knew, she sometimes thought.

Why would she go off in Pete's car? Why, merciful God; why, would she do the things Pete had said? Why had she changed so much so suddenly, so abruptly? Mental illness, a doctor would say. But something deep in her own mind couldn't accept that yet. Couldn't accept that any more than she could accept Bertha's horrible, superstitious diagnosis. Where her daughter was concerned, she couldn't accept anything as different as what was happening to her.

Perhaps she had only gone to town. Perhaps, because of the argument between her and Dale, she had set out to get even and had used Pete deliberately. Though Olivia wished she could doubt his word, as Gene had, Dale's silence in reaction to Pete's accusation, was indication that Dale knew it could be true.

Olivia pressed the lock on the door so that she would not be disturbed or interrupted, and went slowly into the room. A glance in the bathroom showed it to be as neat as the desk. Rene's work again.

She turned and crossed to the closet door. Neatness here, too. Neatness everywhere.

She stood on a bench and looked behind the doors of a top shelf to see if a piece of luggage was missing. But even the makeup case was there. If Peri Lee had intended to run away, to be gone for even one night, then why hadn't she taken an overnight case?

She began to go through the things hanging in the closet, thought it was rather a hopeless job. She didn't really remember all of Peri Lee's clothes, but if anything was missing she couldn't see it. The dresses she wore most often hung neatly in place, probably the work of Rene again. The new dresses were all there too, and the pantsuits. The blouses seemed to number in the dozens. When she stopped to recall what Peri Lee had been wearing that morning, the last time she had seen her, she couldn't remember at all. Jeans? Shirt? Something like that. She didn't even know.

The significance of her thoughts struck her, and she suddenly felt sick and weak. *The last time she had seen her.* It had been a spontaneous thought, as if it came from somewhere deep within, from a knowledge beyond her conscious control.

She sat down on the bench and leaned her forehead on her hand. The tears ran down softly and silently, wetting her cheeks, running into the corners of her parted lips.

"Oh God," she whispered. "Wherever she goes, go with her. Bring her home safely when she's ready to come home."

The sense of hopelessness disappeared and her fighting spirit made a new effort to take a more positive outlook. She got up, took tissues from a shelf and wiped her eyes and cheeks.

"He could be wrong," she said aloud, in self-reassurance. "He could be wrong."

There was no indication that Peri Lee had done anything beyond taking Pete's car for a drive. No indication that she had left home. Nothing.

A knock at the door increased her heartbeat and sent her quickly to open it. On seeing the young, plain face of Rene, she sighed in disappointment. She immediately attempted to cover the sigh.

"Yes, Rene?"

"I just remembered another thing, Mrs. O'Brion. About what I found on the floor, a day or two ago."

"Yes?" Olivia replied, feeling with dread that it might be better if she didn't know.

"Well—her money. Here and there on the floor. Dimes, quarters, half dollars. Change. A big handful of it."

"On the floor," Olivia repeated. "Had it been dropped?"

"Mrs. O'Brion," the girl said shyly, looking as if she were half afraid to say what she thought. "Not close together, you know? I mean, I came to vacuum, and I heard this clink. I began to look and money was scattered all over, even under the bed, as if she had thrown it all around. Just like the papers this morning. Only it was a lot harder to find in all this shag. I had to go around on my knees for a long time. Till Bertha started yelling at me. I don't know if I got it all."

"I see." She didn't want to hear anymore. "I'm sure you must have gotten it all, Rene. Perhaps you'd better go along and help Bertha."

But the girl didn't move. "I put it back in one of her purses, Mrs. O'Brion."

"Oh. Well, thank you."

Olivia put out her hand and gently turned Rene toward the stairs, then walked beside her, silent and thoughtful.

This was not Peri Lee that Rene was talking about. Peri Lee didn't do things like that. She didn't want to hear these alien things about her daughter.

At the foot of the stairs she said to Rene, "You've been very helpful, Rene. Please go and tell Bertha to prepare a very light lunch, rather late. I doubt if any of us will be needing much."

"Yes Ma'am."

Olivia went on to the privacy of her husband's office to wait for him. There was something about collapsing into one of his big, comfortable chairs that made her feel more secure. As if his arms were around her.

Harry drove to town as if he didn't have a passenger. He stared straight ahead, his thoughts to himself. Pete did the same. Without asking Pete where he wanted to go, Harry pulled up in front of the bank just long enough for Pete to get out and get his suitcase; then Harry drove on.

Throughout the afternoon he drove the streets of the town, slowly, covering every block, looking for Pete's car, for Peri Lee. Finally, he parked in front of the police station and sat for several long minutes.

When he got out of the truck and went into the police station he asked to use the phone. When he reached his number he asked only one question. "Have you heard from her?"

Olivia answered in a low, controlled voice, "No. Nothing."

"Then I'm going to report her as missing."

Her control broke and her answer was caught in a sob. "Yes. Please. Oh, please, ask them to find her."

Harry filed the report, a seemingly cold set of facts. He even managed to bring out of his subconscious the number of Pete's car license. "You can't miss it anyway," he said. "It's bright red with three wide white racing stripes painted all the way over the top from nose to tail."

The officer looked at the report.

"You don't know what she was wearing?"

"Uh—she changes so often. No, I don't."

"If anyone in your family knows call back please, Mr. O'Brion."

"Yeah—yeah I will."

"What about money?" the officer asked. "How much of that did she have available to her?"

Harry stared at him, mind gone blank. Money? Money in investments, money in banks. But cash? "Why—I don't know. I think her mother usually handles that. She has charge accounts at the dress shops and stores—she didn't need cash."

"Then you don't know that either."

"No, I guess I don't." Strange, he thought, that money should now become an important issue. Because without money, cash, what would happen to his little girl alone in this world? "I'll go ask my wife," he said abruptly and didn't wait for an answer.

When he reached the house Olivia came to meet him. They went into each others arms and for a moment were silent, then she pulled away.

"Did you report her missing?"

"Yes. Ollie, I can't believe this has happened to us. To our little girl. Did she ever do anything that made you think she wanted to get away from us?"

"Lately, Harry, I just didn't know her anymore. But even if she is different, she's still our daughter and only God knows how much I love her."

His hand squeezed hers painfully, "I know, Ollie. He cleared his throat. "They said they'd find that car, and—but if they don't find her they'll be wanting a picture to send to other places. They'll let us know. They want to know what she was wearing and how much money she had. Do you know if she had any money?"

Olivia too seemed to have gone blank. In a monotone she said, "Rene picked up a few dollars of change from the floor. Peri Lee threw it away, I guess. She might have had some. I don't know. What are the police going to do?"

"Look for the car, I think. Maybe Gene will remember what she was wearing. We'll wait till he gets back before we call the police again."

"But if they find the car they'll surely find her too, won't they, Harry?"

"Yes, sure, Ollie. Don't worry. She'll be home by tomorrow. They'll have that car located in no time. Who could miss seeing a red car with white stripes?"

CHAPTER 8

Gladys smiled in satisfaction, thinking of her escape from the small town—and with the money. The car was her only way out. She had taken time to stuff a few bills into the tight bodice, and the others she tried to hide beneath her vest. They made a knot that looked like another, lower breast, so she crossed her arms over it awkwardly and hurried across the street. An uncomfortable thought came to her. What if she started trailing money behind her? She tightened her arms across the lump on her diaphragm, threw caution to the wind and began to run.

The car was still there, sitting alone under the row of trees, with plenty of room to pull safely and easily back into the street. A couple of cars were coming slowly down the street, and she crossed in front of them. When she reached Pete's red car, she saw she had left the keys in the ignition. She gripped the steering wheel with tight, nervous fingers.

"Oh Gladys," she whispered to herself, "Oh, dumb Gladys! Leaving the keys in the car..."

Working in nervous haste, she pulled the bundle of money out of her vest and stuffed it under the seat. Then, her breath caught, she turned the ignition on. The car roared, and she looked quickly around to see if the noise had caught anyone's attention. No one was in the street.

She lifted her foot from the accelerator until the motor was purring softly, then she eased the shift into drive. The car began to move, toward the trees on her right. She turned the steering wheel frantically, and was back in the street again. Slowly she moved along, twisting the wheel until the car was moving straight down the street. She drew a sigh of relief and pressed gently on the accelerator. Not too much speed, not too much, she told herself severely; just enough to get out of town without being stopped by the patrol.

She knew another moment of near panic when she reached the edge of the eastbound interstate highway and sat with her foot on the brake, to watch the traffic whiz past at top speed. She had to drive onto the highway. There was no way back now. It was her avenue of escape, but how was she ever to compete with those experienced drivers?

She waited for a lull in the traffic, and at last one came when she could see no cars within a half mile. She let the car ease forward as slowly as it would go, got it straightened out and safely in the outside lane. Then she sat back and pressed the accelerator.

At first her breath caught, in her astonishment that the car was staying where she wanted it to. Then came the high. She felt as free as though she were racing through space. She began to laugh, to sing, and to shout. She would like to have removed one hand from the steering wheel and given the car a pat of praise, but she didn't dare.

"I can drive, I can drive!" she cried into the strong force of wind that came through her open window. "Just as though I'd been driving for years. Oh, you beautiful, beautiful car!"

Gliding smoothly along the eastbound lanes of the interstate, Gladys felt a sense of elation and power. Her mind was unoccupied. There was nothing else to do. The landscape was unchanging, nothing but flat fields of green wheat in all directions.

Had Peri Lee driven? Of course she would have. She probably had her own car. Was it Peri Lee who was now doing the driving? Gladys found that thought disturbing, and it sobered her.

She drove for hours, she wasn't sure how long.

. . .

A CAR OF HER OWN... yes, she'd have to buy one of her own, as soon as she reached a town far enough away. The police would be looking for Pete's car before the day was over—or at least by tomorrow morning. There wasn't much chance that Pete wouldn't notice his car was missing. So yes, of course, the answer was to buy her own car. But that would take a lot of money, and she had other plans for the money. Perhaps the best thing would be to drive to an airport and fly away. Yes, far away. Chicago, or New York. And finally to Paris. To the entire world! To the best places... where she could meet really wealthy men.

She saw a truck-stop off the right side of the highway, down a winding ramp, and thought to look at the gas gage. But the red needle pointed nearer full than empty. Good old Pete. He had kept his gas tank full. She could drive until dark with no trouble, and then she would have to abandon the car anyway.

She laughed, thinking of Pete finally finding his car, miles and miles from home with its gas tank empty.

To pass the time she began to plan her future. A town, an airport, a ticket eastward toward total freedom. Or westward? Los Angeles, or San Francisco? How far would the money take her? Far enough, she was sure, to meet the right kind of men.

The sun was far behind her, sending slanting rays into the rear window. It occurred to her she might be listening to music instead of the continual roar of wind. For the first time she took one hand off the steering wheel and reached to dial the radio.

And that was her mistake. She knew it instantly, but it was too late by then. The car jerked to the right toward a long drop down an embankment toward a wheat field. She grasped the steering wheel with both hands and twisted it back again. To her horror the car flipped sideways and suddenly was rolling, over and over, down the bank toward the field. A scream died silently in her throat and she held to the steering wheel in terror as the sounds entered her consciousness; roaring motor, glass crunching, splintering. Then, blessedly, the car stopped rolling and rested on its top. Gladys found herself lying beneath the steering wheel, twisted and smothered. Her thoughts were in abeyance for a moment, then she forced herself to realize her predicament. The car window, now at her feet, was crunched and narrowed by the impact, but still large enough to crawl from.

Slowly, she twisted her body about until her head was out the window. Crawling, wriggling like a worm, she pulled herself into the tall wheat outside the car. She sat up and drew a long breath. She was unhurt. Not even her arms were scratched.

The car motor was still roaring, and above that sound came another that sent goosebumps of alarm over her. *A police siren.*

Oh God, Oh God, she cried softly to herself. Now she was really in trouble. If they found her—*if they found her*—

Even before she consciously planned it, she was moving, slithering on her stomach through the wheat, reaching behind her to obliterate any signs.

She heard the siren stop far above her on the highway. She kept going, out into the wheat field. A strong south wind whistled over her head, making the wheat field a moving sea of rippling grass, concealing her, protecting her.

The roar of Pete's car suddenly stopped, so she knew the highway patrol had reached it and turned it off. She lay still then, pushing her face into the soil, her hands gripping slender stalks of wheat so hard they were crushed.

Male voices filtered to her through the singing wind.

"Where's the driver... gotta be a driver around here somewhere..."

Another voice, closer, called to the first, "I don't see any signs of anyone. Maybe he..."

He. At least they hadn't actually seen her. Only the car.

The voices continued, softer, less distinguishable from the wind. She didn't dare move, not yet, although her body cried for movement, and began a vague aching from the enforced stillness.

She heard a car start, and she realized the voices had ceased to murmur in the wind. Slowly she raised her face, turned and sat up. She had to rise to her knees to see over the waving heads of wheat. A patrol car on the overpass was moving slowly into the thin traffic of the highway, but still she wasn't alone. Wandering about the red, wrecked car, the car that lay on its back with its wheels sticking into the air like a huge beetle, was a man in uniform. He wasn't looking for her, he was looking into and around the car. At that moment she remembered the money.

All of it, or most of it, still under the seat in the car.

"My God!" she whispered, both hands automatically moving to the dip between her breasts. She began to claw frantically at her clothing for the money she had stuffed there, and with great relief found it. She drew it out, three thin bills. In anger she almost threw it into the field. "Three hundred lousy dollars! Damn, oh damn it to hell!"

She had to get back to the car. But how? She couldn't risk being caught, not even for the money. She would wait; maybe the other guy would leave. He had to leave sometime.

But what if more men came to help search for the driver? Wouldn't they naturally assume the driver had been hurt and was somewhere in the thick grass of the field that seemed to go on forever toward the horizons?

She sat with knees drawn up, elbows resting on knees, chin in hands, and thought it over. She came to the fast conclusion that her freedom was more important than the money. With her looks, she'd get along all right. Maybe she'd get to those far-away places on someone else's money.

Now, she needed to get away before she was found. If she could get to the railroad track, then go under the overpass to the field on the other side, she might have a better chance.

The sun had dropped behind the western mountains, creating a bright halo above them. In another few minutes twilight would be on the land. To the southwest she noticed the building of dark clouds, and moving lazily through them brief lines of lightning. Too far away yet to be a danger. But storm clouds could move swiftly.

She began crawling in the general direction of the railroad underpass, going on her hands and knees. The next time she raised to look toward the car the patrolman had stopped looking around and was leaning against it. His arms were folded across his chest, his eyes toward the highway. He was obviously expecting someone to show up, and soon.

Thunder reached her ears then, and Gladys saw the storm had

swept rapidly to cover a large portion of the darkening sky, and the swift, darting lightning was almost continuous. A bad sign.

She had decided to take a chance and run for the railroad when the cars appeared on the shoulder of the highway above. Two patrol cars, and one plain brown car. She lay down hastily, her face pressed close to the soil again, but she was far enough away so that she dared crawl slowly onward.

Dark descended suddenly, and with it came the rain. Sheets of it soaked her immediately and left her shaking with cold. The thunder roared menacingly above and the lightning seemed at times to be reaching for her. Whimpering like a trapped and frightened animal, she tried to find shelter in the whipping wheat.

It finally occurred to her that now, in the darkness, she could escape. She could at least get to the protection of the railroad under-pass. But caution stopped her. Wouldn't that be the logical place for them to look, if they were still looking?

She continued to go in the direction of the railroad tracks, but they seemed to have disappeared into the endless field of rain-beaten wheat.

The highway then, she thought, her teeth chattering helplessly, her body tight against the cold. Yes, the highway, and maybe a ride with someone to a motel. The warmth of blankets, the seclusion of a room, a door she could lock against the world. Nothing else mattered more, now.

She stood up and a flash of lightning showed, in the distance, the rise of the overpass. Nearer, were a few scattered lights of cars or trucks moving on the highway. In the darkness, in feeling her way through the wheat, she had changed her direction. She had put the wrecked car and the overpass farther away, and brought the highway closer. She began to run, the wind-driven rain pressing her clothes tightly to her body.

She reached the highway breathless and nearly exhausted, heart threatening to explode in her chest. The eastern lanes were empty of cars, but just visible was a truck coming on the western lane. Now, without money, where could she go but back to Denver? There, at least, she knew her way around her own part of the city.

She paused only long enough to allow her breath to settle, the pain in her chest to lessen. Then she ran again, across the open eastbound lanes, to the edge of the westbound. She stopped on the pavement where the trucker couldn't help but see her.

"Stop. Oh please stop," she cried softly, as though searchers were still about her in the night.

The truck's brakes squealed as though tortured; the truck slowed, came to a stop beside her. It was a huge insect in the night, standing high above her, but it was her sanctuary.

The door opened and a face looked down at her. The voice said gruffly, "Christ a mighty, girl, what're you doing out in this storm?"

She gripped the door. "May I ride, please? I need to get to a shelter somewhere."

"Well, sure. Come on up. Need some help?"

"No. I can make it."

She climbed, and the man who opened the door moved back to sit under the steering wheel. He looked at her in the pale overhead light.

"Jesus, girl, you're wet."

"I know," she said, settling into the seat, pulling the heavy door shut. "I was caught out in the rain. Could we please go now?"

He kept looking at her with sidelong glances as he shifted, and the truck labored into movement.

"If you don't take pneumonia I'll be surprised," he said. "Where are you headed?"

"Right now, to a motel." She saw him raise his eyebrows, so she added pointedly, surprised at the vehemence of her feelings, "Alone."

The driver turned his face toward the slapping windshield wipers and the rain-beaten road that looked like a glistening black snake in the dark. He shifted twice more and the huge transport truck rolled smoothly toward and past the maximum speed limit. For a while, the most outstanding noise in the cab was the chattering of Gladys' teeth.

He stretched a thick arm toward the dash and pushed a button. "I'll turn the heater on," he mumbled. "Maybe that'll help you. Looks like it's going to rain all night."

"Y-yes," she said, finding talk difficult through her chattering teeth. The warmth from the heater seemed only to increase the shivering of her body that she now knew was caused from more than being wet. She sat leaning forward, her arms hugging her body, her eyes straining through the night ahead for the neon lights of a motel.

"There's a Holiday Inn not too far down the road," he said. "Twenty or thirty miles. Do you want to stop there?"

"Yes. Th-thank you."

"If you should change your mind, well, I'm on my way to the west coast."

She answered him with a mere grunt. She didn't feel like talking, like looking forward or backward. All she wanted was the warmth of a bed.

Far away in the distance she saw wavering dashes of light. But in this flat, wheat-filled landscape she knew those lights could be miles off.

"Got a family?" he asked. "You're not old enough to be married, though, are you?"

"S-sure. I'm—twenty-one. But no, no family. I'm not married, I mean."

"Did you run away or something? I mean, pardon the questions, but you puzzle me. It's not often I find a girl like you standing on the road in the middle of the night, with the rain beating down on her head."

"What time is it?" she asked, hoping to get his mind away from the mystery she presented.

"Eleven o'clock."

"Good lord," she murmured to herself. Had she wandered that long in the dark?"

"Well, that's Central time. I guess we're in the region of Mountain Time now. I'll have to reset my watch when I stop for a coffee break. When we get to the Holiday Inn, I'll buy you a cuppa coffee. That should warm you up."

She didn't answer. She kept her eyes on the lights until they were only indistinguishable blurs, streaked by the falling rain, joined at times by the sweep of lights from trucks on the eastbound lanes.

She closed her eyes finally, and fell asleep. A hand touched her shoulder and she jerked awake to find the truck had stopped beneath the flickering neons that announced, HOLIDAY INN; in smaller letters, *Restaurant*.

"Here we are," he said, and leaned across her to open the door. For a moment he was lying heavily on her, his arms pressing against her breasts.

She tumbled out into the rain again and ran toward the brightly lighted lobby of the inn.

A girl behind the desk watched her approach with curiosity written clearly on her face.

"I'd like a r-room, please," Gladys murmured.

The girl pushed a register pad toward her. Gladys picked up the pen, paused a moment, then wrote *Gladys Swartz*. The tall blonde girl behind the desk silently handed her a key with the number 205.

The door opened again as Gladys turned, and the trucker came in, smiling at her. She saw he was taller and heavier than he had seemed in the huge cab of the truck. He had a leathered face and tousled wheat-colored hair. For a brief moment she thought it might be nice to go on to the west coast with him. But the thought of the bed, of being alone in it, was more attractive. She stopped though, in front of him, and said, "Thanks. Thanks so much. You don't know how grateful to you I am." She knew the girl was listening and watching, so she was careful to say no more. To make sure he said nothing, she pushed on past him to the double doors that led to the galleries of the motel.

She climbed the first flight of steps she came to and found her room without trouble. The key shook in her hand as she inserted it, and a moment later she was in the safety, the privacy, the warmth of a clean, typical Holiday Inn room.

She slipped the safety chain into position, turned on the lights and headed toward the white-tiled bathroom; removing her still damp clothes as she went. In a tub of hot water her chills finally subsided, but she knew she had fever, burning fever.

She went to one of the two beds, dragged the blankets off the spare, then added them to the one she crawled into. With the lights still on, she buried herself under the warmth of piled blankets and slipped into a dozing sleep.

Strange images flitted through her feverish half-waking, half-sleeping mind. She was standing in a field from which the mist of early morning rose; far away, coming nearer through the eerie, moving mist was a tall, wide-shouldered boy whose blond hair was touched by the rising sun, and her heart beat with longing and love. He raised his arms, opened them for her, and his lips silently spoke her name, "Peri Lee...Peri Lee..." She answered, "I'm here. Come and get me, my love."

Gladys jerked fully awake for a moment, and felt the dream still in her, struggling to live, the longing still there. Her body, her heart, her torn mind ached for him, for Dale. She wept dry tears for a love that had not been hers, and in fear she knew Peri Lee was gaining strength in her fever-ridden brain and was crying for her lover.

Gladys staggered from the bed, washed her face in cold water, then with the telephone clutched in trembling hands dialed room service. She saw through a slit between the draperies that day had come. The sun shone brightly on a landscape washed green.

When the voice answered she asked, "Is the bar open?"

"Yes."

"Please bring me two Alka-Seltzers with a double shot of bourbon."

The voice hesitated, then asked incredulously, "All in one?"

"Yes. The room number is 205."

She moved restlessly, but with overwhelming exhaustion, as she waited. She turned off the lights, and in the twilight gloom looked at her face in the mirror. She brushed back her hair with water-dampened hands. The face was pale, large-eyed, sick looking. She longed for bed, for sleep and rest, yet was afraid.

Peri Lee was trying to return. She was bringing into Gladys's mind her own thoughts, desires—or was it memories?

Did she dare sleep again with this strange fever that weakened her? What would happen to her sick body if she left the motel and started walking, hitchhiking, back toward Denver? If she returned to her old neighborhood, would it help her gain control, push Peri Lee away again, this time forever?

She felt a longing, sharp and sudden, for the safety, the security of her old bedroom in the rickety old apartment house, a loneliness for her Mama. Would her mama love her now, seeing she was pretty?

Would she mix a hot toddy for her, strong with ginger and sugar, and tuck the blankets about her in bed?

A knock on the door startled her and brought a low whimper to her throat. She leaned against the dresser in weakness before she went to the door.

She took the glass from the tray that was held by a woman, signed her name, closed and locked the door. She drank the mixture without pausing for breath, then sat on the side of the bed, wanting to lie down, to draw the covers over her chilling body. But the fear was still there, too strong to let her rest.

Her head bowed, her eyes closed, she began to plead softly, aloud, "Oh, please don't. Please don't come back. Leave me alone. Go, and leave me."

She fell back into the bed, drawing the blankets over her head. The visions returned, sweeping like disconnected films, dreams mixed with vague realities. A little girl, climbing onto her daddy's knee, feeling the closeness of someone she trusted. *How's my Kitten today?*

I'm fine. Daddy. Daddy, are you going to take me with you today?

What would your mother say if I took you up where the combines are running.

And suddenly, breaking through from another world like glass shattering, *Mama, I'm sick.* A whine, a pleading, and her mama looking at her in cold silence.

Again she was walking through a house unfamiliar to part of her mind, but warmly familiar to another, deeper part. The house was large, furnished in polished antiques. Dale's arm was around her narrow waist and he was saying, *When Mother was still living she told me she hoped the girl I chose to marry would love this old furniture as much as she did. But of course when we marry the house will be yours, and whatever you want to do with it...*

I'll want to leave it just as it is—Dale, my darling, my love. How could I want to change anything? I want everything to go on always just as it is...

Oh no, no, no.

Gladys pulled herself up from the blankets crying, "Mama. Mama!"

The antique furniture, the papered walls, the heavy satin draperies were gone. The small motel room seemed strange and unfamiliar for an instant, then focused sharply. She wouldn't sleep again. She didn't dare. The memories had to go away—they weren't hers.

Gladys put her hands to her face and found that she was perspiring. The blankets had grown heavy and hot. The fever was gone.

She picked her drying and wrinkled clothes up from the floor and began to dress hurriedly. She had to go on now, quickly, back to the world Gladys Swartz had known.

Where Peri Lee O'Brion could never live.

CHAPTER 9

The wrecker was just hooking up to the smashed red car with the white stripes when Dale Larson left his own car, parked off the edge of the highway, and walked down the hill. He stood with his thumbs hooked in the pockets of his tight jeans and watched the operation solemnly.

The man finished hooking the car onto the wrecker chains and motioned for the driver to lift it. Then he looked at Dale.

"A mess, ain't it? A shame too. A nifty little car. Lucky nobody was killed."

"Yeah."

"They say it's a stolen car. The driver gone, nowhere to be found. Supposed to be a girl, alone. But I can't hardly believe that, can you?"

Dale's narrowed eyes watched the car. He didn't answer the man.

"Well," the man said. "Time to pull her in. You've got a good-looking job up there yourself."

"Thanks."

The wrecker moved out, going slowly and easily around the foot of the embankment. Dale was left alone with the wind blowing the tall, green grass against his boots, and the sound of the traffic on the highway above. Where the wrecked car had been, the grass was crushed. He went nearer.

He stopped in the middle of the crushed grass and stared down, nudging a bit of broken glass with his toe as if somewhere there he could uncover the mystery of Peri Lee's disappearance. The area had been searched, the police said, thoroughly. But it didn't satisfy Dale. He moved away from the chilling spot where the car had lay and began to search the whipping grass.

Yet, if the police had searched they must have searched closely. He began to have a strong feeling he would be wasting time to go over the area himself. He passed under the viaduct, across the four railroad tracks, and came out on the other side. More tall grass, waving in the wind, otherwise undisturbed. Beyond the grass and the tracks were shacky looking houses, and a cafe that was worse. He took a deep breath and moved toward it, walking with long, fast steps.

The interior of the cafe was worse than the outside. A small counter held a few smudged sugar containers, a couple of catsup bottles, a mustard jar brown around the edges, and at least a hundred flies. They crawled over everything. At one end, a man sat over a plate of something greasy and smelly. Dale took a stool at the other end.

"Yeah?" the man behind the counter said.

"Coffee, please."

"Cream?"

God, no, Dale thought, looking at the flies that crawled over the cream pitcher. He said aloud, "Black. Plain."

The coffee turned out just as Dale expected. A week old. He stirred it with a spoon that he first inspected for somebody's leftover supper.

"Were you open when that car ran off the viaduct?"

"Naw. I close at seven. Don't get much business after that, since them sonsabitches took my beer license away."

"What time do you open in the morning?"

"About eight."

"Then you don't know anything about the occupant of the wrecked car."

"Naw. I didn't even know the car was there until someone came in talking about the police being down there. I hear tell the wreck happened sometime around sundown."

"Is there a bus or anything out of here around that time of day, that the driver could have taken?"

"Are you kidding? Buses come through here, but they don't hardly ever stop."

"How about a slow train?"

The man looked interested suddenly. He leaned, down, his elbows on the counter. "Say, I never thought about that. There is an old freight that runs through about three. Ain't that right, Stanley?"

Stanley gulped on a mouthful of runny egg and answered, "Yeah. The damned thing wakes me up every night hooting its horn right outside my winder."

"Where does it go?" Dale asked.

Stanley wiped egg off his chin. "East. That'n goes east. I know. It takes it half the night to get by my winder. It used to go faster, shooting cinders like a possum spitting prune pits, but one night I stuck my hand out the winder and give that old engineer the finger..." He stuck up his second finger. And ever since that bastard has took three times as long, and toots his horn all the way. If I had any place to go, I'd move. What they ought to do is junk both of them. That old engine, and the asshole engineer right along with it."

He sunk his face toward his plate again, and the cafe man said to Dale, "Stanley here, he gets riled up sometimes."

"Yeah," Dale said. "So do I."

The cafe owner leaned closer. "You know that girl or somethin'? I heard she was running away. Maybe you're one of them detectives that rich family of hers hired."

"Maybe."

Dale reached into his pocket for a quarter and paid for the acid-black coffee. His walk back to his car was on the verge of a run. He passed the spot where the car had been, without giving it a glance. When he reached his own car he backed up, pulled into the traffic and headed east over the viaduct.

Where had she gone? He'd follow the railroad, hitting every small town between here and hell if he had to. But he wasn't going home without Peri Lee.

He paused in town only long enough to go to the bank and have the bank manager call his home bank for an okay on a bundle of traveler's checks. There was no trouble, no problem. When he pulled out at last he had enough money to take him halfway around the world.

Two miles east of town the railroad turned and headed southeast, alongside the road. Flat, level country where a pair of good eyes could see for miles. Then, just as he had the car cruising along at a pace that would have attracted anyone wearing a badge, the road turned straight east, leaving the railroad to disappear in fields of waving wheat.

Dale pulled right onto the first dirt road, found he had chosen a mess of ruts and holes. He slipped the car into its lowest gear and roared through, taking off down every road that held toward the direction of the railroad, no matter how small and impassible it looked. After about one hour he came out on a secondary road that once again ran straight as a ruler alongside the railroad. At the first train depot he pulled in, parked, got out and looked around.

Here the wind blew as if it had nowhere to go but on. Like himself. It tumbled his hair over his head and into his eyes. He pushed it back and took a good look at what was probably considered a town. A wide graveled street, a little grocery store and gas station, and another place called an eatery.

The depot was not only closed, it was locked. After trying unsuccessfully to look through the dusty window of the door pane, he turned and crossed the wide, quiet street and spoke to the gas station attendant.

"Pretty busy these days?"

The man laughed. "Population two. Me and my wife. She runs the grocery store. Sometimes a farmer comes in for gas, and a farmer's wife for something she ran out of. You can't compete with these big supermarkets that are springing up all around."

Dale looked around, saw nothing but flat fields, wheat and three far-away homesteads.

The man didn't move. He had a chair balanced on two legs, the back leaning against his small building. "Well. They're around. You just can't see them from here."

"Have you seen a train go through recently? An old slow freight?"

"They're not so slow by the time they get here. The only time they stop is harvest time, when the grain starts coming in. We get a few customers then, too."

"Is the cafe open?"

"No. My wife runs that, too. It doesn't pay to keep it open until harvest time."

Dale turned, hooked his thumbs in his pockets, then looked toward the eastern horizon.

"But is there an early morning train?"

"Yeah. About daylight."

"Do you ever see people riding those freights?"

"I might if I got up that early. No point in getting up, though, just to look for hobos. You looking for somebody?"

"Yeah. A girl."

"Sorry, fella. She's not here. If she was on that train, she's still on it. I suggest you go right along to a town pretty close to the Kansas line. The train stops there, switches, and sets around for a while. You might find out something."

"Thank you."

Dale went back to his car and drove away. But his mind picked up a thought it had toyed with all the time. Instead of a slow freight, going nowhere, a car, going somewhere. A good-looking girl hitch-hiking in the dark hours of the night would have no problem getting a lift from most traveling men. And Peri Lee, now, would have no qualms about accepting a lift like that. She would rather accept a ride with a strange man than go on a slow, dirty old freight train. It would have been just as easy for her to walk up the highway a mile and start thumbing, as to climb into a slow-moving box-car.

He wondered why he had ever considered the train, and couldn't answer his own question; except it had simply been there, available, during the night.

He drove on, found the wide, smooth interstate highway, picked it up on an eastern entry and mashed down on the accelerator, trucking along about twenty miles an hour over the speed limit. He ceased to watch the fields of green wheat. No point. She had gone on, east maybe; he didn't know. All he had left was instinct. Blind instinct.

That night he checked into a hotel in Kansas City, then placed a call to the O'Brion residence.

Harry O'Brion answered on the first ring, with a quick and breathless, "Yes? O'Brions."

"Dale speaking. Any news?"

Harry cleared his throat. "Well, Dale, nothing good. Just something we can't figure out, don't know what to make of it."

Dale felt his throat tighten. "What?" he asked bluntly.

"Summerton called us to tell us Peri Lee had checked out all her money before she left town. She's got something around fourteen thousand, I think. I don't remember exactly. And she's got it in cash."

There was a moment's silence. "Well, that doesn't leave her exactly penniless then," Dale said finally.

"No. And we're glad of that. But what bothered us, Dale, and I don't know what it means, is that the signature wasn't hers. It was entirely different. Yet they swear it was she, all right. Summerton went out and looked at her to make sure. Peri Lee told him that she had hurt her wrist and was practicing a new form of writing. Yet she didn't even spell the name right. So, well, I don't know what to tell you. It looks like she wanted to get away from everything that had even been familiar to her. Even herself. Maybe she can't help it. Of course she can't. We shouldn't have put off taking her to a hospital."

Dale didn't answer. He held the phone and let that latest news enter his mind. There it lay, refusing to fit into anything coherent.

"Dale?"

"Yeah, I'm still here."

"Well, Dale, good luck."

Harry O'Brion's voice had a gentler, fatherly quality then, that reminded Dale of his own dead father. His throat tightened again so that he had to swallow before he could answer.

"Thank you," he finally said. "I'll need it."

"And Dale?"

"Yeah?"

"Don't worry about your farm, Gene will see to it, and I'll be there off and on."

"I'd appreciate that. I've got some good men, though, and I think they'll get along. Just tell them to keep it going and don't look for me until they see me."

"I'll do that. I'll wire you expense money—"

"No. I've got plenty. I'll be calling once in awhile to find out if you've heard anything."

"We'll be around. Waiting."

He spent three days in Kansas City, checked with the police, checked with the O'Brions again, checked with the hospitals as well as he could, and then began to check the bars. With a purpose different from his first. On the fourth day he pulled out and headed for Saint Louis.

THREE MONTHS later his determination had lost itself among the restaurants, joints, dives, nightclubs, long-hair communes, police stations and hospitals all the way to New York City. He drove back into Denver thoughtfully, through streets narrow and crowded with traffic. When he finally located a hotel and a parking space, he pulled in and switched off the ignition.

For a while he just sat. He'd done a lot of sitting lately, sitting in bars and restaurants watching people go by. He wasn't really sure why he chose the bars. Still going on instinct, maybe. A feeling that when Peri Lee changed, she changed completely. Lost. A girl lost.

He got out of the car and reached for the one suitcase in the back seat. He couldn't remember the name of the town where he had bought it. The clothes he was wearing now were for a man twenty pounds thinner.

He checked into the hotel, but he didn't pause to do anything except drop his suitcase on the bed. With the key tucked into the pocket of his blue jeans he went downstairs to the desk.

"Any good places to have a drink around here?" he asked the male clerk.

The man looked him over swiftly. "With girls?"

"Sure with girls," Dale answered casually. He had gotten used to a lot of things lately. "What do you think I'd want? Something less?"

THE CLERK LAUGHED. "Well, some do. There's a place around the corner thataway and down three blocks. Guaranteed to satisfy your eyeballs, at least."

Dale nodded his thanks and went out.

He passed several bars, but there was no mistaking the one the clerk had meant. It had a dark and mysterious looking front that suggested eternal night, with all the delights and dangers that thrive in a place of shaded reality. He pushed open the door and went in. At two-thirty A.M. it was still crowded. A large, smoky, music-filled, people-filled room with tables, booths, bars, and a small band playing under colored, moving lights on a raised platform in a far corner. Dancers moved on a small floor near the band. But most of the people were men, Dale saw, and they all faced toward a section of a bar. Nude girls stood on the counter, wiggling a kind of dance-less dance, so sexy half the men were reduced to a state of glass-eyed misery.

Dale found a small table being vacated by a man and a woman and sat down. He pushed aside glasses and a cigarette-filled ash tray, put his elbows on the table and looked around at the couples. Peri Lee would be with a man, now; he felt sure of that.

While he waited for the waitress he kept looking, but without much hope. Peri Lee hadn't called home once. He had a feeling she never would. One glance up at the girls, far across the room and misted by the smoke, revealed to him that of the five there was only one who was brunette and she definitely was not the girl he was looking for.

But he was about ready to give up. He wasn't even sure why he had stopped at the hotel when another hour's drive would get him back to the valley and home.

Home. He didn't know if he could take it. Giving up a dream, a girl he loved, wasn't the easiest thing in the world to do. In view of the money Peri Lee had taken with her, he had to face the fact that she might be in China for all he knew.

. . .

IT WAS HARVEST TIME NOW. The pumpkins were ripe on the vine, so to speak. Peri Lee had always loved autumn, Halloween, and witches and things.

The waitress came and took his order. When she returned with the drink he looked up at the nude dancers. Lovely legs, all of them. Lovely bodies. Round breasts, dark nipples, small waists. The legs of the one in the middle were shaped something like Peri Lee's.

He put his glass down quickly and leaned forward over the table, staring. He had never seen Peri Lee completely nude, but he had watched the growth of her legs from rather bony and out of proportion to the lovely, curved legs of a beautiful young woman. There was something about her thighs that were different from other girls' legs. They curved out slightly in front, smoothing back into a sexy dip beneath her hip bone. He couldn't count the times past when he mentally had to slap his hands to keep from feeling her there.

His eyes raised quickly to the girl's face, then up, staring. Heavy makeup and thick mascara; eyeshadow, lips glossy with lipstick, hair platinum blond. *Bleached.*

The music stopped and the dancers started drifting back from the floor. Other people got up from tables and went toward the floor. The nude girls on the bar counter gave a last smile and wiggle of well-shaped butts and ran along its length to jump down, out of Dale's sight.

He fought to get past people, swearing because they kept getting in his way. By the time he had caught up with the last of the dancing girls, she was going through a door that slammed in his face. A big arm was raised casually to rest across the door, and big voice growled out a question.

"Where do you think you're going, Charlie?"

Dale forced himself to pause and think. Trouble would gain him nothing. "Are the girls coming back?"

"Tomorrow night."

"Yeah," Dale said. "Look. The one in the middle, the curvy one with the beautiful face. You know her name?"

"Sure I know her name. What the hell! We both work here, don't we?"

"Uh—" Dale looked the big man over. He was a trained fighter with a chip on his shoulder. Otherwise he wouldn't have been hired as a bouncer in one of the toughest joints in the area. He decided to appeal to the soft part of him. Provided he had one. "I was after her because I thought I knew her. She looks like a girl I had once. My first girl."

"Oh, yeah? What was her name?"

Dale grinned and shrugged. "Would you know I've forgotten? I called her other things, like Kitten." That was her dad's pet name for Peri Lee, and the first one that came to his mind.

The man laughed. "Well, that sure as hell fits better than the one she's got."

"What is it?"

"Gladys Swartz."

The frown came automatically, with puzzled repetition, "*Gladys Swartz?*"

"Yeah. Gladys Swartz. Has to be real, don't it?"

"It certainly sounds real. She must not be the girl I was thinking about. How long has she worked here?"

"Ah. I don't know. A month maybe."

Dale turned away.

The man raised his voice. "You want to see her she'll be back tomorrow night."

Dale went on without answering. Gladys Swartz. It had to be real, as the man said. No young, good looking girl, who wanted to make it in show business would fake a name like that. If Peri Lee tried to find another name in order to lose herself in the world, why would she choose that? No, he had simply been too long on the road. All girls were beginning to look like Peri Lee. Especially if they were beautiful, shrouded in the veil of dim lights and cigarette smoke. And the mind-altering effects of straight Scotch.

He thought about it as he walked back to his room. Then he thought about it in bed until he fell asleep.

He would give up and go home. What else was there? The police couldn't find Peri Lee, neither could he. It was an unsolved disappearance, that was all. He had even considered that it might be her way of getting Pete, running away with him. But that had been easy to check. He had found Pete working on a ranch in Wyoming, owner of a new car. But no Peri Lee.

Somewhere around three in the afternoon, he woke suddenly and completely, with a changed mind. He wondered why, today, he felt so positive about the girl. Last night it seemed he had only been seeing a dream. Perhaps because he was more rested, less drunk. He knew one thing: he had to have another look at that girl. Just one more look.

He was one of the first to come into the nightclub, sitting at the bar where the girls would dance, playing with a drink, waiting. The room filled with people gradually, then the gaudy little band came in and started tuning up.

After an incredibly long time, the door opened and the girls came in. But the girl in the middle was missing. The door closed, and four girls climbed onto the bar and began to dance, grinning down at him and other men who gawked up at them.

Dale stared at the door, but it remained closed.

After several minutes he spotted the bouncer leaning against the wall, his eyes roving the crowd lazily. Dale got up and went over to him. "Where's the girl? Gladys?"

He shrugged. "The boss don't like you much, Charlie. You just lost him a crowd puller."

"How'd I do that?"

"When I told Gladys about a big, hayseed Swede being here last night to catch her before she went out the door, she couldn't get out of her fast enough. Whoever you are, she don't want to see you, that's for sure."

"She didn't want to see me?" Dale repeated softly, more to himself than the man.

"Sounded like it. Looked like it. She just grabbed her clothes and said not to wait for her to come back."

"Where did she go?"

"I don't know."

"Well, where does she live, man?"

The tone of Dale's voice caused the bouncer to bristle. He unfolded his arms and prepared them for battle. "Now look. I don't know where she lives now, or where she ever lived. I've got a wife at home. I don't chase broads. Especially this kind. I'm hired to see they don't get raped on the floor here, that's all I do. If they're raped in the alley, that's their business. Once they pass that door they're out of my territory."

"Does the boss know her address?"

"No. If he did he'd go after her. These girls come and go, and you don't know anything about them. For all I know she could be the devil's daughter, and you him. So why don't you just peel out?"

Dale didn't bother to answer. There was no need for him to stay longer. A quiet place was what he wanted now, and a cup of coffee to clear his brain completely.

Because one thing was sure. Gladys Swartz knew him. And that meant... he didn't know what it meant. Was she Peri Lee?

The silence of the little restaurant, compared to the noise of the nightclub, and the sobering effect of the coffee, didn't help much. One fact kept stunning his mind. Was Peri Lee trying to lose herself? Was it possible she didn't want to see him? Ever?

What he should do, probably, was go home and tell her dad, and let them work it out by themselves. Stay out of her life. If she didn't want him, she didn't want him. He thought of all the times before that, when she had turned sweet lips to his and told him in words he would never forget that she had had a crush on him since she was six-years old. No, it wasn't a crush, it was love. Love that was born with her and wouldn't die, ever. Not ever. No one else had ever looked good to her, and no one else ever would. But she wanted to wait for that wedding night, the beginning of a honeymoon to remember, the culmination of their love for each other. Every word she spoke had increased his own love, and he respected her wishes. He wouldn't have forced anything. Sometimes it had been so hard to do, he had stayed away from her completely. Especially when she was still growing up, a sweet and vulnerable young teen who looked at him with surrender glowing in her eyes. Finally, he could date her.

And then came the change. A sudden and terrible change that was not reality for him. Not his Peri-Lee. Not his little sweetheart.

So no matter what he thought he should do, he couldn't bring himself to call home or to leave town. He slept mornings, walked the streets afternoons and evening, then went from bar to bar at night. And looked for her among the crowd.

He changed hotels, moving to a seedier location. So many solitary, young girls began to look like Peri Lee that when he did see her again, just a glimpse from across a crowded street, he almost missed recognizing her. The bleached hair stunned him again, for a moment, giving her time to slip through a door and disappear.

"Peri Lee," the whisper crossed his lips, then he began to run.

He was forced to wait for a light change because of heavy traffic on a narrow, dirty street. When the light turned to WALK he ran again, cutting across between the stopped cars to the sidewalk in front of the small, painted windows of the bar.

The interior was so dark that for a moment he could hardly see, and then he thought he saw her again, going through a door in back of the long, narrow room. He pushed through where small tables crowded closely together, and went out through the door in the back to find himself in a nearly dark, very narrow alley. A few feet away stood a couple in a clinch, and the girl had blonde hair. It wasn't Peri Lee. If she had come out the door she had already disappeared in the maze of back stairways.

He looked up at apartments above. His hopes rose. Perhaps she lived in one of them. If so, there was no hurry. He turned, went back into the bar and took a stool at the counter.

His beer was half finished before the bartender ran out of something to do and came close enough for Dale to casually ask his question. This time he would make sure he didn't scare her away. "Would you happen to know Gladys Swartz?" He hoped that she had continued to use the unusual name. To his surprise the bartender answered him without hesitation.

"Sure."

Dale's heart nearly stopped, then got a fresh spurt with a bang. Keeping his voice lazy, he said, "She lives around here?"

Suddenly the bartender was giving him all his attention. After a long stare, the grey-haired man asked, "You an insurance man or something?"

"No. Why?"

"Just wondered. You plainly didn't know Gladys very well."

"Why do you say that?"

"Well, because she's dead. Didn't you know that she died?

"Dead!" Dale lost himself. He forgot to control his emotions and hide them from the bartender's sharp eyes. He pointed toward the back door. "But I just saw her go out into the alley!"

The bartender snorted. "Man, you're drunk. Or crazy. Gladys Swartz died last spring. A truck hit her when she was crossing the street."

Dale settled down, staring back at him, remembering last spring; a kind of icy awareness that he didn't understand moved over his skin.

"Dead," he said again, softly. "I'm sorry. I didn't know." *How*, he thought wildly to himself, *had Peri Lee happened to take that particular name*? "Did Gladys live in one of the apartments in the back alley?"

"Yeah. Her folks still live there." He nodded back up the street. "Third door. You can get there either way, but Gladys came through here when she got off work and went to that booth way back in the corner. She could hide, and have herself three or four beers. She liked beers, poor girl, about the only pleasure she ever got out of life, I guess." He took the beer he had drawn down to a customer, and came back to lean his elbows on the bar. "Where did you know Gladys from?"

"Uh—I'm not sure I knew her at all. I might have her mixed up with another girl." *Keep the man talking, keep him talking, maybe the answer would be revealed. How did Peri Lee know Gladys Swartz?*

The bartender laughed a short, humorless laugh. "Mix Gladys up with another girl? No, you didn't know her. I can see that."

"I don't get you. Why couldn't I mix her up? Sometimes people look like other people." Dale was digging; he wasn't sure why or for what. But there was some connection between Peri Lee, Gladys' name, and the dead woman. He had to keep the bartender talking. "Especially good-looking girls," he added, in a voice he hoped sounded more casual than he felt.

"Not Gladys. She was one of the unfortunate ones. Crippled when she was a baby. Fell down the stairs, I think. She never grew out of it. She was only about this high; well, she could hardly see over the bar, somewhat bent and twisted. Pour soul, she didn't try to do anything for her face, which wasn't that bad. She had pretty hair. I felt sorry for the woman, but you couldn't get close to her. I mean, no friends, you know? She came in my bar till the day she died, and I don't reckon she ever said more than hello. I got to where I didn't try to talk to her. You know how it is. Some people can take a crippled body and make the most of it, be friendly and outgoing. People like them and forget how they look. The most beautiful people in the world can't go on their looks entirely, they got to give out with some personality. You know what I mean? I'm not very good at this talking business, I usually just listen."

"Yeah," Dale said, "I know what you mean."

"Well, with Gladys, it seemed she automatically expected everybody to take her at face value. She never gave anyone a chance to really know her." He shrugged. "That's the story of her life. When she was about seventeen she went to work in a factory across town and never missed a day that I know of, and never missed a day coming here for beers and going to hide in that corner booth. I kept papers and things over there to keep it reserved for her. I don't mind saying I missed her a lot, you know, the way you miss old street cars going by a certain time of day. I thought about her a lot afterwards. Well. That's life and death, I guess. Anyway, she's gone now."

Dale licked his dry lips. "How old was she when she died?"

The bartender frowned at the ceiling a moment. "I don't know for sure. In her middle thirties, I'd guess."

"Well, she's not the girl I knew, that's obvious."

Somebody down the bar called and the bartender moved away. Dale finished his beer, waited for another. A bit of the information the man had given him settled naggingly into his thoughts. *The Swartz family lived three doors down the street.* If Peri Lee had in some way known Gladys, the Swartz family might know Peri Lee. He had to find out. It seemed incredible that Peri Lee would be living up there. He hadn't seen her go upstairs, he had only assumed it.

The clock above the mirror on the bar said seven-thirty, and Dale decided to not wait for another beer, it was not too late to visit the parents of Gladys Swartz.

He went out through the front and found the third door. There was no lobby of any kind, only a narrow, steep stairway that went upward toward a dim light. Among a dozen mail boxes hanging on one wall he found, in tiny, typed, faded letters, the name Swartz. Apartment Three B.

He climbed the stairs, glad that he would have only three flights. It took several moments for someone to answer his knocks. The door opened as far as its chain would allow and a thin, wrinkled face peered through the crack.

"Mrs. Swartz?" he asked.

"Sure."

No friendliness there. "I realize you probably never heard of me, but I'll introduce myself if you have the time. I'd like to talk to you about your daughter."

"Which one? I got two."

"Gladys Swartz."

The tone of the voice changed to a puzzled. "*Her*? She's dead."

"I know. I'm sorry."

"Better off," the voice said, going back to its monotone. "What do you want to talk about her for? What'd she do?"

"Nothing. I—" Dale couldn't think of a reason that would interest the woman. "I'm from an insurance company—" He hated lying, but he could see that money would mean something to these people. Later he could mail them a check and it wouldn't matter to them if it was a personal check.

"Oh," she said, opening the door wide enough to let him into the bleak little room. "I've been wondering if I'd ever get anything out of that accident. I went to a lawyer and he said I couldn't because it was her fault, but he said he'd write a few letters. Are you coming about that? She walked right out in front of the truck, spectators said. But I don't believe it. I don't know why she'd do a thing like that. Come in."

A man, who looked very much like Mrs. Swartz, sat in a rocking chair near a large color TV. He nodded at Dale.

'Turn that thing off," Mrs. Swartz ordered. "This man is from an insurance company." Then to Dale she said, "Gladys didn't have any life insurance. Not even enough for burial. It's all poor people can do to keep hospital insurance paid. They took that out of her pay-check."

Dale sat on the chair the woman pushed out for him. He took from his pocket a small notebook and pen he always carried. "I'm interested in her life, if you don't mind. How old was she when she was killed?"

"Thirty-three."

"Was she your eldest? Your first daughter?"

"No. My third."

"She had an older brother and sister?"

"No. Two older sisters."

Dale paused. "I understood you to say you had two daughters, so—"

"Well, Gladys is dead."

"I see."

There was something flat and cold about the woman's eyes that surprised him. "Was she born crippled?"

"No. She fell down the back stairs into the alley when she was a baby. Mashed her face up, too."

"Oh. That must have been terrible."

The woman ran the tip of her tongue over her lips. Then she said, "Well, she was always sickly. There was always something wrong with her. I don't know what."

"You didn't take her to a doctor?" What he was hearing didn't seem possible. He looked from the woman to the man.

"Huh!" The woman answered, making a sound like a contemptuous snort. "When she started school they tried to do some things. I always knew it wouldn't do her any good. She just never was right. All it did was cost us money we didn't have in the first place. How could we help her without money?"

Dale began to feel extremely sorry for the person who had been Gladys Swartz. No love in her life? The woman looked as disgusted as she sounded, and the man sat as if he still was watching television. His own personal escape from life. "I understand she was never married," Dale said, looking at the woman now.

"Her? Who'd have had her?"

The man spoke up. "She got her kicks from a bunch of trash novels we found after she was dead, and from guzzling beer in the bar downstairs—"

Dale glanced up to see Mrs. Swartz direct a hard stare at her husband. The man hushed up immediately. Dale wanted to get out. But there were two more things he needed to know, for sure. "It must have been terrible for you to lose your youngest daughter in such a way."

"Oh it was, it was," the woman said, nodding. "And I think we ought to get—get—what do you call it? Money, anyway, from that."

"You'll get compensation, I'm sure. Do you live here alone now? Or do you have a renter?"

Surprise showed in Mrs. Swartz's voice. "A renter?"

"Yes. I thought perhaps you might be renting out your daughter's room."

"What has that got to do with money from that trucking company?"

"Nothing, of course. You aren't renting it then? I was only wondering about additional income for you, now that your daughter is gone."

"No. We don't rent it out. We use it."

Dale drew a long breath. He felt as if he wore blinders. "Now can you tell me please the name of the cemetery where she was buried?"

"It's one on the other side of town. I think they bury—uh—welfare people there a lot. You know, the county. Some kind of Memorial Gardens they call it. We didn't have the money to put her anyplace else."

"Thank you." A cab driver, or the bartender, Dale thought, would probably know more about it than Gladys's mother.

He was so glad to get out of the apartment that the stairs looked beautiful. He had gotten a couple of confusing answers. Gladys Swartz had never been loved in her life, not by anybody. She therefore had never been taught to love, never had learned to love. And the Swartz' did not rent Gladys' room to anyone. Not to Peri Lee, not anyone.

On the street he paused. The connection bothered him. Gladys Swartz. Peri Lee. How had Peri Lee learned of Gladys Swartz; why should she take her name? Why did she come to the street where the woman had lived? He didn't know what he was after, but he felt the answer had to be back upstairs in that awful, depressing atmosphere. Not even sure of the question he wanted to ask, he retraced his steps up the stairs and knocked on the door again.

Mrs. Swartz took the chain down the moment she recognized him. "Did you forget something? Come in."

He didn't accept her invitation. "It will only take me a moment, so I won't come in this time. I was just wondering if you have recently seen or met a young lady with pale blonde hair and very dark eyes. A very beautiful girl. She's about five-feet-four and weighs around one-ten."

"Well, maybe. There's one girl sounds like her who's around sometimes. I think she's moved into the house because I keep meeting her in the hall. I noticed her because she kept watching me. Odd person, too friendly. Just today she spoke to me and asked me about my daughters. I told her, and do you know she went running off with tears in her eyes? She didn't even let me finish. There ain't nothing about my two daughters to cry about. And she was the one that asked, I didn't offer!"

"Do you know her name?"

"No. I don't know nothing about her. I first saw her about a week ago, right here in the hall. What on earth has she got to do with Gladys?"

She had begun to frown suspiciously, so Dale was afraid he had gone too far. Here was a woman who wouldn't hesitate to call him a rapist and have the police after him. He had to think of something.

"We believe she had some connection with your daughter. For some reason she's been using Gladys' name."

Mrs. Swartz stopped looking suspicious. Bewilderment crossed her features. "That's crazy. Why would anyone do that?"

"That's what we'd like to know. The insurance company," he added, to keep her on good terms. Keep money in her mind.

Mrs. Swartz snapped her fingers and her eyes glittered. "Fraud!" With a second thought she asked, "Fraud?"

"For what possible gain?"

"You're right." Mrs. Swartz pinched her chin thoughtfully. "No telling then. I thought right off the girl was a kook of some kind. The way she run off crying after asking me herself. She was the one who asked. I told her about Marian and Clarissa."

"Could she be a friend of Gladys'?"

"Who knows! Gladys got to where she was gone more than she was at home on her days off. When she was at home she read books in her room that—" the woman hushed suddenly. Then she eagerly said, "If she had friends I didn't know it. If she did, and chose the kind of people who liked to read what she read, it might be a hunch of witches. What're they moving in here for? What did I do?" Fear was creeping into Mrs. Swartz's eyes and voice.

"Witches? Why do you think that?"

Her hand motioned in the air as if knocking an insect away. "This one book—she'd read it a lot I could see that—was about witches. These books are on the *occult*." She spoke the word as if it were synonymous with danger, evil, death.

Dale hadn't realized he was holding his breath until it burst out of him. "Could I see the book, please?" he asked, with a rush of out-going breath.

"Uh—it wouldn't keep us from getting some money out of her accident, would it?"

"No, of course not."

"Well," she said. "We don't have it anymore. We put it in the trash where it belonged."

"I see." He looked at his feet, feeling a need to leave now, and think this over. "Thank you. That was all, Mrs. Swartz. You understand we have to ask a lot of unimportant questions to find some answers to the accident."

He left again, wondering what Mrs. Swartz had said to make Peri Lee run away from her with tears in her eyes. Was it because she hadn't mentioned Gladys among her daughters? The last he had seen of Peri Lee, she seemed to have lost all sensitivity and sympathy. Maybe she wasn't totally lost after all.

It was rather late in the day to enter a cemetery, but he had nothing else to do, and he wanted to see the grave of Gladys Swartz.

Why? He asked himself the question. He wasn't sure why. He

wondered at himself, at his purposeless wandering. It seemed as though a curtain had closed off part of his mind, and the answer he so desperately sought lay just behind the curtain. If he could only push it aside. Make the connection. The connection between Peri Lee and Gladys Swartz.

The answer hadn't been upstairs in the apartment after all. He doubted if it lay in a still, voiceless cemetery. It seemed a waste of time to go there; but he had nothing else to do at the moment, and the cemetery drew him like hands beckoning from the other side of the dark curtain in his mind.

He stopped a cab, told the driver where he wanted to go, then rode for several minutes before they reached the gateless cemetery. He told the driver to wait, and walked to the edge of the small city of stones. A street light behind him threw his own long shadow to lie among the shadows of the older tombstones, while the rest of the cemetery faded into the darkness of unlighted night.

He saw how impossible it would be to find her grave now, without even a flashlight. A grave that probably didn't even have a stone. He returned to the cab and gave the driver the name of the bar where he had seen Peri Lee.

For the rest of the night, until it closed at two o'clock, he sat in the booth where the bartender said Gladys had hidden with her many beers. He sipped one beer after another, slowly, and stopped trying to think.

Wait. That was all. Wait, and she might come back. He sat on the side of the booth from which he had a view of the entire room, but he didn't see the blonde girl again.

When he had to return to his hotel he slept a few hours, then went back to the cemetery.

The day had dawned cold. Frost still lay on the grass, but the sky was a perfect blue and the sun promised some warmth later. Dale walked for a while among the graves, and finally decided the only solution was to use his head a little, if he ever intended finding the one he wanted. There was something increasingly eerie about this, something that struggled for recognition in his mind. Whatever it was had to be known by himself only.

Peri Lee. Gladys Swartz. Books on the occult. On ESP, on out-of-body experiences, on reincarnation. And a book on witches.

He frowned and shook his head against the worm in his mind. Witches were a bunch of fanatics who practiced ancient rites. There was no power, no truth in it. But reincarnation? That was a religion, a belief. One of the strongest, most powerful and persistent religions in the world. Reincarnation.

Why did it keep burrowing into his mind, to join the girl with the pale, bleached hair with a handicapped girl he had never known? A girl who had died.

He went on reminding himself forcefully to note the names on the gravestones. The grave would be a more recent one, one that was still marked only by a small metal and plastic marker stuck into the ground. If he started at the right hand corner and walked the rows, stopping at the recent graves, he was bound to find it before the day was over. Just what good it would do when he did find it he hadn't figured out, but it seemed important that he should find it.

He began to walk, passing the graves marked with stones, then pausing to read each small metal marker. He noticed that only cheap plastic flowers adorned these graves. The remembrances of poor people. He felt a tug in his heart when he thought of the poor and the burdened. He had been born one of the lucky ones; the fortune was made by his great-grandfather, a pioneer in Colorado. But he was conscious of it, and tried to earn all his own money. He was lucky because the farm he owned had been left to him by his father and mother. The money by his grandfather.

He had read perhaps a hundred grave markers when he found it, down near the end, by a dirt road. His eyes caught the name, Gladys Evelyn Swartz; the dates were November 13, 1945-May 25, 1978, then he saw the flowers.

His attention was captured by the flowers, and amazement grew in him. Where all the other graves held plastic flowers, or none at all, this one was decorated beautifully with yellow roses combined with delicate lace fern and white iris. A large and expensive bouquet, so fresh it had not wilted at all. He bent down to sit on his heels and touch the long stem of one rose thoughtfully.

Whoever had brought the flowers had brought them early this morning before his arrival. They had not been touched by frost.

There was no doubt who had brought the flowers; the very cost of them shouted Peri Lee O'Brion's presence.

The puzzling thing was: how had she known about Gladys Swartz? He looked across the cemetery to the row of spruce trees on the far side. To the mountains that lifted white caps toward the sun rays that sparkled on the new snow. But his mind stayed with Peri Lee and her strange connection with this woman who had died so unloved, in the springtime.

May twenty-fifth, day of death.

Now that he had found it there was no use in hanging around. The more he learned, the less he knew. But at least he now knew approximately where Peri Lee was.

He returned to her apartment house and checked the name plates. No new arrivals listed. If she had moved in, using her own name, her name wasn't here yet. He climbed the stairs to the second-floor apartment that belonged to the manager and knocked until his knuckles were red and his temper short. Finally a puffy-eyed woman, in a robe and hair that was wildly uncombed, opened her door and glared at him grumpily.

Everybody who lived here was soured on life, he decided, and his temper softened. No wonder, what dreary surroundings! He would probably sour early too, or at least be wild to get away.

"I'm looking for a girl, and I've been told she recently moved into a room or an apartment here." The woman began to shake her head before he was half through. When he started to describe Peri Lee, the woman interrupted him.

'No. No. No. Nobody. All of my apartments are full and have been for a year. Some of them for several years. I keep my rent down."

"Well, has anyone tried to rent?"

"No. No. No. You've got the wrong place."

"Her name—"

The door slammed in his face, so he had no choice but give it up. He went downstairs and into the bar next door. Chairs were still stacked on tables, but the bartender was there.

"Man, you start early, don't you?" the bartender said, not sounding happy about it.

"Well, your door was open."

"Yeah, sure. I open up for the early ones. The alcoholics. What'll you have?"

"Just a beer."

"What kind?'

"I don't care what kind. Whatever you've got on tap, whatever's closest. The main thing I want is a little information. I'm looking for a girl."

The man behind the bar laughed. "Ain't we all?"

"This one," Dale said, unamused, "Is built like a sex goddess and has bleached blonde hair. Her face is the most beautiful face that ever was, and her eyes are dark. I saw her come in here last night."

The bartender put the foaming glass in front of Dale. A grin lingered on his face. "Was that the girl you thought was Gladys?"

"Uh—yeah."

"Boy." He shook his head.

"Do you know her?"

"Well, let's say I do know who you're talking about. She's been coming in here for two or three months, and doing the same damned thing Gladys did. Hides herself in that back booth. When I tried to talk to her she cut me off so fast that I didn't try any more. I didn't see her at all last night. Are you sure she came in?"

"Yes, I'm sure."

"If so, she didn't stay." The man leaned an elbow on the bar. "Where'd you get the idea her name was Gladys Swartz, anyway?"

Dale wiped foam off his upper lip. He was beginning to wonder the same thing, it was all such a mess. "Damned if I know," he said. "Look, would you do me a favor?" He pulled a twenty-dollar bill from his pocket and lay it on the counter. "If she comes in, call me at this number. If I'm gone at the time, just leave the message." He wrote his hotel phone number and room number swiftly on a sheet of the note paper.

"I don't know," the man said, looking at the numbers. "What do you want with her?"

"I won't hurt her, if that's what you're thinking of. I happen to love her very much and—"

"And you don't even know her name?"

Dale got up. "Look—just call me, all right? I'll pay you for your trouble—*after* you call me."

"Well, I guess so."

Dale left and walked the streets, looking among the crowds. In the evening he went back to his hotel long enough to check for messages, bathe and change. On his way back to the bar he stopped for a sandwich. At last in the bar, he chose a stool at the end of the counter from where he could watch both doors and the half-hidden booth.

Hours dragged slowly by, the room grew noisier and grey with smoke. But Peri Lee did not show. Not even for a moment.

When the bar closed Dale went back to his hotel, but he set his alarm clock for five. He had a feeling that she might go back to the cemetery. At least, since she had gone once, she might go there again and he would be present.

Dawn was just a pale touch of pink toward the east when he got out of the cab; the cemetery a silent, shadowed place where cold wind moaned softly around the stones. Dale walked straight through to the grave of Gladys Swartz and stood looking at the flowers. Dead too, they had wilted with the brown of frost bite.

He crossed the cemetery and went into the grove of spruce trees, where his presence was shielded from anyone who would enter the cemetery, but where the tiny marker of the grave was still visible to him.

The sun rose and shadows grew behind the stones and moved with the sun, shrinking and changing. The silence in the cemetery remained. Dale shivered in the cold shadow of the tree, and wished he had remembered that it was the time of year when coats were sometimes needed. At one o'clock she still had not arrived. No one had. He had never known before how lonely a cemetery could be. The forgotten ones. Or, in most cases, the unreachable ones.

A small figure on the far side of the cemetery caught his eye. She was wrapped in a coat, with a scarf covering her hair, but his heart caught. Peri Lee.

She cut across into the cemetery, walking straight toward the grave. Today she had no flowers, though. Her hands were pushed deep into the pockets of her coat.

At the grave she turned, facing the road, and raised her arm. Dale stood very still, watching as she motioned for someone. A moment later he heard the low whine of a truck. It came slowly in view, driving up the narrow dirt road that surrounded the cemetery. A sign on its side said something about monuments.

Dale watched in bewilderment as two men got out, opened the rear doors of the truck and began moving out, on a dolly, a rather large stone. Even after the stone was in place, and the men were going back to the truck with the dolly, he didn't move. Nor did she.

The truck left, coming on around the road between Dale and the edge of the cemetery. Once again silence settled around him. Peri Lee stood looking at the stone, and for a reason he couldn't have defined he stayed hidden, watching her. Then he watched her slowly leave the cemetery, coming around the road close to him, her head down against the wind.

There was no doubt now that it was Peri Lee. Her face was clean of makeup, the way he had known her. The bleached hair was covered by a black scarf. But she raised her head once and he glimpsed within her eyes a certain far-away sadness that he did not remember. He wanted to rush out and pull her into his arms and hold her, to tear away the unhappiness in her eyes. But he remained where he was, unmoving, his heart crying silently, *My Peri Lee, what has happened to you?*

Then she was gone; and after a few minutes he stepped onto the road. But she was going out the far end of the cemetery, and she didn't look back.

He waited a few more minutes, then he crossed to look at the new stone. His mind was disturbed, his brain stumped in confusion again, as if it was growing a fungus that interfered with logical thinking.

The stone was white, much larger than any nearby stone, and on its top stood an angel with face uplifted toward the sky. Dale went around to the other side of the stone to read the inscription Peri Lee had chosen.

Gladys Evelyn Swartz, born November thirteen, nineteen-forty-five.

The crawling, worming coldness started on his face, spread downward over his arms and chest, to a quivering knot in his stomach. *No death date.* The curtain lifted from his mind and he was staring at something that seemed impossibly incredible. The answer hung in the air about the stone like the fragrance of perfume—or a thought cast out to be taken in by another's mind.

"It can't be true," he said aloud, but he knew it was.

He backed away, his eyes still on the stone. Things like this just didn't happen, he thought wildly. When people die, they die; they don't remain to take possession of living minds and bodies. They just don't.

But he found himself staring at the spot where he had last seen the girl who had gone away, the girl he hadn't attempted to stop. The eyes were different. The whole personality was different. And the change had come last spring, after Peri Lee's week of terrible fear.

Suddenly he was seeing her again, lying in the driveway after she had fallen off her horse, the night she had run from something he couldn't see. Clearly her words came back to him. "Dale, help me! Save me, oh God, save me. Dale, something wants me!"

The scenery around him blurred, went out of focus as his mind returned to pick up the bits of evidence that Peri Lee, the girl who had changed, hadn't known she was giving. The day after Hamilton committed suicide. The day he took her for the drive into the mountains, the last time he had been with her; it was the way she made love to him. No, not love. Just a feverish and animal sexual act. Now he wondered—was it the only way she knew?

And she hadn't known who Butchy was. She hadn't known the name of her own pet dog.

He felt sick, to his roots. If Peri Lee had been possessed by this person who claimed herself not dead, then where was the Peri Lee he had known and loved? She was still in existence, somewhere. Her personality couldn't be entirely suppressed. Or destroyed. My God, could it? If he went to a psychiatrist and told his story and asked for help, they would probably be convinced that he was hopelessly insane. He knew what a doctor would say. Peri Lee O'Brion had heard of the woman, Gladys Swartz, and in her own paranoid mind she became the woman.

No. He didn't believe for a minute that it was so. Therefore, there was no one on earth to whom he could talk. Ever. Especially her family. No one.

He walked away from the stone, pausing only to look again at the date of death on the small, discarded metal marker. May 25, 1978.

He struggled to recall the first change in Peri Lee, the beginning of her fear. The night they had gone to young people's meeting at the church, when she kept looking backwards into the night? About the first of June. The week before that, though, they had parked at the river and she had been melancholy, afraid they were going to be separated.

"My God," he said aloud.

There was nothing more to do but go somewhere and get drunk. What else could be done? He was helpless against something like that.

He went back to the same bar, the same secluded little corner where Gladys Swartz, the real Gladys Swartz, used to sit. He ordered straight Scotch.

"Not your usual beer?"

"No. Scotch. Just bring me a bottle."

"Not even water?" the amazed bartender asked.

"No, Goddamnit!"

The bartender whistled under his breath and said quietly. "Bad temper this evening. A bottle coming up. I'll donate a glass."

Just get drunk, Dale thought as he swallowed the first drink, wishing he had let the guy bring water too. But it didn't matter. What mattered?

Peri Lee mattered to him. But Peri Lee was gone. Gladys Swartz was there now, the girl with the unhappy eyes; the girl who had never been loved in her life, who didn't know how to love. Yet she was still his girl, this wild and rebellious spirit that called herself Gladys Swartz. He would win her over, gentle her as he had gentled frightened antelopes that sometimes were caught in the fences.

If he could.

He left the bottle, nearly untouched. Though the bartender stared at him, Dale didn't wait to tell him he could have the bottle back, plus money paid. He left the bar with no intention of ever returning to it.

At the corner pay phone he called a cab and waited for it impatiently. But he might as well learn to be patient, he told himself, because this was going to require patience. A wild antelope trembled when you tried to get close to it.

When the cab arrived he asked the driver to take him to the office of the largest newspaper in town and then hang around, because he wanted to go to every other newspaper also. Even any underground papers that might exist.

At the first office Dale went through a procedure that he was to follow in every newspaper office that the cab driver could think of. Girls in ad rooms behind desks smiled and asked, "May I help you, sir?'

"Yes. I'd like to write a message for your personal column."

She pushed pad and pen toward him, and he wrote the message swiftly.

"I want you to keep it running, until I give you the word to end it."

Still smiling, the girl answered, "Yes, sir."

Dale gave her enough money to cover a month, then he went on to the next newspaper office.

CHAPTER 10

G ladys dropped a dime into the phone slot, then dialed the number of the manager of the apartment house. The answering voice was sullen, just as she remembered.

"Would you call Mrs. Swartz to the phone," she ordered. She had never liked the manager anyway, and wouldn't have said "please" to her for anything.

"Who?" as if she hadn't heard.

"Swartz! Swartz! She lives across the hall, you know. Longer than you do."

"Yeah, well, hold on."

"I intend to," Gladys muttered when she heard the phone thump onto the desk.

Time passed, and finally her mama's voice said eagerly, "Yes?"

Gladys knew. She was thinking it must be one of her two precious daughters. "I just called to tell you it's urgent that you come to the cemetery."

After a pause her mama asked in a strained voice, "What cemetery? Who is this?"

"You don't know me. But you should know what cemetery I'm

talking about. The one where your other daughter is buried. It's urgent you come. Right now."

"Why?" The tone had changed, sounded almost scared.

"Come," Gladys repeated. "Hurry, there's a message here for you."

"But how can I?" her mama cried. "I don't have a car."

"Call a cab. It won't cost you much, and I'll pay you back when you get here. If you're so afraid to spend your own, use a couple of the bills you've got hidden in that vase on the top shelf of the kitchen cabinet. Money that your *other* daughter gave you, for fifteen years of board and room."

She had regularly given her mama over half her paycheck, and she knew where it was kept. In fat green rolls, because she didn't trust banks.

The voice at the other end of the phone was completely silent. Gladys knew why. No one, not Marian, not Clarissa, not even her dad, knew about the money. Gladys knew, and her mama knew that Gladys knew. She had seen it, just a few days before the truck business and her mama had clutched it away. Gladys had gone on to get a drink, pretending she hadn't seen. But her mother knew.

"Who are you?' the voice hissed into the phone, "How did you know about that? *Who are you?*"

Come to the cemetery," Gladys repeated. "It's urgent that you come. You'll find out who I am when you get here."

She hung up the phone and turned away. That took care of her mama. Not even remembering she had once had a third daughter! She'd remember now, forever, and be afraid every time she heard a voice because she would think that Gladys was still around somewhere.

Only she wouldn't be. She had said her final goodbye that day in the hall, when her mama stood bragging about her *two* daughters.

Gladys went out into the street and began to walk, back toward the hotel where she had a room, stopping at a bar where she could find a place to hide awhile and drink a few beers.

She wasn't going back to the cemetery again. Her mama would go now, she knew; but not today, not alone. She would wait a few days, thinking about it, and then she would call Marian or Clarissa and ask to be driven over.

That was all Gladys wanted. She wanted them to see the stone and her message to them. Forgotten maybe, but not gone.

She didn't have to pay for the beers; she never had to anymore. The bar maid brought a second one, unasked for, saying, "This is from the guy at the counter. He wants to pay for your first, too."

Gladys looked up. One man at the bar was watching her. He smiled when her eyes met his. She gave him a quick once over, though it really didn't matter. She had discovered looks didn't have a thing to do with how well a man made love. Nor, in a lot of cases, did age. She returned his smile, and he got up to come toward her.

Smiles, talk, leaning closer to her as the afternoon progressed. He was free tonight, he said. Well, she was free too; free to see if he was the one who could at last satisfy her longing. It was taking all fun out of being alive. All of it.

In the beginning, there had been excitement in the attention that came from men. But even that had palled as she began to realize that something was missing. She tried to find it in work, the only kind she had found exciting. She drifted from one cheap dive to another because all she had was looks. No talent. Sometimes, instead of dancing or stripping, she simply served drinks, usually in topless places. But the hands that reached for her, as if she were only a thing to be handled, became too damned much. The bosses didn't like it when she slapped a customer's hand.

The man who paid for her beers talked, telling all about himself. She looked through him and thought of the months past. His words began to pass over her like that intangible thing called happiness.

She left him at one o'clock in the morning, while he slept in the cheap bed he had rented. He was nothing at all. She hurt somewhere inside, in her heart, her mind, as if something were pulling her apart. He hadn't been able to help her.

She continued the walk back toward her hotel, closed into her coat, her head down. She was ignoring the hands of stray drunks as they reached for her, ignoring the small clusters of long-haired young guys who grew silent as she passed them. She wasn't afraid. What was there about them to be afraid of? They couldn't do anything to her that hadn't already been done short of murder—and at times she felt she would welcome even that.

In a small bar near her hotel she stopped and bought three bottles of cold beer to take to her room.

"Hey, you're not leaving," a male voice said.

"I was thinking about it," she answered without looking at him.

"How about a dance or two, first?"

She looked around. "Where?" On a table?"

"We could find somewhere," he said.

She laughed at him over her shoulder as she left.

The little room she had rented for a month wasn't worth the money, but it was a place to hide. She put the beers on the vanity-dresser, took off her clothes and stood a moment looking at herself in the mirror. It was a fairly long mirror, and showed her reflection down to her knees.

The excitement didn't come. Not anymore. Hadn't, for a long time. Just a body, that was all it was. There were lots of bodies in this world. Too damned many.

She pulled her thoughts away. She couldn't give up yet. Surely, somewhere in this world, she could find fulfillment. Surely, somewhere, there was a man who would love her.

She went to bed nude, drank the beers quickly, one after the other so that she could get some sleep. Sleep without dreams, that was what she wanted.

She slept, but the dream came. In the midst of the dream she saw him; his blond hair sun-bleached to a pale platinum, his dark blue eyes narrowed and watching her, his shoulders square and broad and covered loosely by his shirt. He didn't move toward her, and she couldn't move toward him. Her body remained as stationary as his, and he was so far away that the mist sometimes nearly obscured him. The yearning was deep inside her, growing stronger, aching and hurting. The soft weeping came up from deep inside her too, and she heard it, but still she couldn't move toward him. Though she knew that if she could, the weeping would stop and the hurt would go away.

The weeping woke her. She sat up in bed, her heart beating slowly and heavily. Not her heart. Peri Lee's.

Gladys pressed her hands between her breasts and moved them up to press against her throat, pushing back sobs that belonged to the dream.

Why should she cry every night for Dale Larson? He was nothing to her. It was Peri Lee, still in the depths of her own brain, continuing a weak fight against her, coming out only in dreams.

Gladys threw back the blanket and got out of bed. It wasn't even daylight yet. A neon light that blinked maddeningly from across the street kept her room in a state of dark, light, dark, light. It was about to drive her crazy.

"One more night in this damned hole," she said aloud as she went to the wall switch, "and I'll go up a wall. Or out the window."

The ceiling light didn't help her feelings much, but only showed better the size of the nine by twelve room. The scratched and chipped old vanity dresser, and the bed with the blanket that looked as if it had been washed ten thousand times, but needed another washing.

She sat on the stool at the vanity, the only chair in the room, and looked at the face in the mirror. The hair needed bleaching again, or something. It was artificial, like a doll's hair. She would have preferred leaving it the soft, shining near-black it had been. But in order to conceal the identity of the girl the O'Brions were bound to be looking for, she had been forced to bleach her hair. Way back in the summer, a few days after she wrecked Pete's car.

She thought of Pete, and his car, and a slow grin replaced the scowl on her face. Served the sonofabitch right. She hoped he was as poor as she, and not able to buy another car. Whatever made him think he deserved a car like that anyway? A guy from the wrong side of every-thing, like herself.

Three days ago she had one thousand dollars. Money she had earned and saved. Then she bought the tombstone. It had taken all her money except a few dollars. She didn't care. She would need another job soon though. Very soon.

And that reminded her again of Dale Larson. Persistent devil. She hadn't seen him that night. There were always so many men around that place, but when the heavy described him to her she knew that it had to be Dale Larson.

She hadn't lost any time getting out of that part of town, but she still hadn't gotten away from him, not really. Because it was then that the dreams had become so intense. Every night he was there, and something within her was crying out for him. It was a hopeless kind of yearning that was worse than anything she had ever felt.

She longed to go back to her old hiding place in the bar beneath her old home and drink herself to sleep on beer. But the last time she had gone there, she turned to look behind her and there he was, coming in the door.

How the hell had he found that crazy little bar? Was there no getting away from him?

If she had the money she would go to Los Angeles, or New York City. She had been on her way to New York when she ran the car off the viaduct. In a way it was funny. Funny enough to laugh about, even in this dirty hotel room. She had forgotten she couldn't handle a car worth a damn. So she ran off the viaduct.

She fingered her hair, wishing she hadn't been afraid to go to a professional to have it done. Because she hadn't really known what she was doing, so she used too much on it. The girls, snooty because none of them was as beautiful, always made a point in asking where she bought her wig, even after they knew damned well it wasn't a wig.

She hated them. All of them. People had been nicer to her when she was ugly and shapeless.

Except men, that was. They were something else again. But they were a bunch of cheaps too. They wanted everything for free, and she was getting sick of it. But she'd be damned if she'd sell it. For spite, if nothing else. *That* for them.

She picked up her wrist watch and looked at it. Five o'clock. Naturally. Her alarm had gone off regularly, for over fifteen years, at five o'clock, and her mind just naturally clicked at that time. Even when she worked most of the night, or otherwise played around, it never failed that her mind went click at five a.m. So she'd get up, go to the bathroom and then go back to bed. She'd sell it first, before she would go back to a factory.

She wasn't sleepy now, though, and she was sick of the room she had rented. She went to the tiny stall where there was a smelly toilet and shower.

She showered anyway. She chose tight pants and a warm, tight sweater with a high rolled collar and long sleeves. So she wouldn't have to wear a coat. Later in the day she would have to look for a job, but right now she wanted to find a cafe and get a cup of coffee.

She walked, until she spotted a cafe that was open. It was beginning to get light from a sun just below the horizon. The cheap light of the cafe sign looked as sick and purposeless as she felt.

A man that reminded her of Hamilton came out of the cafe picking his teeth, saw her and stopped to grin suggestively at her. His eyes explored her body voraciously.

She felt even sicker, thinking of Hamilton. The damn fool, hanging himself like that. She didn't want to think of him. But for some reason his memory was staying with her lately. She passed by the man without giving him more than a glance.

In the small cafe she chose a booth with her back to the wall, then looked at the other people. At the counter sprawled one man, his legs spraddled, his chin leaning over his plate, asleep. Sneaking a nap over his breakfast before he went on to work. In a booth, by the windows, sat a young couple, side by side. They seemed to be paying more attention to each other's noses than to whatever was in front of them.

A fat waitress came and grunted at Gladys, her small eyes trying unsuccessfully to find fault with the figure beneath the sweater.

"Coffee," Gladys said so shortly it was almost a grunt. The woman hated her because of her good-looking body, Gladys could see that. But instead of getting satisfaction from it she felt vaguely disturbed. When the woman came back with the coffee Gladys ignored her.

After a moment she began to watch the young couple. Their lips touched lightly, gently. Gladys wondered how it felt to be in love like that. The lonely feeling that had begun to plague her so much lately felt stronger, turning her cold.

Someone to love. She couldn't remember the number of men whose lips had touched hers in the past three months. If she had learned anything from it, it was that beauty didn't seem to be enough. And another thing—they might have loved Peri Lee, but they could never love Gladys Swartz.

She wished she had worn a coat after all.

She finished the coffee and left, slowly walking the seven blocks back to kill time; stopping only to buy a six pack of beer. In her room, her door locked, she drank the beer and tried to make plans. The taste of luxury she'd had left her wanting more, but that took money, and lots of it. To be quite frank with herself she didn't know how to get it. Her brain was geared to seventy dollars a week at monotonous labor, one bolt here, one bolt there, and she didn't know how to make more than that. Even the money she had made dancing, so boring after the first week, was little more than seventy dollars. In fact, it sometimes dropped lower because every penny depended on tips from the men who gawked up between her legs and drooled down their chins and pants legs. She hated them.

The boss had suggested she could pull a hundred or more a night, and he'd get work for her. On the couch in his office he had suggested that. Part of her was willing and raring to have a go at it, and part of her balked. The longer she lived in this body, the more she found that men were no novelty for a good looker, as they called her. In fact, the panting of one was just like the panting of another, and when it was over they pulled on their pants in the same way. No one ever ended up loving her. Oh, well.

She slept awhile after she finished the beer, then she made up her face, wore a black dress that was slit so low in front it not only showed a third of each breast but her belly button top, wrapped a fake fur around her shoulders and went out to look for a job.

If she had to work she would choose a bar. At least she might get all the beer she wanted to drink.

The high-class bars made her feel conspicuous, so she carefully avoided them. When the people in those bars looked at her, she felt they were criticizing rather than admiring. She had to admit she just didn't fit in as Peri Lee O'Brion. That was one reason she would never be able to go back, even for the money.

Not unless she got so broke she would be forced to return. In that case, she already had a plan of sorts. She would hook the old man out of enough money to take her to Europe, in style. Why not? She pushed aside the feeling of something not right and tried to pull her thoughts away from the O'Brion family.

Only briefly did she wonder about them, how they were getting along without the daughter they had loved so much. Was the O'Brion home sad and lonely these days?

Sad and lonely. It was a state of mind that seemed to exist for everyone in one way or another. Peri Lee had been happy once. So had her family and her lover. Maybe, Gladys thought without wanting to, she should have left them alone. It was too late now. She wouldn't think about it anymore.

She walked a street that was not lit by street lights and touched by beckoning bar signs. It reminded her of her own street, and the loneliness grew so sharp she felt like crying. Even now, when she knew that her mama had never wanted her, had not even counted her among her daughters, Gladys felt the need to go to her and say, "I'm sick, Mama." Even though she knew she would hear a long sigh, and a disgusted, "Well, go to bed, Gladys."

Gladys walked on, her head down, almost forgetting what she was after. The memory of meeting her mama in the hall those days, then finally getting her to talk, of asking her if she had any children; then hearing her reply, "Oh yes, I have two lovely daughters—"

It made her want to run again, wet and messy tears on her face, streaking her mascara and making her ugly, to hide herself in the booth downstairs and drink herself to sleep. The loneliness she thought would be gone when she was beautiful, the aching sadness she couldn't explain, the yearning that had no object, not only lived with her night and day but was growing worse.

"Hey, beautiful!"

The hand touched her and she looked up into a face she didn't like the looks of, a face that seemed vaguely familiar. Someone she had shacked up with a few weeks ago?

"Wanta go play around awhile? You look like you need cheering up."

She pulled away, saw the door and went in.

At the counter she took a stool and waited for the bartender to come her way.

"Are you old enough to be in here, honey?" he asked.

"Sure. Bring me a glass of beer and tell me where the boss is."

"I'll tell you where the boss is and I'll give you a glass of beer when you can show me your ID."

"Well, *I* want to see your boss. About a job."

His eyebrows raised. "What kind of job, honey?"

"Serving drinks. What else do you think? Washing glasses?"

"A girl like you wouldn't have to work serving drinks or anything else. I'd pay you just to lay around the house."

"Under you, I suppose, for fifteen bucks a week." she said angrily. The whole thing was beginning to irk her. "Are you going to bring me that beer or not?"

"Not."

She shrugged, and the cape fell of her shoulders. She slid off the stool and bent over to pick it up.

A hand was in front of her, reaching the cape first, and bringing it up. She straightened to see a guy holding the cape. His arms went around her just long enough to put the cape in place on shoulders. He pulled it close together in front, covering the slit in her dress.

"You'd better keep that thing on, you'll catch cold," he said gently.

The first thing that entered her mind was, He's nice. Behind him another man, about the same age and size, approached with a smile.

"This fellow is my buddy. We were just having a drink, but we're willing to leave it and go someplace where you won't have to prove anything."

"Sure," Gladys said. "Why not?"

They had their own car, and as soon as she was settled in the front seat between them, the one who had picked up the cape and the driver began giving names.

"I'm Blake, that's Frankie. Okay?"

"All right by me. I'm—" She felt compelled to use her own name, or abandon someone who was already forgotten by the rest of the world. "I'm Gladys Swartz."

They laughed. "You're kidding."

"No."

The one called Frankie laughed and put his arm around her shoulders. "Really?"

"Really," she said, and she didn't think it was funny.

The driver looked searchingly at her even though he was pulling into heavy traffic. She could see in his eyes that he didn't give a damn about his buddy trying to kiss her neck. "The only place I know of where we can take you without an ID is our pad. We're a couple of free men. Okay?"

His eyes asked more than his question and she knew what the deal was now. She felt a little letdown. She had a notion to tell them to stop the car and let her out, but then she thought what the hell. A new experience. Two guys at once was reported to be pretty good stuff. It was about the only thing she hadn't done.

She said, "Sure why not?' and repeated under her breath, "Why not?"

"Champagne for you," he said.

"What for?'

The guy leaned forward and looked around her at the other guy. "Champagne for this doll, eh Blake?'

"Sure. Whatever she wants. For the rest of her life."

"All right then," she said, "make it beer." For the rest of her life? That meant she probably had a deal offered to her before the night ended. To live in and be a kind of unmarried housewife for two men. It would be the closest thing to marriage, so far. It might work out. Maybe somehow, with two instead of one, she could find security and love.

At least one guy had been very gentle when he put her cape on her shoulders. Polite, too. She liked that.

"Beer?" in astonishment.

"Yeah, beer," she said, on the defensive again. She liked plain old beer. "Champagne tastes like vinegar and I don't like it."

The guy shrugged. "Okay. Okay."

The word seemed silly to her. She didn't like it, but couldn't think why. She didn't feel very happy or thrilled about either guy all of a sudden, and didn't feel like talking either. But she had an almost frantic, desperate need to lie close to somebody. When they asked her a question, which they finally stopped doing, she let them know that nothing was any of their business. It didn't matter where she was from, how old she was, where she lived, or anything else.

"Here in town?" one of them persisted.

"Out of town," she answered shortly. Then added, "Way out." And a smile spread into a soft giggle, as she thought of what would happen if they knew the truth about her. They probably wouldn't be able to bail out of the car fast enough. She began to laugh in a kind of low-toned evil glee, visualizing the two of them taking off in opposite directions.

Her laughter sobered them, though they tried to laugh with her. They looked uncomfortable, as if they knew she was laughing at them. She had to stop laughing before it turned to hysterical weeping. She had to make up with them so they'd let her live on with them as their *wife*. Maybe, if she didn't laugh at them, they would love her.

She put her arms around the necks of both men and kissed their cheeks, and their discomfort was gone. The one who wasn't driving bent over her, pushed her cape and dress aside to bare her left breast and put his mouth on her brown nipple. Then slowly, one hand moved up under her dress.

The driver kept glancing at his partner, smiling. To Gladys he said, "You're going to work out fine, honey. We like you."

"I like you too," she said. She had to like them. Maybe someday, she could love them.

The rest of the way to the apartment house was done rather quietly, with more play than talk. There was only one stop at a liquor store for the beer.

The minute one of the guys had locked the door the other one took her cape and tossed it to the floor, then slid the dress off her shoulders. It fell to her waist. Something inside her crawled and twisted against the eyes and reaching hands, but she lost it immediately. She kissed them, hard kisses that made her feel better. One mouth was softer than the other, she noticed. One pair of hands was gentle. But here at least was variety, if she wanted to look for unusual advantages.

They had forgotten to bring the beer up from the car. A whole case of it in the truck. Gladys decided to forget it for the present, because she wanted to observe how two guys made love to one girl at the same time. She had read about it in novels, but she had no first-hand knowledge.

They didn't fight, they didn't even argue. The other one reached out and pushed the dress on the floor, and with it went her nude pantyhose and her shoes. As if they were used to cooperating, the first one carried her to the bed.

The conflict began to creep in on her again. The dirty words that poured softly from their mouths, their attention only to her body, as if she didn't exist as a person. Their doing to her things a man had not done before. She finally asked her own questions, when they suggested the ultimate.

"At the same time? Now look, I'm not about to be sandwiched between the two of you. Where the hell do you guys get all your ideas?"

"We're creative," said one. . .

She didn't know which was which. Why should she worry what they did to her, this wasn't her real body.

"Just do it, baby, and you can live here as long as you want."

She didn't answer, but she thought about it. Here was her offer. The one she had expected. It might be better than any job. All she'd have to do...

"You expect me to wash your dirty shorts?'

"Who wears shorts?'

"Well, socks, then."

"No. Promise. All you have to do is be a nice little girl, eh Blake?'

"Uhn," Blake answered.

"Yeah," she said. "Like a piece of meat on a spit."

They liked that description well enough to laugh at it.

"Go get me my beer," she demanded, just to see if they would.

"Now?'

"Yes, now, damn you. Don't you guys ever quit?'

So one of them took a long breath and said to the other, "Get your pants on and get the goddamned beer."

She sat in the middle of the bed, her legs spread and bent for balance, and drank two beers like water when it was brought to her. It began to help a little, and she didn't mind so much then.

But as hours began to drag, she discovered how two men can make you feel. Not only like meat on a spit, but choked, used and burning sore. She took it because she wanted to stay. Their apartment was comfortable, good-looking, and at least they had enough money so that she wouldn't have to search for cheap jobs all the time. And someday they might love her.

They finally went to sleep while she lay in the middle and stared at the ceiling. No one had turned out the light, and she didn't want to risk waking them by crawling out to turn it off. Her skin felt as if it had been gone over with sandpaper, and she was tired of men. She felt gagged and she hurt all over, front and back; she had been used *but good*, as the old saying went. But she had found a home.

Yeah, she thought, when a woman has a body, and is not fussy about how it's used, she can always find a home.

She closed her eyes and let the beer carry her into a light, half-sleep. She wanted to sleep. Wanted to so badly that its dark comfort seemed just beyond her grasp. When she made an effort to reach it, it only slipped farther way. But then the mist began and grew, she saw that strange and unreal world of dreams. The yearning in her reached toward it, as her brain had reached toward the oblivion of sleep. Then she heard the weeping.

The sound grew and after a while she was able to see into the mist; lying limp, nude, used, torn, on the ground, the body of Peri Lee. But it wasn't Peri Lee who wept. The weeping came from the curtain of white mist that moved over the body. *The essence of herself.*

She woke screaming.

She found herself sitting up in bed, staring straight ahead, the two naked men coming up and shaking her. She saw them, saw they were strangers, but someone she needed. She clawed at them, begging them to help her. They both slid away from her, off the bed; one of them said coldly, "This bitch is crazy. Get her out of here."

So the other one took her by the arm, pulled her off the bed and stumbling into the living room. He shoved her toward her clothes. "Get them on. Get out of here."

Sobbing, she pulled on the dress and grabbed the cape. At the door she turned back and put her bare feet into the shoes. Then she ran out and didn't pause to wait for the elevator. She wanted only to get away from everything, to walk the deserted sidewalks, to breathe. To escape the dream.

Not until she stopped at a pay phone in an all-night drugstore to call a cab did she notice that she had left her handbag, and all her money, in the apartment.

For a moment she was stunned. Not even a dime for a phone call. Not even a dollar for breakfast. And certainly nothing to pay a cabbie to take her back to her hotel.

She started to go back to get her money, then stopped on the sidewalk, looking around. Rows and rows of apartment houses, blocks long. She didn't even know where the place was. Would they even let her in long enough to pick up the small evening bag? More important—could she face them in her shame? No.

She couldn't face anyone for a while. She needed to walk. To think. To go back to her hotel and try to scrub away the filth of degradation and rejection. She went back into the drugstore and asked directions to her hotel, then she began to walk.

It was much farther than she remembered. In the early dawn factory workers hurried toward bus stops, their chins sunk into their collars the way she used to do. She began to see that most of them walked as she had walked, dreading the day at a boring, low-paying job. Maybe some of them carried in their minds the guilt of trying in some wrong way to escape the sameness of an unhappy life. Just as she now did. Was there no answer to any of this?

She felt a hand touch her arm, close about it with a firm grip, drawing her to a halt. She looked up, startled, nervous now, wary of any touch. The eyes she saw were bluer than the sky, warm and bright, as though tears never to be released gathered beneath the surface.

She heard her voice gasp softly, "*Dale.*"

She started to pull away, to turn and run, forever. But the slow pounding of her awakening heart stopped her.

A faint smile touched the corners of his lips, but it was brief and sad. "Have you had breakfast?" he asked.

His voice was low, and beautiful. Gladys felt the yearning of her body toward him, the strength of attraction that was new to her. A love that filled her body, her heart, her mind. She felt she should pull away, reject him in order to save herself, to save Gladys Swartz, but she couldn't. She merely shook her head.

He kept his hand on her arm. "Let's walk over a few blocks. I saw a pretty good restaurant around there."

She walked in silence at his side, expecting him to begin the questions she would find hard to answer. But he too walked in silence.

His hand moved down her arm, touched her fingers. She felt a natural reflex in her hand as she slipped it into the warmth and security of his. Fingers tightened, entwining.

"How have you been?" he asked after a while.

"Okay."

Another silence. With him she felt shy, nearly tongue tied. She wanted to talk, but what could she say? He thought he was walking by the side of Peri Lee.

They reached the restaurant and he held the door for her, his eyes on her face in serious contemplation, as though he wanted to say things he wasn't sure of. It was as though they had just met for the first time.

At the table he started to take her wrap, but suddenly she was ashamed of her cheap, revealing dress. She clutched the cape at her throat.

"No," she said. "I'd rather keep it on."

He smiled, and pulled out a chair for her. "Had you been walking long?" he asked. "You must have become chilled."

"Yes. Yes, I did."

She couldn't meet his eyes. She felt the night behind her, the obscenity of it, the degradation. She didn't want him to see. She wished now he could remember her as she had been, before the day in the mountain glen. She wanted him to love her, as he had loved Peri Lee.

She raised her eyes to his at last, and found she couldn't look away.

A waitress came and gave them menus. But the thought of food choked Gladys.

"I'm not hungry," she told him.

"You need to eat," he said. "You're thinner."

"So are you."

"Then I'll make a deal with you," he said softly, smiling at her, reaching across the table to take her fingers in his. "If you'll eat, so will I."

She nodded. "Okay. Scrambled eggs?"

"And raisin muffins."

"Yes. And coffee."

"And orange juice," he said. "And then—we have a short day before us. What would you like to do?" Her lips parted, her smile died. Hope rose, trembled, and died. Was there a chance for love with Dale? Was there a future? Or was there only today? He thought he had found Peri Lee—

"You will spend the day with me, won't you?" he asked.

She bit her lower lip. "I—I don't see why not. I don't have anything special to do."

He seemed relieved, yet his eyes continued to watch her, as though she were a mystery to him. At times she grew uncomfortable, and wished he would voice the unspoken questions in his eyes. She was puzzled that he did not mention the past in any way, nor Peri Lee's home and parents.

"Where would you like to go?" he asked. "How about a drive up into the mountains? We could take a cab back to my hotel so I could pick up my car. Then, well, the world lies before us."

"You mean just go and never come back?" Eagerness was in her voice.

"Something like that. You don't have anything to come back here for, do you?"

She drew her hands away from his as the waitress placed bacon, eggs and muffins in front of them.

To go and never come back. With a man she loved, who loved her. It was all her dreams combined. But sadness rose above the hope in her heart. It was Peri Lee he loved, not Gladys Swartz. "How did you find me?" she asked.

"I just kept looking, and kept looking. I would never have stopped."

She glanced up at him and spoke without thinking, "I would like to have a man like you. I would like—" she bit her lower lip again. What was she trying to tell him? Why was she betraying herself, when all she had to do was reach out for him?

"That's a strange thing to say."

Looking into his eyes she knew he was right. Peri Lee would have had no need to speak those longing words. She had not known what it was to not have Dale. Did she know now?

They ate in silence for awhile. Neither of them finished the food on their plates. Maybe, oh God, maybe she could go with him, live her life in the warmth of his love. But first, she had to be alone. To try to understand this strange and powerful love that had possessed her.

She rose suddenly. "I have to go change first," she said. "I can't go up to the mountains in this dress."

He rose too and caught her hand as though never to let her go. "Don't worry about the dress. When the shops open we'll get you something else. I don't want to lose you again."

She pulled away from him. "No. Please. It's not far to my room. It won't take me long."

"Let me go with you."

"No, please. Wait. Just wait for me."

His hand dropped away from hers, and when she reached the door she looked back. The sadness in his eyes tore into her heart and burned in her breast. She wanted to rush back to him, put her hands on his face, her lips on his and say, "*Don't, don't hurt so much my love, my Dale. I never meant to hurt you. I had never loved before, you see, to know that your hurt is my own.*"

But she ran on instead, into the crowd of nameless people who hurried along the walk. A strange and disturbing thought entered her mind. Not once had he called her by name. Not once had he said Peri Lee.

She walked for hours, down one street, up another, trying to sift through the levels of her mind. She longed to return to Dale, to see if he still waited at the restaurant, but something drove her on out of his life.

The sun was far to the west when she reached her room. After bathing for a long time and dressing in pants and a jersey top, she went down to the desk.

"You got a paper I can borrow?" she asked without enthusiasm. The time seemed to have come when she had to return completely to her allotted place in life. Nothing, neither beauty, nor the attempt at possession of another girl's life, could keep her from eventually returning to her own.

"Which one?" the clerk asked, giving her his very friendly grin.

"I don't care. A big one. I have to look for a job and another place to live."

"Sure. Here."

She took the rolled newspaper and went back upstairs with it. She sat cross-legged in the middle of the bed and spread the paper out before her, discarding all but the ad section.

There seemed to be about a million jobs, but none that she wanted. The ones that sounded really attractive she knew she wouldn't be able to do, like accounting or secretarial work. The waitress work required experience in almost all cases. Factory jobs... she couldn't face them yet, though she knew she eventually would. The beauty would fade— as the flowers she had placed on the grave.

But if she dared dream a while first. What kind of job would she really like? She chewed her fingernails and thought. Dancing again? For pennies, crap. All she could do was wiggle.

She looked at the paper again. Cab drivers! Under women wanted? She looked at the ceiling and laughed, trying hard to bring a touch of gayety back into her life. "That's the one for me!" she said aloud. But the laughter didn't last. She felt low, depressed, and tired. And very lonely.

How about modeling? Nothing offered. She would like modeling, she thought. Wearing beautiful clothes all the time. But no offers in this paper.

She pushed it aside and got off the bed. A glass of water for her empty stomach. She remembered that she hadn't eaten a thing the day before, and the breakfast with Dale was like a dream that hadn't really happened—not to her. There was a good chance she wouldn't be eating much tonight. Her stomach felt like an empty bag.

"Empty beer bag," she said, another attempt to cheer herself up, to cling to her own identity.

But it was no use. The water tasted awful. She went back to sit on the bed. Idly, her eyes read words on the paper. Then three words in capital letters, pushed out from among the other ads. A name GLADYS EVELYN SWARTZ.

She grabbed the paper up and peered closely at the name, and the seven words that followed it. *I love you. Come home with me.* Followed by a contact number.

She threw the paper down as if it had turned into a serpent in her hands. But the words were still there.

Gladys turned her back and went to the little wash basin for another glass of water. Her teeth chattered against the glass.

She went back into the bedroom and looked at the paper. A kind of calmness came over her and she approached the paper with timidity and shyness slowing her steps.

Standing away from it she read the words aloud, softly, barely above a whisper, "Gladys Evelyn Swartz. I love you." Then again, more loudly. "Gladys Evelyn Swartz, I love you."

She pressed her hands together, entwining her fingers, because she didn't dare to touch the paper. If she did, it might turn out to be a dream too, a drunken dream caused by the water from the dripping tap.

"How did he know?" she said to the paper, to herself. How did he know about Peri Lee, about Gladys Evelyn Swartz? He knew, and it meant that he accepted her. He loved her, too. Gladys Evelyn Swartz. He knew she had been a cripple, he knew she had died. And he knew she had done them all a great injustice—a terrible thing—a tragic thing. Still, he was telling her he loved her.

"Gladys Swartz," she said aloud, again. There was a beauty in the sound of the words that was almost like music. She hadn't noticed before how beautiful her name really was.

She lay down, crossways on the bed, her head resting on a pillow she pulled down from the end. She looked at the message he had sent to her. She looked at it, but she didn't move.

Hours later there was a knock on her door. She went to answer it and saw the clerk grinning in the hallway.

"Did you find what you were looking for?" he asked.

"Yes," she said quietly. "I found it."

"Oh." He looked uncomfortable suddenly. Then, "I'm going off duty in a couple of hours. Would you like to go out to eat with me?"

Was it that late? She had forgotten that she had ever felt hungry in her life. "No." Then she added, because it sounded too short and unfriendly, "I'm not hungry, thanks anyway."

"Are you through with the paper?"

"I'd like to keep it."

She closed the door and locked it, and went back to stand beside the bed. The paper blurred before her eyes. Pictures in her mind now; green fields and cold mountain water in irrigation ditches, a mother and a father who loved, deeply. Home. Dale's home, where he would take his bride. Peri Lee in white. The virgin Peri Lee.

And Hamilton. Hanging from a rope in the barn loft.

The closed suitcases held a box of stationery she had never used, and a delicate, gold pen she had never used. She pulled it out, took one envelope and a sheet of paper and went to the vanity.

Fear shook her hand as she wrote, but she paused only to steady the hand. On the outside of the envelope his name, Dale Larson, and beneath it the phone number.

On the sheet of stationery she wrote four words. *Thank you. Forgive me.*

Her thoughts finished the unwritten words.

Thank you for telling me you love me, but I understand. It's Peri Lee you love. It's Peri Lee who belongs there, not Gladys Evelyn Swartz. Forgive me for needing your love before I could go on to my ultimate destiny. Forgive me, Peri Lee. I meant you no harm. With God's blessing you will not remember me.

She sealed the envelope and pushed it down into her bra. They wouldn't miss finding it there.

From another suitcase she got her small razor and removed the blade, then she sat down on the bed and held the blade against her wrist. This was the only way. Through Peri Lee's weakened body she had entered; so it must be through the weakened body that Peri Lee could return and Gladys must exorcise.

What would happen to her? She knew, and she shook with fear because now the time had come, and she must go on. But it would be easier now, because she had been loved. Could her exorcism bring back the girl whose body she had used? Or had she destroyed her forever.

She bowed her head, closed her eyes and whispered, "God, forgive me. Help me. Help her come back."

The pain was sharp and burning, and the tearing of the flesh made her gag and vomit. But there was only water from her stomach to mix with and weaken the red blood that spread over the newspaper. Quickly, before she dared think of the pain and the nausea, she sliced the blade into the other wrist.

With her eyes closed, her face upward toward the ceiling she waited, sobbing softly in pain and terror. When the dizziness came she got up and took the three steps to the telephone to call the clerk downstairs. She kept her eyes closed so that the mirror didn't sway and make her feel that she would fail and it would be too late. Too late to help Peri Lee.

Answer the phone, my God, answer the phone!

"Yeah?" the clerk finally said into her ear, sounding far away.

"Listen... I have... cut my wrists—"

"What?" he yelled, "On purpose?"

"Listen..." the weakness was coming too fast. She clung to the phone desperately as she went down on her knees. "Send an—ambulance. Hurry. Before this body... dies."

For one moment, she saw the layered mists of the inner world of Peri Lee's mind. She saw it fold away and disappear beyond the mists, blending and receding as the consciousness of Peri Lee began a strong surge upward.

Gladys saw the outer world then; saw herself fall, the body limp, lying on its side, blood gushing from both wrists, the skin growing grey-white in frightening contrast.

Hurry, hurry, hurry, she was screaming. She realized there was no sound now from her voice, or from the body on the floor. She had separated from it, without knowing it had happened. Disembodied, nothing now but a helpless, hovering mist of sorrow, she floated above the still body on the floor.

Someone at the door turned a key in the lock. The white face of the clerk looked in, "Jesus!" He withdrew. A moment later the shrill cry of a siren grew louder and louder. Even after it stopped in front of the hotel, the siren sent out its scream of warning.

Gladys watched the white-coated men rush in. They went down beside the body and one man swiftly wrapped tight bandages around the wrists and arms of the girl, while the other listened to her heart with a stethoscope and drew a sample of blood into a needle. He nodded, and they lifted her onto the stretcher.

They drove into the emergency section of a small hospital and ran with the pale, limp body into a room that was filled with surgical equipment.

Gladys floated closely above them. It couldn't be too late. Had she waited too long to call? No. She had seen her return. But would she die now?

Blood transfusion equipment was being hooked up on one side of the body, even while a nurse spread a sheet over the body and began to remove all clothing. When she came to the bra, she silently handed the envelope to one of the nurses standing nearby.

They stood watching the girl, silent, waiting. Gladys watched too. She didn't know what they knew. She didn't know if a heart still beat there.

The color of the skin seemed to be changing, then Gladys saw the sigh. The rise of round breasts under the white sheet. The parting of pale lips in the drawing of a deeper breath.

Gladys turned and huddled into a corner, as far away as she could get without leaving the room. She quivered with the aching of tearless, voiceless weeping, the weeping of gratitude.

Peri Lee lived. That was all that mattered now. Someone in the room said, "She'll be all right now. She seems to be sleeping normally."

"The envelope, Doctor. There's a name and a phone number."

"I'll see if he can be located. Stay with her." They all left the room except one nurse who remained standing by the bed.

Time passed slowly. The nurse finally sat down, and Peri Lee lay without moving. Only the slow rise and fall of her chest showed that she had not died.

After a time the door opened and a doctor entered, and behind him walked Dale Larson. His face was even more pale than Peri Lee's. When he crossed the room to stand beside the bed and take up the girl's limp hand in his, Gladys saw that the envelope was in his pocket.

He leaned down and kissed her forehead tenderly, and she opened her eyes. For a moment she looked at the faces as if there was no recognition in her mind, or perhaps no mind at all. Then her gaze went back to Dale and remained there.

He said softly, in a voice deep with emotion, "Gladys?"

She frowned slightly and stared at him. Her lips moved and after a moment she whispered, "What? Who? Dale, where are we?"

Suddenly, crushingly he began to sob, his face hidden against the sheet that covered her. It was terrible to hear, and reminded Gladys of Hamilton. But this time the man's tears were not born of unhappiness. Peri Lee was conscious; she didn't know where she was; she would never remember the past few months. They were not really part of her.

The doctors would call it amnesia and let it go at that.

GLADYS MOVED SWIFTLY, a silent, wingless bird in flight, out the building and into the blue sky. An exhilaration possessed her. She felt her freedom with an appreciation she had not felt before. A wish, and it was so. The conflicts, the unhappiness, the prison of a biological body, gone. Why had she wanted to live again?

She wished to be back at the farm, and the wish was done. She was there, among the leaves of a tree, looking down upon a scene.

A beautiful woman, Olivia O'Brion, getting into the car; the door held for her by her husband. He ran to the driver's door, and the car sped away, fast.

They had received word from Dale that their daughter had been found. Safe. No longer lost. It was written on their faces.

Silence, that seemed more profound than usual in contrast to the noise of the city, was left behind on the farm. A peaceful silence, a place where Peri Lee could live, laugh and love again. And be loved.

Gladys moved slowly toward the barn. There was another thing that she had to do. Ask Hamilton to forgive her.

She rose into the highest peak of the barn, among the spiders that didn't see her, webs that remained unbroken by her presence. There she stopped, afraid to go farther, to face the mysteries beyond death.

Courage. Here, more than there, she needed courage. She knew now that she had been a coward. Too afraid to face life, afraid to face death.

She raised her voiceless cry toward the vast and frightening ways of outer space, screamed from the depths of all that she had ever been. *Help me, oh help me. Take me with you.*

She waited for the music, the reaching down, the lifting up of the soul, of everything that passed beyond life. But nothing came.

Silence. Only silence? Was this her doom then, her punishment? To be left alone, never to know what had once reached for her to carry her on. Never to see if Hamilton would forgive her.

The spiders moved about her, nestling into the deep, dark crevices for protection from the cold of a coming winter. Gladys grew silent too, as silent as they, the weeping gone, acceptance closing her in.

She would wait, here against the rafters where Hamilton had chosen to die. Wait forever, for eternity, beyond all but hope. Wait for the music to return for her, to carry her away to the fulfillment beyond life.

She would wait.

OTHER NOVELS BY RUBY JEAN

1974 The House that Samael Built
1974 Seventh All Hallows' Eve
1974 House at River's Bend
1975 The Girl Who Didn't Die
1978 Child of Satan's House
1978 Satan's Sister
1978 Dark Angel
1982 Hear the Children Cry
1982 Such a Good Baby
1983 The Lake
1983 MaMa
1985 Home Sweet Home
1985 Best Friends
1986 Wait and See
1987 Annabelle
1987 Chain Letter
1988 Smoke
1988 House of Illusions
1988 Jump Rope

1989 Pendulum
1989 Death Stone
1990 Vampire Child
1990 Lost and Found
1990 Victoria
1991 Celia
1991 Baby Dolly
1992 The Reckoning
1993 The Living Evil
1994 The Haunting
1995 Night Thunder
2022 Bear Hollow Charlie
2022 Cry of the Soul
2022 Pride of Bella Terra

www.ingramcontent.com/pod-product-compliance
Lightning Source LLC
Chambersburg PA
CBHW060603310726

48982CB00008B/1215/J